PRETTY MUCH TRUE

A NOVEL

by

KRISTEN TSETSI

PENXHERE PRESS

Connecticut

PRETTY MUCH TRUE

by

Kristen Tsetsi

PRAISE FOR PRETTY MUCH TRUE

"What I love about this story is that there's nothing the least bit sentimental or saintly about Mia, the narrator. It's a fascinating study of how the casualties of war extend far beyond the battlefield that is also incredibly funny in places. Great book." –*Russell Rowland, author of* In Open Spaces *and* High and Inside

"The trauma of battle can be felt far, far from the battlefield. If the oft-repeated claim that soldiers never feel so alive as they do in battle is true, then *Pretty Much True* shows that the ones they leave behind never feel so dead to the world as they do waiting for their loved ones." –*Lee Giguere*, Journal Inquirer

"Kristen Tsetsi's book does what the best books do—it hurls you into a world only think you know or understand and makes it living, breathing, and absolutely engrossing." –*Caroline Leavitt*, New York Times *bestselling author of* Cruel Beautiful World

"Kristen Tsetsi writes about the hidden conflict a world away from the big one with style, heart, and a profound reality." –*Phillip B. Persinger, author of* Do the Math *and* Tools of the Trade

"*Pretty Much True* brings the war home in a way no news report or even memoir could have done." –*R.J. Keller, author of* Waiting for Spring

"I got so caught up in this story I forgot myself. Kristen Tsetsi's writing is hypnotic. The characters sing off the page." –*Kathleen M. Rodgers, author of* Johnnie Come Lately

"Kristen Tsetsi is the rare sort of writer who can satisfy both emotionally and intellectually. *Pretty Much True* is a moving novel whose emotional and intellectual complexity demands much of the reader but offers much more in return." –Small Press Reviews

"One of the most powerful and brilliant books I have read in a long time." –*Joseph Dilworth Jr.*, Pop Culture Zoo

"*Pretty Much True* reads like a long-form haiku written by Charles Bukowski in collaboration with Ann Beattie. Almost every paragraph is a stand-alone gem of insight and observation." –*Rick Shefchik, author of* Rather See You Dead *and* Everybody's Heard About the Bird

"Completely engrossing. A totally spellbinding escape into another world." –*Stacy Leiser,* Leaf Chronicle

"There are many novels about war, most from the battlefield where there's page-turning tension and drama. But there are few stories written from the point of view of a loved one back home waiting, and waiting some more, not knowing if or how the soldier will return home. Perhaps that's because so few have found an interesting way to write such a story, but that has changed, thanks to Kristen Tsetsi." –*Carol Hoenig,* Huffington Post

"An intensely intimate and affecting story. I was 100 pages into *Pretty Much True* before I looked up." –*Steven McDermott,* Storyglossia

"Kristen Tsetsi tells a war story unlike anything readers have experienced." –*Molly Callahan,* Journal Inquirer

"You get the sense Tsetsi has been careful with every word and that no sentence has been wasted. A great novel." –*Henry Baum, author of* North of Sunset *and* The American Book of the Dead

"From beginning to end, Tsetsi's novel is loaded with foreboding." – *Owen W. Gilman, Jr.,* The Hell of War Comes Home: Imaginative Texts from the Conflicts in Afghanistan and Iraq

"An engaging, realistic portrait of a lover's life at the homefront." –Bookpleasures

"Mia's narrative voice holds us to the spot."—*Bill Wolfe,* Read Her Like an Open Book

For Ian

"I want you to feel what I felt. I want you to know why story-truth is truer sometimes than happening-truth."—Tim O'Brien, *The Things They Carried*

"All this happened, more or less. The war parts, anyway, are pretty much true."—Kurt Vonnegut, *Slaughterhouse Five*

PROLOGUE

I tug on my jeans, cover up with my bra. He is asleep before I put on my socks, naked on the couch with one bent leg propped against the back, the other flat and angled open. Even drunk, most people would be self-conscious. Most would have pulled something on first thing. Were he anyone else, I would be embarrassed for him, would find a light blanket, or a robe or a bath towel, to drape over him.

I sit on the floor and run my fingers over his body, the tissue-soft skin of his inner thigh, the sparse hair curls on his lower abdomen, the dark hollow where neck pools into collar bone, and I wonder if I could ever be comfortable enough, trusting enough, to sleep this way, watched, the way I am watching him.

We kissed at midnight, the way people do, but we must not have had time to say Happy New Year before kissing was more than kissing. I don't remember either of us saying it.

JANUARY 1, WEDNESDAY

The phone rings and neither of us moves.

"What time's it?" he says.

"I don't know."

He looks at his watch and wipes his face and picks up the receiver. "Yes, sir. Yes, sir." He hangs up. "Date changed again."

"Surprise." I hold my head.

"By changed, I mean, we're not going."

"For sure? For real?"

"Not going." He rolls over to face me and the tags clink on their chain. Toe tags, really, no matter what they call them.

"Why aren't you smiling?"

"I don't know, M. I wouldn't get too excited."

Chancey jumps on the bed and Jake strokes his tail.

"Why?" I say.

"It's just—there's a lot in the news, and people are saying things."

"What things?"

"Just…something. I don't know anything for sure, so don't get—don't get the way you get."

"Who's saying it?"

"It's not that it's being said—not by anyone reliable, that is—so much as people think Iraq's next."

"It's just talk, though," I say.

"Yeah. Just talk." Chancey flattens between us. "It wouldn't make any sense."

FEBRUARY 27, THURSDAY

From our window, I watch him stuff his bags in the trunk, LAKELAND black-lettered on the sides. He looks up once, then goes back to punching his duffel to wedge it in a side nook. When he finishes, he holds out his arms in the snow and smiles up at me. There's been a lot of snow, for Tennessee. The first we've seen in the year we've been here. He writes 'come play' in the dusting on the roof and I put on my mittens and hat.

· · · · ·

He holds me in the kitchen in front of the open refrigerator. His sweater, wool, scratches my forehead.

"I don't know if I'll write you," I say. "I may not write you at all."

"Come on, M."

"I won't know what to say."

"Say whatever you want. Say you woke up at seven to go to the bathroom and then went back to bed."

"Stop it."

"You'd rather fight about it again?"

"No."

"Then write that you love me," he says.

"Do you?"

"Don't be an idiot."

"Well?"

"Why don't you…You could write notes like the ones you wrote me in high school."

"I hate it when you do this."

"It took me two weeks to figure out who you were. Remember?"

"You're pissing me off. And you didn't figure it out. I told you."

"And when you told me, I figured it out."

"You know it's not some girl thing, right? That I'm not one of those girls who grew up dreaming of some over-the-top princess wedding? I don't even like wedding dresses. It's just, if we—I can't help wondering what I'm doing here if you're not sure."

"Oh, no no no. Don't do th—"

"Besides you—and not even you, pretty soon—what's here for me? There's no work, Jake. Why am I here?"

He leans into the fridge and pulls out the orange juice. "I guess I don't know what else I can say."

. . . . .

The curtains billow in the wind and we are under the blankets, neither of us with a foot on the floor. His last breath is quiet and he falls beside me. "I'll miss that," he says, and I tangle my legs and my fingers in his. He says, "Promise me you'll take care of yourself while I'm gone."

"We've already done this," I say. "I feel like we're in a bad movie."

"That's not what I mean."

"What do you mean?"

He slides his fingers from the knot. "I'll show you."

. . . . .

Janis Joplin says there is no tomorrow, that staying up all night means today never ends, so while Jake sleeps, I sit at the kitchen table and listen to the helicopters flying the pattern. Listen to the artillery exploding at the weapons range on post, five, six miles away. I open the window, smell the snow, listen to the cars on the main road, trucks wheezing up the hill, bass rattling in the window-tinted Lincoln that rolls down our street every night at eleven sharp.

Ten hours.

Ten hours to count or to enjoy, but not both.

I close the window.

OUTSIDE, COOL AIR blows sharp and hard and the snow is sun-bright under flat clouds.

People brush past, arm in arm, sniffing, blowing, consoling.

I squint, but it doesn't help. My eyes ache. Shapeless white-gray clouds go on and on and the sun and the snow and the clouds together are all too white and I don't remember where we left the car. Jake and I had leaned against the trunk after dropping his duffel in a pile, and we'd talked about something, surely, standing out in the lot. Maybe fast food, maybe the weather, while waiting for the call to go inside, for his mother to catch up from where we'd lost her at a red light. I remember running my finger over the raised letters on his breast pocket and reading the name.

This must be what it's like when someone dies. They're here, and then they're not.

"Hon, why didn't you wait for me?"

"I'm sorry, Olivia. I didn't see you." Her hand grips my arm. I tug free and her long nails zip on nylon.

"I called your name."

"I'm sorry," I say, "I didn't hear you," and when a salt-stained minivan pulls out of its spot I see our car, overdue for a wash, a radio station sticker in the corner of the rear window.

"Where's your ribbon, hon?" she says, squinting at our bumper. "I thought you'd have one by now."

We—Jake and I—have one bumper sticker: MARRIAGE = LOVE + LOVE. The message was crossed out by a vandal, the streak extending to the bumper, the ink a permanent, ugly smear on white paint. I tell her, "They were out." Too many—Olivia included—slap on the yellow ribbons in perfect alignment on trunks and bumpers, the more the better. Her SUV boasts six, three on either side of the license plate. She fits right in, in this military town, where a bumper without ribbon magnets is a rarity. Jake and I call the people magnet-junkies and even found, online, a bumper sticker reading, I SUPPORT OUR TROOPS MORE THAN *YOU* DO.

We didn't buy it.

His mother nudges me, pushing me to walk with her across the lot. "There's your car," she says. "I parked just a few spots away." She links her arm in mine and says, "I can come over."

"Oh, no. That's—I'm not going directly home. I have to…" and then I mumble something. I have nothing. Nowhere to go, nothing to do, until Monday.

"What was that, hon?"

"I have to pick up cat food."

"That won't take but a minute. Let me go with you."

We reach our car—mine and Jake's—and she stands in front of me, keys dangling from her fist. Dried tears stripe her cheeks.

"I have so many other things to do." I wipe my own cheek even though there is nothing there and tell her, "You have something…" and point until she scrubs at her skin.

"Gone?" she says.

"Gone."

She pulls me to her and clutches me tight—so tight my nose is stuffed into the fake fur lining of her hood and the perfume collected there makes me sneeze—and then releases me. "Well. Call me, hon." I watch her go, wait for her to close the heavy door of her SUV and disappear behind tinted glass. She honks when she passes.

Cold wind cuts through my sweater.

I zip my coat.

My head hurts. All that brightness.

I check my coat pocket for the keys, hoping Jake has them. Maybe he held on to them and they're in his—

—but I find them in my jeans.

Denise—I'd looked for her in the hangar after Jake and William and the rest of them were marched away—now pulls out onto the street and rolls down her window. I see her light a cigarette.

I drop my keys on the floor and stand in the middle of the living room. We left the tree lights on. It wouldn't matter if the tree were fake, but it's real, and I don't remember the last time we watered it.

The last time I watered it. Jake didn't water the tree because he wanted it gone. "Even New Year's was almost two months ago," he said, but it was doing well, staying green. "Not yet," I said.

Chancey rubs against my ankle. I didn't feed him this morning, I remember. Breakfast was rushed. Jake had wanted eggs and pancakes and bacon and grapes, anything he wasn't likely to have for a while, and we'd forgotten about the cat.

He leads me to his bowl in the kitchen. Jake's coffee cup sits near the window on his side of the table, his cream and sugar spoon ready on the edge of the sink for the second cup there wasn't time to drink. I pull the cat food from the cupboard and pour some into the bowl on the floor.

Chancey's crunching sounds loud.

I leave the bag on the counter and go to the bedroom. Jake's towel from his shower half-covers a torn condom wrapper on the unmade bed, sheets and comforter flung to the center. I pull up the blankets so Chancey doesn't drag litter where I sleep and throw the towel in the closet.

Jake's blue flannel pants lie on the floor, knees bent, running, his dirty socks on top. I pick them up and fold them, then drop them back on the floor and, sweating in my coat, kick and drag the legs and waist, slide them around on the floor until they look the way he left them.

I sit on the bed and pull out the letter he handed me before walking away.

Don't let it ruin us, M. You know I love you. You know it. Take care of yourself and know that even if you don't write me, I'll be writing you. -J

I read it, then read it again.

Some time later, still wearing my coat, I fall asleep.

FEBRUARY 29, SATURDAY TO MARCH 19, WEDNESDAY

THE NEWS IS on, the anchors' dramatic and rolling inflection reduced to gibberish while I wait for something to happen.

The news is always on, at home and in stores and in bars and everywhere, while everyone—guessing and second-guessing— waits for something, for anything, to happen.

Talks go on and deadlines leapfrog, and I expect Jake to be home before the end of March. I expect he'll call any time, now. "Aren't you glad we didn't do it?" he'll joke. "Now we're stuck."

Shellie tells me I don't have to come back to work until I'm ready, and that my cab is out for a new fuel pump, anyway. She says she and her dog, Puddin', are thinking of me.

I wash one plate and one glass and either watch television or stare out the window at the snow and then the rain and sometimes the sun. Rarely the sun. I vacuum the throw rugs and wash the gray ring around the bathtub and drag the sponge behind counter appliances. Microwave. Coffeepot. A pile of dried and burned crumbs have collected under the toaster, enough to make a mound the size of a small anthill. I sprinkle them over Chancey's hard cat food, and he sniffs them, then eats them.

A helicopter *whomp, whomp, whomps* over the apartment and my chest thuds. I go to the window to watch the Chinook's dark, flat underside pass over the trees. "Apaches have to fly in the back forty clear on the other side of post," Jake said when I asked why I never see his helicopter—only Chinooks and Blackhawks—pass over the apartment. "I'd fly over, if I could. Drop a message in a bottle, or something. A hamburger, maybe. No one's done that before."

Denise and I sit—breathing, waiting—on the phone while we watch the first bow of white light streak across our screens and land somewhere in the center of the city. Beautiful, if there's no real thinking about it.

"That's it," she says. Something goes clink on her end, reminding me to refill my glass. "We just watched the beginning from our living rooms. Hey—what do you think they were doing in their living rooms?"

I stay up long after we get off the phone, until the bottle's empty, and check the line every now and then for a dial tone.

March 19

Jake,
Howe area yhou righkt now;?
Don't type trunk. Drunk/
Howareyouhowareyouhowareyou
Alive,righat? Alive, I hope. I'ma sure you war.
Are!
What the hellk.
Lksdoihoagfnlkaglkd

DENISE'S KITCHEN WINDOW blinds slap in the wind and midmorning sun catches floating skin and particles and dust. A fruit fly dives into my cup of tea, no longer steaming.

She fiddles with an arrangement of fat daisies in a vase on the counter, cutting stem-bottoms and twisting stalks so the faces point outward. Her black hair shines blue and she might have forgotten to close a shirt-button.

"You could have told me you don't like tea," she says, and when the flowers fall the way she likes, she sets the vase on the center leaf and tucks in her shirt with one hand and sips from a cup with the other. "I have coffee. Soda. Water. Anything?"

I say, "Tea's fine."

She tells me she'll be right back and her hips carry her out of the room.

Her apartment is warm. She doesn't have the air on. It's cool for late March, but not that cool. I make a streak on the table with my finger, then another, the wood shiny and lemon-scented. Through the archway, in her living room, vacuum cleaner stripes make a palm-leaf pattern on beige carpet.

She calls from somewhere, "Are you going back to work tomorrow?"

"Probably." I try to picture her bedroom. Jake and I were here only once before, for a battalion party. Someone was leaving or someone new was coming, and they grilled ribs and burgers in the light of tiki torches speared into the lawn at the edges of their patio. Coolers held the beer, so no one went inside unless it was to use the bathroom, and because their toilet paper has—or had, for the party—one piece of trivia per square, every return trip was announced by the sharing of a new question. Jake jumped through the sliding patio door and quizzed me on the state flower of Alaska, and when I had exhausted my guesses, someone else—Ben? some B name—said, "Forget me not." Denise looked at him and shook her head, just a little, and then cheered loudly and said, "Good job!" William kept his eyes on the grill and flattened burgers with a spatula, making grease drippings pop in the fire.

I fish the fly out of my mug and drop it on her table. Dead, probably. I scoop it from the puddle with my longest fingernail.

"You must drive some interesting people," she says, but her consonants sound funny. Must be putting on mascara.

"I don't know," I say. "Sometimes."

"Anyone ever hit on you?"

"They're really only interested in a ride."

"I'll bet."

"Well, there was this one time when…" But I stop. I'm not interested enough to follow through with whatever story would come.

"What?" she says.

"Nothing."

She comes out, feeling her clothes and touching her hair. "Ready?"

I pick up my cup to bring it to the sink, but remember the fruit fly and first check the tabletop. The tea puddle is still there, but at some point, the fly had dried off and flown away.

"It's like summer already, isn't it?" Denise rolls down her window, then closes it after the crosswinds blow her hair in her eyes. Low, roadside cliffs support ashy, leafless trees. Water drips from crevasses, and weeds bust green from the rockface. The loveliness of it, the fresh smell of damp soil and—somewhere—fresh-cut grass makes me feel sick.

Denise punches radio stations with nails that match her lips. I look at my own nails, clear and unpolished.

"Deer." Denise points out the front window.

I scan the treeline on both sides, look for a deer eating grass or waiting to cross. Then I see it, just short of the median, head yanked from its body and resting a few feet up the berm from the rest of the carcass. Bright pink blood pools on the pavement and loose meat hangs from both segments. I've seen dead deer before, contorted or crushed or one portion flattened and mutilated, but the head on the road has a round, black nose and alert-looking eyes under a light brown brow, and the body is full. Headless, it might still get up and bound into the trees.

I look away.

Denise adjusts the rearview mirror. "I've never seen anything like that. Wow. What do you think hit it?"

I tilt my head into the wind and laugh. "A fucking big truck."

She looks at me, then changes the station again and sings along with a song. I close my eyes. The breeze fans my eyelashes and rakes my hair and I pretend the wind is Jake's fingers tugging at the ends.

She says, "My mother in-law is coming over tonight before she leaves town."

"Was she here? I didn't see her in the hangar."

"Oh, no. She didn't get to come to the hangar. That's a rule." She lights a cigarette and uses her tongue, pointed and flexed, to remove congealed lipstick from the corners of her mouth, then opens her window and asks me to close mine. I crank the knob. "She actually waited at our house for me to get back and made a list on our grocery pad so I could send a proper care package. Then she made sure the shelves were dusted. She said, 'You must keep the house immaculate.' In case they come to tell me William's dead, but she didn't say that." She flicks her cigarette outside and closes the window. "Too humid." She turns on the air. "I don't think they care what your house looks like, personally. Do you keep yours—" She taps the wheel. "Sorry."

I wonder, anyway, what they would think of my apartment. Maybe she's right. Maybe they wouldn't notice or care. But, maybe they would. Maybe they'd eye the underwear on the floor, or Chancey's vomit on the cat tree. Their first time doing it, their first time making that walk from the street to the front door, maybe they see nothing but the doorbell while they sturdy-up, prepare themselves for angry tears and wonder whether they'll be able to push out that first word. When the door opens, maybe they stand there, their first time, and hope they don't give in to nervous laughter. That they don't stutter or, in a moment of freak empathy, cry.

But after the fourth or fifth time, maybe they notice the weeds alongside the driveway haven't been pulled, that the yard isn't taken care of nearly as well as Mrs. Smith's, whose house they visited last week, and that some doors have doorbells and some have knockers and others have neither but are thin and hollow and sound like empty cigar boxes, clak, clak, clak—

"Which entrance?" Denise says.

—when they rap them with their knuckles.

"Whichever."

Denise flits from store—jewelry—to store—interiors—and I follow. The mall is crowded, loud, filled with weekend couples and mall-walkers. A teenage boy and teenage girl stand hand in hand at a belly-ring booth, thin fingers tightly woven—it will kill them to let go—while they choose from the gemstones in a revolving display. The boy's thumb strokes the girl's palm and their whole life is about this day and one another and a new belly ring. If one of them were shot where they stood, how long would it take for the other to walk away after their pinkies unlinked?

Denise is looking for a lamp for her hallway table, and she finds one quickly. While she pays I wonder about purchases, new favorite things that will end up lost or broken or taken for granted within the year. It won't be long before she'll need something else, some new color.

Denise trails her finger under her lampshade fringe on the way to the car and says something about how the sunlight makes it sparkle. She's decorated, too. Prettied-up in glinting red dangles and a white cotton tapestry, her legs upholstered in denim. Her new necklace, platinum, dips between her breasts, expensive garland. While the jewelry store cashier rang it up, Denise had winked at me and said, "Hazard pay."

A passing man in the parking lot smiles at her and Denise smiles back, says "Hi."

Her "hi" sounds single.

I get out of her car into the dark and a cold rain, a prelude to Tennessee's tornado season. She pulls away and honks before turning the corner.

Inside, dim light falls on a black cat sitting on the first landing, and I recognize it as the one belonging to the woman in apartment three. I've seen her take it out to the side lawn and walk with it in the grass on sunny days. I pet it, scratch its chin, and knock on the door and continue up the stairs. The sound of the door opening is followed by laughter, "Hi, Frankie!" and "Paul, look who's here," then a clicking latch. Once inside my kitchen, I hear them through the floor talking to the cat, asking where it's been and why it never called to say it would be late, and more laughter, all of it muffled but intelligible. I try to be happy that they sound happy.

Chancey meows from his food dish and I feed him before turning on the TV. The screen fills with tracer fire blazing over a city in shades of black and green, and a newsman wheezes into his microphone from inside a gas mask. "A serene, quiet day, to start," he says, ". . .but then, these brave men and women, stoic and professional, closed in on the city. As night fell on the soldiers, the action intensified something fierce, Janie and Tom, with multiple calls for protective and chemical gear. It was a race to the bunker, and, quite literally, it was a race for our lives." He promises nonstop, twenty-four seven coverage and says, optimistically, that this is just the beginning.

"Stay safe, Joe," says Janie.

"Seven more killed in the city of—" says Tom, before the station breaks for a commercial advertising heartburn medication.

Jake and I bought a lot of alcohol a week before he left to make sure we drank until we were good and drunk, but we were tired the night we tried and fell asleep halfway into the second glass, head-to-feet on the couch. The next morning Jake said, "We're a poor excuse for a young couple."

I should sleep, but I find orange juice in the refrigerator and smell it and check for mold before mixing two parts vodka with one part juice. I drink it, and many more like it, in front of the TV.

March 23

Jake,

How am I?

I try noit to lookg at youir pictures. Becaus, what if I jinx thingfs? When all you have is picctures, it starts top feel likje you're looking at relics or dead relatives, you kwno?

I smell yoru shirt sometimes, but not foten. Ofetn. Often. What if I sujck it all out? It's the one with the blue stripe anad th

laksdiojanfajgnoiglkjsdf

MARCH 24, MONDAY

SPACE HEATERS WARM the smoke-filled, bedroom-sized cabstand at the bottom of the Dunlop Street hill, and the air is thick and stale, trapped by plastic sheeting covering the windows. The door stays closed to keep in Puddin' and the dramatic lines of an eighties show bounce off grime-coated walls.

I cover my nose with my sweater cuff, pretending it's for warmth, and eye the remote control sitting by Shellie's phone.

"It was a long damn night," says Lenny, a night driver. "Day'll be worse." He counts money from one rolled bundle and pulls a separate wad from another pocket. He strips off a few bills and adds them to his fare pile. "Damn crackheads'll make me broke. They can all get AIDS, every one of 'em."

"We must find the size nine shoe," urges a TV detective.

Paula sets her cigarette in the ashtray and cleans her glasses with her T-shirt. "They get AIDS, they'll just give you AIDS."

"Paula, whyn't you—listen here, Shellie. Don't be lettin' 'em in here no more to sell their shit." Hay sticks to the bottom of Lenny's right sneaker and a condom box squares his shirt pocket. He takes it out and pretends to look for something on top of the file cabinet while tucking the box behind a stack of adult magazines, checking the window when headlights glow outside. Everyone but Paula pretends not to notice. "You get caught with one o' them whores and Georgia'll kick your ass and take those kids," she says.

"I ain't goin' to get caught, woman. Whyn't you mind your own damn business and worry about that kid of yours and how she's goin' to find out who her baby's daddy is."

Shellie picks up the remote control, turns up the volume, and sets it back down. It's closer, now. Just at the edge of the table.

It wouldn't kill her to watch the news for ten minutes.

"Oh, we know who he is," Paula says, "and he'll pay up. Believe me."

"Prob'ly will, poor bastard."

"Bastard is right." Her voice is smoke-scratched. She takes a drag from her cigarette and exhales over the table toward Shellie. Behind her on the bulletin board, yellowed edges curled since Shellie's return after her angioplasty, hangs the notice ordering all smoking to be done outside. "How you doin', Shellie? How's your heart?"

"Still tickin'." She holds up a fare sheet. "Lenny, you only gave me seventy-seven, but on your sheet, here, I got eighty-seven. Now, I can figure it again, but I already done it three—"

He digs in his front pocket and pulls out a ten. "Got stuck in my change pocket."

"M-hm. Try that again and Lionel'll get his foot stuck in your you-know-what."

Paula says, "Shellie, you're so polite, the way you talk. Come on. Say 'ass' for me."

"I don't want to say 'ass,' or I'd have said 'ass'," she says.

"Mia's sittin' over there thinkin' we're crazy," says Paula. "She ain't been around long enough yet to get used to us. Ain't that right, Mia? She's used to those college kids. Look at her all curled up on the couch. Girl, I know you gotta be on crack, you're so skinny. I can hardly see you in that couch. It swallows you up. Look at her, Shellie."

Lenny drops in a chair and throws his feet up on the table. "*She* ain't on crack."

Shellie winks at me. "You on crack, Mia?"

I have kept quiet because talking makes the sick feeling worse, but I say, "Do you mind if we watch the news?"

Shellie glances up at the TV, then at me, and says, "Well, I s'pose not, but this is almost over. Can you wait?"

A call comes in and she points at me and says, "Forty-eight Maple." I look at the TV. A villain topples over a balcony railing after being punched in the shoulder and Shellie says, "I know'd he was gonna get caught. He stepped in all them tomaters."

"It's tuh-may-*toes*, Shellie. Damn."

"Tomaters. That's how I say it."

I start to reach for the remote. Just two minu—

"Forty-eight Maple, Mia," Shellie says again, and Charlie— another day driver—says, "Did y'all hear about the Apache that went down this morning? It was just up there, up by Pembroke."

thank you thank you just Pembroke Jake's not in Pembroke

"Some kind of trainin' or somethin'. No one knows what happened."

They look at me the way people look at the sun.

Charlie plays with a book of matches. "I don't envy anyone over there, or anyone who's got someone over there, know what I mean? Too many of them boys don't come back."

I grab the cab keys from where Lenny left them on the table and gather my travel mug and fare-sheet clipboard. I pass between them, shoving Puddin' back with my foot to open the door.

The air smells like snow and soil, and the sky is near black with smears of clouds. A plump moon whitens the treetops and glimmers in the spiderweb crack on the window of car number seven, my car during the day, Lenny's at night. I climb in and step on hay—there's hay on the passenger-side mat, too—and turn on the radio and travel through the stations. Music, music, music, news!—but, it's local. Music. Flip to AM and there's nothing. I punch the buttons and the ashtray falls open and sitting there inside, a fat, half-smoked joint.

It's been years, but I haven't forgotten. Sweet, sweet apathy. Random, fading tangents.

Peace.

I pull it from the ashtray and hold it to my nostrils and close my eyes. It smells like nineteen, like the summer before my sophomore year in college. I would smoke in my living room and walk to the river and lie on my back under the sun. Grass poked through my hair and, behind me, bicycle wheels ticked past and the hum of distant conversations came and—

There's a loud rap on my window and Lenny's face is in the glass. "Gimme that."

I jump. The window doesn't work with the car off, so I open the door a crack.

"What the hell are you sniffin' it for?" he says. "You never seen a joint?"

"Is that what this is?" I knock a hand against the window and the half joint breaks into two white stubs, one falling to the floor of the cab, the other dropping on damp gravel.

Lenny says, "Aw, hell, Mia. That's just great."

"Oops."

He takes off his baseball cap and tugs at his hair and puts the cap back on. "You're lucky I got more," he says, and I say, "Or what?" but he ignores me and slams my car door and goes back into the cabstand. I pick up the half from the car floor, open the door to get the half from the ground, and put them both in the ashtray before pulling out of the lot. I drive under the tree canopy leading away from the cabstand. In the rearview mirror shine the taillights of Lenny's wife's Cadillac parking in the spot I left, his children's heads silhouetted in the back seat.

Forty-eight Maple is a two-story house in the nicer part of the not-so-nice side of town, so I don't mind waiting on the street in the dark. Still, I lock my doors.

A shadow appears on the other side of the fogged glass and knocks on the passenger window. I push the lever to "unlock."

A man, late fifties, maybe, slides in and closes the door. He wears faded jeans and a black T-shirt with a hole in the neck seam. He smiles, says "Mornin'," and I move my knees left. Fares sit too close, so close I can smell their breath and see the creases in their fingers and the yellow of their nails. This one has clean fingernails, a little long, and the skin on the back of his hand is like paper draped over his veins. I say "Morning" back, and he says, "Mind if I smoke?"

"If you don't mind opening your window."

He lights his cigarette. "Smells like liquor, in here. You smell that?"

"No." I hadn't woken up with time enough to shower.

He gives the address of a construction site ten miles out. "I'm supposed to be there at seven," he says, and it's six fifty-five. "Y'all usually get here faster."

"There was some confusion with the shift change."

"Charlie on a run, or somethin'? He usually drives me."

"I was up."

He holds his cigarette close to the window and exhales into the wind. "I'm Donny," he says. "Donaldson."

"Donny, for short?"

"Nope. Donald Donaldson." He salutes. "Doctor."

"Mia," I say, not curious. I tilt the vents to blow the smoke toward his window.

"You coulda said you don't want me smokin'," he says. "I can wait." He takes a long final drag and flicks his cigarette outside. "This'll be a good job. I needed it. Been out for a while 'cause of my back, but it's time to work again. I was goin' crazy sittin' at home, you know? Got to spend time with the wife, but I just had to get out an' do somethin'. I get stir crazy."

The sun is in the rearview mirror, a sliver of fire over the trees.

"I'll finally be able to pay to get my jeep fixed," he says. "The wife's car works, but she has to use it, you know. If our schedules worked out better she'd drop me off, but she don't got to be at work 'til nine, and she gets home real late, sometimes. So she's tired in the mornin'."

I say "Mm" and think about where I'm dropping him off, try to remember if there are any shrouded areas, secluded roads, empty lots to park in.

"Next week's our four-year anniversary," he says and lights another cigarette. "Don't feel like it, though. Feels like we just got married. I love that woman to death." He holds his pack out to me.

"No, thanks."

"She's an angel. A beautiful angel. She's hangin' in the hallway." He laughs. "Her portrait, I mean. *She* ain't hangin' in the hallway." His laughter fades. "You might be pretty, but it ain't goin' to do you much good if you don't got a sense of humor."

"Pardon me?"

"Pardon you. You didn't laugh. It was a joke." He slaps his knee. "You didn't think it was funny?"

"Sure it was funny."

"Most people laugh when they think somethin's funny. What're you, havin' a bad day already at—" he looks at his watch, "ten 'til seven?"

"I'm fine."

"Don't get mad," he says. "I'm happy Donny. Donny Donaldson. Happy." He smiles and his thick mustache hangs over the corners of his mouth. His hair, graying slightly and curling up over his ears and at the base of his neck, is messy from the open window. Thick lenses magnify brown eyes.

I ask, "How long did you know her before you were married," and open my own window.

"Forever." He waves a knobbed hand in front of him. "Friends since we was kids, then started seein' each other some years back. Used to go out together, you know, to the bars, but after we got married she liked to stay home, didn't want me goin' out after work. I did for a bit, but it got to be a hassle. I don't want to fight with her. She's my life."

"But you'd think you could go out every now and then."

"What do you mean?"

"Just that—"

"You don't know what I should do, and you don't know nothin' about me or her. I wasn't sayin' nothin' bad about my wife. Got that?" He raps the dashboard.

"I get it," I say, and I want to ask him to please not be mad at me. I open my eyes wide and blink and blink.

"Well, I know where you was goin' with it. It's okay. I understan'. But you don't know us. She was an angel when I met her and she still is. She was sick and I helped her. Doctor Donaldson." He gives another soldier's salute, fingers stiff and straight, then tosses the filter, all that's left of his cigarette, outside. "I go home after work, nowadays," he says. "Which is all fine, if you think about it, 'cause I get to see her more. Plus, we keep plenty of beer in the fridge."

We reach an intersection near an industrial construction site. "It ain't that one," he says. "Take a right." I turn into the suburbs. After a few blocks, I see it. Three houses are being built in a cul-de-sac as an addition to an established neighborhood. Red clay, soon to be topped with sod, surrounds the two-story structures.

"I'm at the second house," he points.

It could be any one of the town's middle-class developments, each house modeled from one of three basic designs and plotted in a simple type A, type B, type C-and-repeat pattern, with one or two façade variations. Brick here, siding there, yellow shutters on one, black on the other. Lawns like putting greens, flat-topped hedges, and no trees other than one or two saplings planted out front in a circle of pink bricks. Jake wants to buy a house one day and would take me to these neighborhoods to windowshop. He'd pause at the ones with tall doors, white pillars, and impossibly round shrubs, and I told him once I wanted an old house with roots growing up through the basement and slanted floors and a jungle for a back yard. "Back yard jungles have spiders," he said, "and you hate spiders as much as I do. Besides. Do you know how much it would cost to repair a cracked foundation?" And he was right. We agreed to meet in the middle, between a museum and a shack, between a sparse, manicured garden and an acre overrun by ivy and weeds.

"Here's good," Donny says and hands me a twenty. "Keep it."

"It's only thirteen."

"Don't want the tip?" He takes the bill from me and pulls a ten and three ones from his wallet and winks, puts it in my palm. "A lesson for next time. I'm sure I'll be seein' you," he says. "Smile more. It's a beautiful life." He slams the door and walks into the clay and I notice for the first time how short he is.

I'm wrestling with the shift lever to slide it into 'reverse' when he comes back to the car and leans into my window, one hand resting on the roof.

"You off at six?"

"Yes."

"Whyn't you come on back at five-thirty," he says.

A berry of some kind, dried and brown, falls from a branch hanging over the hood of the cab, *plank*, and rolls off and lands in tall grass. It's quiet here, minus the birds. Two of them splash in a puddle in a dip in the dirt road, the first turnoff from the two-lane highway out of town. A cluster of trees, blossoming green, shades the path with narrow veins and almost hides my cab parked at a slant on the shoulder, half on the path and half in the ditch. If a police car should come by, I'll say I was sleepy and couldn't drive without a nap. The smoke is going away, the last bit of the first half burning to ash in the ashtray.

"Mia, girl—you hear me?"

Usually, from this far out, Shellie can't reach me. I consider not answering. Charlie disappears for hours at a time, and we all know he's just pretending to be out of range.

The mic won't be wedged off of its dashboard clip. I lean forward until my lips touch the black holes and press the button and say, "Yes."

"You 'bout ready to clear?"

I look at my watch. It's been twenty minutes since I left Donny. "Almost. He's checking on a ride. He might want me to come back for him."

"Well," she says, "if he takes much longer you tell him to call back, or start chargin' him. I need you to go to 124 Lincoln."

"I'm way out."

"I don't got no one else," she says. "Tell me when you're on the road."

I lean back in the chair and close my eyes. Ten minutes to be hypnotized by blowing grass that sounds like rain, to lose myself in the words of a teenager singing about lost love and life choices, her voice too thin for such a subject.

Over the radio Shellie says, "The weatherman just came on my tellie and said there's a tornado watch. Be careful. I'll tell you if it gets to a warnin'. Mia, you clear, yet?"

I reach out and press the button. "No."

"Well, give it another minute and then come back in. Lincoln's still waitin'."

The sky lasts forever. Fast-moving clouds slide by and wind snaps in the window and I wonder what it would be like to be taken by a tornado, where I would land, if it might drop me on a different plane, somewhere more colorful. The breeze is warm and shadows slide across the windshield like snakes, the movements as unpredictable as my future with Jake, here and gone, and Jake is like the shadow, the snake, a crease in my life, a long, shiny snake climbing his tree above the dirt whipping up from the base of the trunk and spraying against the windshield.

"Mia. I need you, girl. You clear?"

The rain comes, heavy drops pounding the roof, dripping on my thigh through the crack in the windshield. I lower the visor to catch the water and tug the mic from the base.

"Yes," I say. "Clear. Thirteen dollars."

"One twenty-four Lincoln," she says. "Hurry so we don't lose him."

By three o'clock, the storm threat has passed and calls have slowed and I can stop for lunch. I pull into the lot of a diner across the street from the river and the song I was listening to is replaced by the day's news.

Fighting in a province earlier today—Jake's evening—included an air strike. The woman says in her even and lulling voice that there were eleven U.S. casualties.

I listen for more, but she's on to approval ratings and then the goings-on in China. This, the only station airing news, and it also happens to be the only station on the radio that cares what's going on in any country anywhere in the world that has nothing to do with America and this goddamn war in Iraq and she's talking about China. I cram my thumb into the buttons, one through five, but it's all rock and country.

"What'll it be?" Her apron brushes the table and she waits with no pen, no notepad.

They have a TV in the corner, but it's not on. "Can you turn on your TV?"

"Sorry, hon. Broken. Get you anything to eat?"

"Do you have a radio, or…?"

"Sorry."

I look out at the car. "Just—just eggs, I guess."

"Omelet? Scrambled? Fried? We have lots of omelets on the menu, with—"

"I don't know. Fried? I don't know."

"Over easy, over hard, sunny-side up?"

"An egg is an egg, isn't it? I mean, isn't it? I just want an egg or a piece of bacon. A slice of cheese." She opens her mouth and I say, "Sorry. Just eggs. And toast. With some different jellies."

"How d'you want—"

"Over medium, please." And sleep, please. A long, black sleep, and hold the dreams.

When she walks away, her reflection in the glass is transposed over the passing cars on the street and the slow-moving river behind the trees on the bank. Jake took me there, to the Scenic Walk—a quarter-mile, pink cobblestone path along the river—when I first moved to town. "See?" he said. "It's not all franchise restaurants and pawnshops."

There's not much of the side of town L.D. Cab caters to that I haven't come to know uncomfortably well. Juniper runs into Golf Club runs into Crossland runs into Lily. Mike, the divorced events director for the downtown museum, lives on Juniper, and he spends the night with a tired twenty-something woman in her run-down apartment on Golf Club. She uses L.D.'s for a ride to Crossland, where she buys drugs from a man who calls at a quarter to seven every morning for a ride to work at the car wash on Lily.

Now and then, I've found myself looking for hints of the town's inner loveliness.

The waitress sets a blue plate in front of me and uncooked egg white oozes onto the chipped porcelain. Cold pats of butter top each toast triangle and a small bowl holds a pile of square, plastic jelly packets, all grape.

"Is there any way to avoid—you list'nin'?—to avoid, for just one day of our lives, wishin' we were the bleached blonde, forty-somethin' drunk livin' in a basement apartment? Now, I don't want to be no woman, don't get me wrong, but this one lives under me and she don't leave 'til noon, and when she does she comes back 'bout ten minutes later carryin' some kind of bottle in a brown bag, the top all wrapped 'round the neck, like she'd been twistin' it the whole way home." A new fare, he sits in the back but leans forward between the two front seats, his left hand trapping a single strand of my hair while he grips my seat. His right hand, cigarette between two fingers, is slung over the back of the passenger-side headrest. "I mean, what would our responsibilities really be then, aside from tryin' not to get beat up? Her boyfriend kicks her 'round, some, sure—you would, too—but 'side from that, what? We'd eat mac and cheese, drink gin, and take naps 'til it gets dark, and the next day we'd start all over again." Ash falls on the seat and he says "Sorry" and leans over to swipe it to the floor.

"I'll get it later."

"I mean," he says, "look at me. I work at a damn grocery store. Worked there for years, probably since before you were born, and long as I can remember this fat man comes through once every three days buyin' the same thing every damn time. TV dinners, chicken with mashed potatoes and a brownie for dessert. Four seventy-five, four seventy-five, four seventy-five. 'Jesus,' I said to myself when he come through today, 'don't this guy eat nothin' else?' Four seventy-five, four seventy-five. Liked t' drive me crazy. And then there it was. A sack of potatoes. 'Thank God,' I said to myself. 'Potatoes!'" He laughs and lights a new cigarette with the dying butt of the other. "I got to deal with this man every three damn days with his stacks of chicken dinners, and that woman downstairs don't have to do nothin' but get drunk. That'd be the life," he says. "Wonder where she gets her money? The boyfriend don't do nothin' that I know of, so they must get their money from the state. Damn beggars. Got to get off the booze and get a damn paycheck. Y'hear me?"

"I hear you."

"Worked hard my whole life," he says. "Raised my three boys when my wife left me and never got help from no one, never complained. Got no reason to complain. I love my boys and took good care of 'em." His fingers curl, uncurl. "Damn good care.

They're grown, now. Gone." He slides back in his seat and stares out the window.

I don't know what to say, so I ask him if he likes any particular kind of music. "Naw, it don't matter," he says, and I turn it to a country station. He moves his mouth with the words to a song I've never heard.

When I get him home, it's ten past five and afternoon traffic slows the drive to the construction site. At a red light I take the second white stub from the ashtray, twist the end tight, and when the signal turns green I lower the windows and light it.

The construction site looks vacant when I get there, so I park and—having given up on getting anymore news—sit back and change the radio station to something less dead-dog *saaaaad*. Scattered footprints flatten the patch of clay, such reddy-orange clay and so bright under my headlights, and what was this morning a popsicle-stick construction is evolving, growing. A toddler of a house. Sheets like corkboard fill the gaps between beams and I can see the makings of the cul-de-sac's pattern: B, A, C, this one. I press the horn, forgetting it's broken, then open the window and yell, "Cab!" It's so *dark* out there.

I flip down the visor and turn on the roof light and check my hair in the mirror. Messy from the wind, and mascara blurs the skin under my eyes. I lick my finger and rub at the smear and tuck my hair behind my ears, but there is no difference. My face is pale, skim-milky, and the gray under my eyes won't be wiped away. Whatever prettiness he saw earlier is gone, long long gone, covered by hours and street grime. I scrub harder, until the skin turns red, then slap up the visor and watch the trailer and lock my doors, because who knows what lurks out there at the edges? I open the window again, scream "Cab!" and close it again and wait. The trailer door opens and a hand emerges from the darkness, one finger held up. *Wait.* I slide down the window again. "I have to go," I yell, my voice frantic instead of strong, and he steps-one, steps-two down the stairs with his free hand clutching the railing, then staggers to the car with a beer can, his boots dragging through the clay.

He gets in and slams the door, slurps his beer. He smells, not like smoke but like the inside of a smoke-filled lung, like skin saturated with the straight nicotine of one hundred cigarettes, and when he turns toward me his head lolls like a baby's. "Hi, beautiful," he says, and his breath carries vomit.

Orange streetlights pass over the hood, the windshield, Donny's hand. His fingers tap his thigh to the music on the radio. His other hand holds his beer against his stomach and the aluminum makes hollow popping sounds under clenching fingers. "Good day," he says. "It was a good day. Sheathin' today, trusses tomorrow." He looks at me. "The roof."

I nod and smile. "Right." I turn up the radio.

"You're very pretty," he yells, and "very" and "pretty" run together to sound like "vurpurdy." His head falls on a shoulder and he watches me.

"Thank you," I yell.

"You don't mean that."

"Sure, I do," I say.

He shakes his head. "Nah. You don't mean it. You—hey, you wanna turn that down?"

I turn it down.

"Hurt your ears, that way, music so loud you can't hear yourself talk or nothin'. What I was sayin' was, you said—what was…? Yeah. You said 'thank you, oh thank you, mister Donaldson,' like you— you looked at me and saw…you didn't look at me, but I saw your face, and you didn't mean it. You said it like you're a robot, or like you think I want to have sex with you just 'cause I say you're pretty."

"Like a robot?" But that *is* what I think when they're drunk, when they slur *Gee, honey, you must make a lotta tips*, or *You sure are a bitch, ain't you?* It's what I think when they won't just sit there and look straight out the window.

"A robot," he says. "No emotions." He pounds his chest. "You say thank you but you mean Fuck you, you old man, you pervert. Sure, I'm old. Older than you, seen stuff you'll never see. But not old, not an old person. So what if I say you're pretty?" He tips his can into his mouth, but it's empty. He sets it on the floor and holds it between his feet. "You're beautiful. What's wrong with sayin' that? It don't mean I want to take you home, don't even mean I like you. Everyone has beauty." He presses his palm to his chest. "There's beautiful people all over. It don't mean Donny's sayin' 'Fuck me'."

"Okay. I get it."

"It don't mean I think you're more beautiful than no one else. I knew this ugly woman once—no joke, she was damn ugly—but she was still the most beautiful person I ever met. Ever. You ain't got nothin' on her." He shakes his head and picks up his can again, tries to drink from it, and puts it back between his feet. "Stop at that gas station there so I can get some beer." He slides his window up and down. "If I'm to put up with this bullshit I need some beer."

"What bullsh—"

He pounds the armrest. "You don't know what I seen, don't know what kind of man I am, but you sit there and think I'm tryin' to get you into my bed, just a kid. What're you, twenty?"

"Twenty-six." I pull in and park by the door.

"Don't know nothin'. Don't know me or what I seen and you think you can judge me. I'm old enough to be your daughter." He picks up his can and gets out of the car, and on his way inside drops it in the trash.

I check the dashboard clock—five fifty-two—and pick up the mic. "Shellie."

"Yes, little miss Mia?"

"We stopped at a gas station, so it'll be few more minutes."

"Okey-dokey. Dollar for the stop. Tell me when you get your gas."

Donny's house is on the way to the cabstand, so I drive over to the pumps and stand by the trunk while the tank fills, hands in my pockets to keep warm. The night air is a strange mix of cool and muggy. Inside, the gas station looks inviting, warm and alive under bright white fluorescents. A girl in short sleeves mops the back of the store near the coolers, behind the bright reds and blues of chip bags and cracker boxes and sacks of candy. She steps aside for Donny and he lifts his six-pack in a thank-you, carries it to the front and stands in line behind

Jake

it has to be Jake same height same uniform jesus oh god there he is it looks just like him

a man in BDUs, just some man. One who hasn't left, yet, or who's come back, for whatever reason. He pushes open the door while stuffing a chew tin in his pocket and the door swings closed behind him. He stops to put on his hat and nods at me and smiles. I turn away and pretend to check the dollar amount on the pump and lean, not entirely steady, against the car and touch my face, hot. Sweat stings my hair follicles. If my heart keeps doing this I'll have an attack and fall dead at the Yancy Street BP and no one will know but Donny—Donny and L.D.'s, because Lenny will come looking for the car. Jake is my only emergency contact—that needs changing—so no one will know who to call and my body—

"What the hell!"

—will be left in a Dumpster behind the gas station.

Donny cuts across the way with his arms held over his head, one of them dangling silver and blue cans.

"I look out and you're gone and I don't know how I'm goin' to get home!" He laughs. "Damn, girl, I thought you left me. Thought I was goin' to have to call Lionel and tell him to fire you." He winks and gets in the car and I finish up and pull back onto the road.

"You saw that man?" he says.

"Mm."

He salutes. "That's me. Donny Donaldson. Airborne. Vietnam," he says. "*Doctor* Donaldson. I took care of 'em. You know." He holds out his arm and pushes up his sleeve and uses an invisible needle to push an invisible injection into a shockingly dark blue vein. "Gave 'em morphine when they needed it. Saved their lives. Some of 'em young, younger than you, for sure. Eighteen, one of 'em. Can't remember his name. I try, nights, but I just can't. 'N' somethin'. Nesbitt. Nelson. Nur—Nur-somethin'. Don't know. Don't know, don't know, and you'd think I'd..." He draws a set of stripes in the fog on his window. "I come back here, and..."

I ask because I think he wants me to. "What?"

"Never came home," he says. "Not here. No one saw Donny, no one was there, didn't..." He trails off and pokes at his can. "Bullshit!" He leans close to the window and his hair leaves squiggled lines on the glass. "Hurry up. I don't feel like talkin'."

It takes about a minute to reach his house. At the curb he says, "Come in with me."

"I can't. I have to get the car back."

"So what? Get the car back. Then come on over in your own car. Have a beer."

"Thanks, but I have to get home. And your wife..."

"What 'bout my wife?"

"Well, I mean—she must want to see you, because you said that she's—anyway, it's dark out, and everything."

"So what if it's dark?"

"I should get home, is all."

"She'd love you," he says. "I want you to meet you. Aw! Hear that, what I just—sometimes, I just don't—what it was, what I meant to say, 's that I want *you*… to meet *her*."

"Sorry. Really. I can't."

Donny rubs his feet together to break off some of the dried clay. "Well. Another time."

"Mm."

"You're an angel. Now, don't look at me that way. You are. A beautiful angel." He digs in his pocket. "How much?"

"Same as always."

"Well," he says, "I don't remember right now how much that is. Whyn't you just tell me, goddamn it?"

"Thirteen," I say, and that heat comes back to my eyes, so I pretend to scratch them. "I mean, fourteen. It's fourteen. Because of the stop—dollar for the stop."

"A damn dollar for a stop? Charlie don't charge a dollar. What the hell's goin' on, over there? I got to talk to Lionel about this." He hands me a twenty. "Keep it this time." He wipes the window with his sleeve and looks out at his house. One room, the one with the largest window—living room, probably—shows light behind the curtain. The rest of the house is dark. He pushes open the door and gets out, leading with the beer. "Careful out there, y'hear?"

Lenny takes ownership of the cab with a football team's jacket slung over his arm and, "How'd you enjoy that joint? Don't even pretend to be miss perfect, 'cause I know you kept it and smoked it. I shoulda charged you for the damn thing," before getting in the car. He opens the window to yell, "Next time fill the damn thing up all the way, goddamn it! I'm bringin' it back in the mornin' a quarter tank gone."

As soon as I'm through the door I ask Shellie to turn on the news, and I watch it while she collects her money and Lionel's money and the government's money. I leave with fifty-one dollars and fifteen minutes of a news fix, just enough to assure me Jake is safe. His unit wasn't part of the air strike.

I try not to divide fifty-one by twelve, try to fight the instinct to calculate the day's earnings, but I can't help it. On the way home I don't stop at the drive-through coffee shop for my day-end treat, and I don't stare out at the glimmer of the lights reflecting on the black, rippled surface of the river. Four twenty-five an hour is what I'm thinking. I take the roads by rote, stop reflexively at stop signs and red lights, brake for a loose dog without flinching and toss the bills in the air and watch them fall on the floor, flutter to rest under the emergency brake handle, make a star on the passenger seat.

At home, Chancey's food bowl is empty. I fill it. Slime layers the bottom of his water dish. I rinse it and pour him fresh water. I close the curtains. Rinse my travel mug for morning and set it beside the coffee pot. Straighten throw rugs. Slide the left corner of the oversized chair an inch forward because it isn't in line with the rug. Turn on the news, and it is a brown morning and four are reported dead from a firefight. Look at the machine for a blinking message light. The window displays a rectangular, red '0'.

Hum-de-fucking-dum.

Sleep doesn't come. One in the morning and the room is television-blue and my legs make shadows like waves under the comforter. Chancey lies curled between my feet, a furry raft. I flip over and he readjusts. I flip again and he jumps down and waits on the floor, watches me punch my pillow into shape and jerks at the high-pitched squeal of the television turning off.

I turn it back on and make sure nothing happened in the seconds it was off and find a volume that isn't too loud, but that I don't have to strain to hear.

Blankets tangle down at my feet and I hold his shirt close with one hand, eyes closed tight, and I think so hard the pressure pounds my ears like wind. Trying too hard, trying too hard, and it never works that way. "Just relax," he would whisper with a soft touch and then go back to it until, indeed relaxed, I finished. But this is different. This is…if I could just separate, split myself in two, or lose my mind entirely, I could do it. If, if, if.

I stuff his shirt under his pillow and pull up the blankets, cold now, and press the volume button.

"…saying 'No' to any hostage negotiations. And in Minnesota, truckers driving, on average, ten miles over the speed limit. See how this could affect…"

MARCH 26, WEDNESDAY

March 26

Jake,

I hate this fucking war. I hate the President and I hate congress and I want each of them to wonder if it's possible that the one person they think they couldn't live without died an hour ago. No, three hours. And all that time, those three hours, they'll have gone on with life as usual and with no idea they should be mourning. (It's strange, you know, to think that you could die and I could not know. How could I not know?)

It's just today. I don't feel like this every day.

But you can't know that.

So I guess I won't send this one, either

eijgjklkjlskljsfd

March 26

Jake,

Hi! How are you?

Okay. So I lied. I'm writing.

Chancey and I are great! We watch the news together at night and he snacks on the Christmas tree during the day (I'm working toward taking it down). Driving is the same as ever…some good money days (someone needed a ride to the airport yesterday, so I brought home $100), and some bad (the day before: $51). I'm still thinking about quitting, so I hope the offer you made before you left was serious. I might need your money!

I see Army men walking around, every now and then, and every time I do, it's like…it's…I don't know if you can know what it's like; you won't until you see a brunette girl about five feet tall wearing an orange t-shirt like mine, jeans like mine, and sandals like mine.

Somehow, I don't think that'll happen where you are. But it's nice to think I see you!

I hope you're doing well! Six months won't be so long, really, if we just take it easy.

Sorry this is short, but I just got back from work and you know how tired I am when I come home.

More soon!

Love love love,
Mia

A DENSE CLOUD cover darkens the stairwell and the automatic lights are hours from their timed lighting, so the passageway is quiet, as if abandoned, and I feel like a ghost or an intruder. Halfway to the ground-floor mailboxes, I smell a thick spice, curry maybe, and something clanks behind number three's door—a spoon in a pot?—and then there is chopping, chopping, something on a block, and humming that matches the smell of whatever it is she's cooking. And then there is another—familiar—odor.

Just one would be all right. Just one cigarette after all that writing, or to celebrate sleep, maybe. I've been good, and a joint doesn't count.

I knock on the door.

"One minute," she says, and after a second or two opens the door. Two brown braids, hanging from underneath a yellow scarf tied around her head, fall just to her shoulders. "My upstairs neighbor," she sings, hands held in front of her, palms up, touching nothing. Two cats, one black and one gray, sit at her feet like statues with tails curled around their hind legs. Behind her in the kitchen, a mosaic of foods in cubes on the counter.

I sneeze from the curry.

The gray cat creeps toward the door and she nudges it back with her foot. "I am Safia," she says.

"Mia."

She waits and I stand in the hallway. Cigarette smoke snakes through the air from somewhere inside.

"Is there something…?"

"Oh, sorry," I say. "I just—I was making sure you had your cats. I was the one—"

"You knocked on my door!" She bends to pet the black cat with her wrist. "Frankie. Always breaks free!"

"Well—okay. I mean, good. Frankie is here."

"Yes," she says, "but he gets no more treats." She stands again and waits again and sniffs and rubs her wrist under her nose. She steps back and waves and says, "Thank you," and closes her door.

I take the stairs down and leave my letter to Jake on the shelf for outgoing mail.

Back in my living room, the message light blinks '1.'

Jake.

I sit at the desk, but I can't, so I stand, leaning close to the machine to miss nothing.

"Mia," says the voice that isn't Jake's. "Donny. Donaldson…You home? Issa weekend. Saturday. I need a ride." The sound of a lighter lighting, an inhale, an exhale. "I don't need a ride. . .Where are you?. . .I, uh…no one gave me your number. I got it from the book. Remembered your name from that card…You know, that…your ID, on the dashboard. Anyhow…I won't call again…But I wanted to tell you. Party tonight. You know where…Come over. Bring friends…Or don't. This is Donny. Bye."

I press the delete button. It doesn't register. I push it again.

"To delete all messages, press the 'delete' button again."

I press it again.

"All messages deleted." A steady red '0'.

Something glimmers, sparkles, takes my attention away from the desk. Balls. Four of them, silver, dangle from stiff branches the color of rust. The rest have fallen. Slipped off when dried needles snapped. Batted down by Chancey and soccer-kicked around the apartment until they were lost to the dark spaces under furniture. A single light strand droops between boughs. The tree leans left and the skirt is a bundled mess of fake velvet. Chancey sleeps curled around the stand.

Across town there is a party. A strange house filled with strangers, secret smiles and private jokes. No phone—not mine—to wait for, and watching TV would be considered poor form.

I put on a different pair of jeans, clean and smelling of a fabric softener, and brush my hair and draw on a layer of lipstick. I look in the mirror and wipe it off, but it stains, in a nice way, I suppose; like my lips, if lips could be, are flushed. I turn on the TV to watch a little, just a little, with an equally little drink, and not a strong one. Not too strong. I bring it to the living room and sit down, and on the screen a sun as perfect and white as a hole punched from paper balances atop the sharp point of a mountaintop.

"Another morning here," says a man's voice from behind the image, "and another day for things to go extraordinarily well, or to go horribly, horribly wrong. With each sunrise there is new promise, but that can be a promise of something good or, as we know too well, Janie and Tom, it can be an omen. Yes. A promise of another kind, of something terrible to come." A red filter covers the sun in blood. "After last night, we could sure use a good day. An intense battle raging for five hours, both in the air *and* on the ground, losing a reported twenty-five soldiers and marines, and killing approximately one hundred of theirs. And, as you know, Janie and Tom, that's the highest death count we've had on our side in one day since the start of the war." Janie says they'll get back to him after these messages, but his voice carries on in my head: *Your soldier— that's right, yours!—could be one of the dead. Tune in at six to find out if you're today's winner of an elegant trumpeted service and a brand new, gen-you-ine American flag courtesy of the American Honor Guard!* I wonder if they have a board marked up with tally lines, "their side" and "our side," each soldier a Roman numeral one. Jake. I. William. I.

I. I. I. I. I. I.
I. I. I. I. I. I.
I. I. I. I. I. I.
I. I. I. I. I. I.

Jackasses.

I finish my drink and follow it with another, stronger. Tie my hair in a ponytail. Change from jeans to Jake's flannel pants and a T-shirt. Give Chancey water. Sit in front of the TV and watch more news and make another drink. Each one tastes more like orange juice, so I add more vodka, and more vodka, and the treetop leans closer to the floor and the balls hang in a smile. A popular sticker comes to mind, a yellow smiley face with a bullet hole in the forehead dripping red. Kids in school, the smokers, would wear them as patches on their jean-jackets when patches and pins were in. I had one, too, ironed onto my jacket's shoulder like a tattoo. Because cool kids burned things, I would hold the cherry of my cigarette to the bullet hole until, over time, a real hole burned through to denim. "Nice dimension," Jake said one day during our lunch break, his smoking habit new, the cigarette still awkward in his fingers.

I leave my glass on the floor and hug the wall on the way down the stairs to apartment three. I rap one, two, three, four tim—

"Who is it?"

"It's Mia," I say.

"Who's 'me'?" says the voice.

"No," I say. "Mia. From upstairs."

"Ohhh," he says, and the door opens. He has the hair and complexion of a Viking, an interesting contrast to the thin-stemmed wine glass he holds with graceful fingers. "Hello," he says. Safia comes up behind him cradling a half-empty fishbowl, the goldfish skimming a thin layer of green and blue rocks. It swims left, sucks at the water, then swims right.

I ask them for a cigarette. "I would buy my own, but I quit smoking a year ago, and if I buy a new pack, I'll smoke them all by midnight, and I'm just having a really—"

"No problem," he says, and to Safia, "I think they're on the kitchen table, doll." She looks at him, then carries the bowl away.

"Thank you …"

"Paul."

"Mia."

"I know." He smiles.

Safia reappears with the pack in her hand, one filter poking out. I take it, say, "Thank you both so much," and ask for a light. Paul gives me one from his pocket and tells me to keep it.

When I'm inside, home with the cat and my walls, and my door is closed and I'm sitting on the floor beside my drink, I take the first drag, deep. The smoke is thick and rough in my throat and the lightheadedness that comes halfway through mixes with traces of nausea. Chancey crawls out from under the tree and lifts his nose to the smoke, then recoils and leaves the room.

Jake wouldn't like that I'm smoking. Even so—or as a result, what the hell—every drag is better than the last. I blow the smoke at the tree and envelop it in fog, in lake mist, in the cloud that precedes a charging fire. I picture the toxins filling my lungs, damaging the cilia, leaving a black, ashy film on what it took me so long to re-pink. Months of smoking four a day, three a day, to none. Before today, I hadn't smoked a cigarette in six months.

Maybe he'll get shot down this year, and maybe I'll get cancer. The odds have to be weaker against both of us.

DENISE PULLS ASIDE the dressing room curtain and waits in a floor-sweeping red gown for me to say something. She reaches behind her neck and gathers her hair in a loose nest. "It's so expensive, but I just love it."

"Are you buying it?" I wonder where she'll wear it, what plans she has.

"It'd be silly not to. It's perfect." She shakes out her hair. "Aren't you going to try one?"

"I don't think so."

"Oh, come on. I saw a yellow one I think would look stunning."

She grabs my wrist with one hand and raises her hem with the other. "This way." She stops at a rack of satin and sequins and drapes my arm in something yellow, then shoves me into a dressing room and says, "Don't come out until you have it on."

The bench in the dressing room—a closet, really—is a hollow plywood box that creaks when I sit. On the floor: a price tag, a knotted piece of black string, and a white button. I pick up the button and put it in my pocket, then hang the dress on the hook and take off my pants and sit in front of the mirror. The lighting they use drops shadows in dimples in my skin that never show in the mirror at home. The hanger spins and spins around the rod when I yank off the gown. I slide it over my naked legs.

Out there, between dressing rooms or in a room near mine, two girls—teens, I judge by their 'likes' and 'ums'—talk about jeans, which ones the boys like, which ones they won't buy because boys don't ask out the girls in the jeans that sit too close to the belly button. One of them says *tell me about it*, and the other says she and Bobby had sex for the first time two nights ago, so she thinks she's ready for the really low waistline because her mom always said super-low-rise jeans were for *those girls*, and now she, finally, is one of them.

The friend says *omigod*, because she and Daniel had sex for the first time two months ago, and she had thought *she* was way behind.

They bring to mind my own first time, years ago, in a one-person tent on a lakeside sand-and-gravel clearing. Pit-sparks popped and fireflies blinked and dead-skunk smell drifted over from the highway behind the trees. I remember his name, but it—he—is little more than scenery in the larger memory. When it was over, we went for a walk. "Was everything…all right?" he said. Fine, I told him, wondering what "all right" would have been.

One of them squeals at something and the other says "Oh my god!" but I don't find out why. Only giggles follow, and whispers.

I don't really want to try on the dress. Where to wear it, anyway?

The satin falls in waves to my ankles. I rub it, take it between my thumb and fingers and slide one layer against the other, feel the ribbed resistance in the fine grain. Silk-smooth and slippery.

My first efforts had failed because—maybe—the blankets were too heavy, or the air too cold. The cat was making too much noise or the downstairs neighbors would hear or I couldn't stand the way my own hands felt because they shouldn't have been mine.

But here in this nowhere, I am nobody. All memories exist on the other side of the curtain.

And that's all it takes, really.

"Is it on, yet?" Denise's voice comes from somewhere down the line of dressing rooms.

The first time we kissed, his hair was long and thick and my hand caught in the coarseness of it circling my fingers like netting.

"Not yet," I say, and I hope she doesn't come in, but to make sure, I say, "Don't come in." I get up only to slide my jeans beneath me, then sit back down, barely feeling the seam that presses into the skin on the underside of my thigh. My body surprises me, the reaction more immediate than I would have expected, and the rest comes just as quickly, my breath held.

We stand in front of a three-way mirror. I can't deny the yellow is flattering.

"You look gorgeous," she says.

"So do you." And she does—a Renaissance-era painting, full and rosy and dark. Her eyes are narrow and as dark as her hair. "Yes," she says and turns to me. "You should get yours, too."

"I thought you were buying the other one."

"I'll get both."

I show her the price tag hanging from my strap.

"And? Mine's four twenty-five."

"Which one?"

"This one. The other one is only two hundred."

"You can afford those?"

"Hazard pay." She spins to make the dress fan. "He said he wants me to keep myself happy while he's gone. He didn't say how." She bends forward, inspects her cleavage, uses cupped hands to nudge them high. "I might need this taken in, some. You think?"

"I don't know."

"I think I will. I don't want to look saggy like his mother. Did I tell you she called?"

"No."

"Does Jake's mom call you?"

"No. I mean, sometimes."

"William's called yesterday," she says, and then, "Come on." She leads me back to our dressing rooms. "And every few days before that. 'Have you heard from William?' 'How's the house?' What does she mean, 'How's the house'? What could happen to it?" She holds my arms straight out. "My god, it really is stunning on you, just like I said it would be. You have to buy it, and you have to come with me to the party. Look." She pushes me past the curtain and holds me in front of the mirror. I don't know that 'stunning' is the word, but I do like what I see, for a change. The way the padded bodice adds more than a cup size. The way the rest clings to my hips and waist. I swivel to this side and to that side and the bottom sways. I am a bell, a wind-dancing daffodil.

"See?" She sticks her face in the mirror, then opens her mouth and digs clumps of lipstick from the corners with her fingernail.

"What party?" I say.

"Some of the ones still here thought it would be fun to have a formal. Or maybe the idea came from their women friends, or their wives. I really don't know. But it ended up sounding like a good idea. Don't you agree?"

"Sure."

"It's not until next month, but that allows time for alterations."

I look at my watch. Twelve thirty-three. It's been dark for Jake for a couple of hours, now. "And they expect a lot of women to come alone? I mean, it won't be—People won't look at us funny?"

She pulls away from the glass and studies the points of her shoes. "I won't be going alone. But you can. What I mean is, no one will think anything of it. You can ride with us so you're not by yourself."

"Us?"

She slides off her shoes and picks them up and holds them by their ankle straps. "Me and Brian." She looks again at the mirror and plays with her dress straps. "He's Rear-D. Rear detachment? He almost doesn't want to go because he's afraid he'll have to see some of the wives who call him. You wouldn't believe. 'I have a cold! So, like, my husband needs to come home!'" Her wife-voice is high, nasal. "From *war*, Mia. Are they serious?" She shrugs. "Anyway, the Rear-D guys are good for a party." She swings the curtain shut and the rings knock the wall. "Hurry up and change, okay? Want to get a coffee?"

I let the dress fall off, let gravity pull it down over my skin, and it feels like slipping out of a bath. Naked again, or nearly enough, in front of the mirror and the shadows emphasize the tonelessness of my arms, the lines between my ribs. It's no wonder clothing stores are so successful. In this light, anything looks better than naked.

"It's not as if I never looked for a job," Denise says, "but you know how it is. Why would you drive a taxi unless you had no other options?" Rain streaks the window behind our table. Air-conditioning season, now, and it's on southern-standard high. I fold my arms to cover my nipples. Denise sits back in her chair, hands flat on the table, and I try not to look at her shirt.

There were options. Like teaching.

"Did you graduate from high school?" she says. She sucks latte foam through the hole in the plastic cover.

I tell her I did.

"College?"

"Sure."

"See? But that doesn't mean anything here. There's nothing," she laughs, and not with much humor, "we can do with our degrees. I applied to every major hotel in town. Not one of them contacted me. When I called them to follow up, they said they were looking for cleaning people. Front desk clerks. And I didn't even try at some of the smaller places. Have you seen them? The one-floor wonders on the side of the road?"

I have seen them. "I drop people there, sometimes. What about them?" Blackout curtains stay drawn across small windows, and doors open a sliver when cars pull into the lot. People live in them, not stay in them. Tourists and visitors are steered to hotel-city, a two-block cluster of accommodations just off the interstate.

"Mia, they should be condemned. The lobbies are ten feet by ten feet, the grounds are littered, and," she shudders, "they're scary. I checked the papers for a month straight for other jobs, so it's not like I'm not looking. I am. And do you know what I found? Telemarketing. In a cubicle! I wouldn't even get to be a supervisor. 'We only promote from within, sweetie, and it's based on seniority.' Luckily, my husband understands. I told him after the first month of living here and looking for work that I can't—cannot—settle. It sounds selfish, and maybe because it is, but that's just the way it's going to be. I don't want another job. I want a career." She blows into the cup. "William knows. When the right thing comes along, I'll take it."

I know what I'm supposed to say. That it's his fault, really, because he brought her here, and that if she can't find work, William can't blame her for holding out for something better. It's technically true, but more than that, it's convenient, so I say everything I am supposed to say, the way people do.

"It must be a little harder for you, not being married. You two don't get the extra pay. Do you have health insurance?"

"No."

"What happens if something happens to him over there?"

I look at my cup. "It's okay. It's taken care of."

"He put you down as his beneficiary, right?"

"I guess. Sure."

"Still. Just because you're not married doesn't mean you should be stuck driving a cab. I assume you moved here to be with him, so…Wait. Unless you like driving a cab, of course! It's just so…It's so…What is it?" She looks to the beamed ceiling. "Something. No offense."

I want to tell her that offense is taken, if even just a little, and that I drive by choice, not by necessity. I was a professor, an adjunct, but telling her that would sound like a defense of some kind, and she would ask *Why? Why don't you teach anymore?*

"I was no good."

She looks at me. "What was no good?"

"Pardon?"

"You said something was no good. What was no good?"

"Um…the school," I say, and then I tell her I used to teach and add some things—anything—about the school, about the students not knowing the basic sentence structure they should have learned before being admitted to college ("I didn't sign on to teach basic English"), about school politics, scheduling conflicts, a lack of opportunity for tenure, low pay, a poor paper supply that left the copiers empty just when I needed them for handouts, warm water in the drinking fountains.

I finish off with a complaint about bad parking and the price of lot passes, "Which, if you consider what we're paid, is stupidly expensive."

"You gave up a job as a professor—a *professor*—"

"Instructor. Adjunct."

"—to drive a taxi?"

"I thought it would be fun," I say, which is true, "and it is," I say, which is not.

She smiles. "Wow."

"What?"

"I have this weird kind of respect for you now. To give up something like that. Are you going back to it when you two move to a place with a better school?"

I say, "Oh, definitely, you know, for the money," and, "Did you know they have art here?" I point over her shoulder at paintings hanging on the far side of the room.

"Mm," she says. "So, when *are* you and Jake getting married?"

I tell her, "Some time after he gets back," and sip coffee. Admitting there are no wedding plans will plunge us into the inevitable woman-talk of stereotypical men dragging their feet toward marriage, the *Us women* (when it should be 'we' women) *need to push them into things like that or they'll never commit; you know how men are*, eye-roll, and *Amen, sister.*

The paintings must be originals. Typed labels display…something too far away, too small to read…beside the unframed canvasses. It is the white one—a white house covered in snow—that grabs me.

"Excuse me."

I get up to read the tag.

Emily's at Dawn, 1981. G.D. (Oil.) The house is old, chipped paint giving way to dull wood, the structure itself slanting rightward with the shallow decline of the snow-draped yard. The sky is winter-morning gray, but early sun shines through the haze and catches the shadow of an adjacent shed, spreading it across the undisturbed driveway. White sheers fall behind long, wood-framed windows, and the distinct, warm, brightness of dawn (but controlled—no brash oranges and golds, here) touches the half of the house closest to what would be considered the back yard, the slope, and inside is, must be, a woman, *Emily*, who would be middle-aged, yes, with long, wavy hair and wearing gray wool socks and a flowing white bathrobe. Happy in her kitchen, warm in her winter house. Brewing coffee, probably, unaware of the adoring man standing at the end of her driveway and watching her house morning after morning, who painted this rendering of his love, 'pure as the undriven snow,' no doubt, and like the house, worn but warm, hidden, the way she is hidden behind the windows to—

"What a dingy old house. You can drive five minutes from here and take twenty pictures of houses like that, and that's art?" Denise says, passing on her way to the counter.

—her kitchen. No light comes from inside, but sunlight stripes the sheers and must (must!) spear through them and across hardwood floors, patching the wall, setting fire to Emily's hair when she passes. The floorboards are deep mahogany and the distressed kitchen table holds dried flowers in the center in a crude pottery vase and there's bright sun porch just past the kitchen and—

—and I have to have it. Have to possess it.

I check the tag for the price.

Denise, behind me with her refreshed cup, says, "One *thousand* two-*hundred? Dollars?*" She adjusts the cardboard sleeve. "It must be a typo. Excuse me," she says, turning to the girl behind the counter. "Is this one *thousand* two-hundred dollars, or a hundred and twenty?"

The girl comes out from behind a grinder, twisting a rag in a carafe. "It's twelve hundred."

"Who's the artist?"

"Doesn't it say on the label?"

"Yes, it says on the label, but they're just initials. Is he or she famous?"

The girl twists and twists the rag. "No."

"Then what makes him…or her…?"

"Him."

"What makes him think anyone would buy this…house…for one thousand dollars?"

"It's not a house," the girl says.

"It's not a house?"

"No."

Denise points at the canvas, her finger touching oil siding. "This isn't a house?"

"Please don't touch that," the girl says. "Yes, it's a house. But the painting is not a painting of a house."

Denise cups both hands around her latte. "Well, I guess I'm ignorant then, aren't I?"

Twist, "No, ma'am," twist.

Denise leans in to me. "Would you pay a thousand dollars for this?"

I look at the girl. She sets the carafe on the counter and waves the rag in the air. I follow Denise outside.

Before pulling away from the curb in front of my apartment, Denise tells me she'll call in a few weeks about the party and suggests I think about wearing "some kind of pretty yellow flower, but a small one," behind my ear—"It'll make you look so feminine!"—and adds that I might not want to mention the party in a letter to Jake. "Sometimes it just makes them feel worse when they can't be a part of something," she says.

APRIL 8, TUESDAY

HOT TODAY. Heat dances on car tops. I watch the mailman come and go, his bag weighing heavy. When he's rounded next door's lilac bushes, I go down to check my box. Two envelopes, one of them a letter from Jake. His name, rightward slanting and angular, in the return address corner. The envelope is fat—four pages, at least—and by the time I reach my door it's torn and the letter is out, fanned wide in my hands, and it's not four pages, no, but six. Six! I open the door and slam it shut behind me and accidentally kick Chancey on the way to the chair, stuff myself into a corner and read.

March 1

Mia, Mia,

I miss you crazy for only having left yesterday.

I'm still on a plane. Or, I'm on one again. We had a layover at an airport with a bar, but we weren't allowed to drink anything but water or Coke or whatever because we were in uniform. Doesn't war mean anything to anyone, anymore?

We've been flying for five hours this time and pretty much everyone is sleeping, except the guy next to me. He's reading a book, The Executioner's Song. *I guess that's interesting. I don't want to say the title works because I don't want to give you the impression that I feel like I'm heading for my death, but it does. It works. And part of me does feel like I'm heading for my death, but not in a real way. I can't explain it. I suppose when you know you're going to war, you know there's a chance you'll get killed. I've heard people say the chances of getting killed where I'm going are about the same as they are at home, but at home I'm reasonably confident that people aren't trying to shoot me down while I fly the traffic pattern. Which still makes me sound scared, but truthfully Mia, I'm not. I'm sad, though. Leaving you was tough. I can't believe I can still count how many hours it's been since I was holding you.*

Twenty-eight.

We had to go back into the hangar after we'd all gone outside to get on the plane, which turned out to not be ours. I went out to the lot to see if you were still there, and I saw you at the light at the end of the street, so I was waving and jumping up and down like a crazy man, but I was too late. If I'd come out just one minute sooner! Damn it!

Anyw

March 8

Well, we're here. Sorry that last bit ended so abruptly, but I got tired and passed out without even knowing it. At least I finished the sentence. I woke up with Smythe (the guy reading next to me) punching my arm because I guess my head fell on his shoulder. He said I was snoring and that I drooled on him. I didn't, though—he was kidding. You know I only drool for you, baby.

'Here,' by the way, is a place in the dirt with some tents and stuff. Not much else. If you want to know what I've been up to, I'll tell you: a whole lot of nothing.

March 18

Hey, you. We moved again. Looks the same, though. Brown. I got to take a shower three days ago—that was good. The water ran dirty. Have I mentioned we're all a little anxious? No one knows what's going on or if this thing will even start. I hope it doesn't, but I think it will. Something needs to happen one way or another, though.

March 21

Ask and ye shall receive.

So, we still don't know much, and we weren't part of it, but there's been a ton of movement and we've moved again, too. Supposedly, the next place (up north is all I can say right now) is where we'll be for the long haul. How long of a haul? Don't know. Wish I could tell you.

As you know by the time you get this, the war is on and…the war is on.

We got here yesterday. It's not bad, geographically. Nice scenery. Big sky. All the textbook components of a desert environment. Ah, Mia. I could write pages about where I am, what I'll be eating, what I have in my tent, when I think my tuff box will get here, how long I think it'll be before we go on a mission, but even thinking about sharing all that feels like a waste of time. I don't know if wasting time is what I want to do.

I love you, M. I love you like I've never loved anyone or anything else, and it feels like I've been without you for months, already. What's it been, three weeks? Every day at mail call I hope for something from you, but I don't count on it. I don't even know if they know where we are, yet (only because we just got here), so they're probably holding onto mail for a while longer. If you've mailed

42

anything, that is. But I don't think you have. I hope you know I understand. I hope you know a lot of things, like…like, I know you lie to me. It was hard not to laugh when you said you didn't mind my mom coming to the hangar. I know you hated it, but you have to understand I just couldn't say no. I hope you're not still mad at me personally. And M, I'm sorry she got the last hug. I didn't think she'd come back in. She just kind of ran at me, and what could I do? I guess maybe she shouldn't have come. No. You're right. I know she shouldn't have. But you know how she can be.

It's hard not to think of you at night. It's so flat you can see…well, as far as your eyes'll let you… and the sun goes down over this ocean of brown, the edges kind of melting out onto the sand, and it makes me think of you because I know you'd want to see it. I got a shot last night with William's camera (Denise made him take along about three disposables to last until they buy a digital), and when he sends the roll home he said he'll add a note to make sure you get it. He's already taken a ton of pictures, so it should be done soon, and he writes Denise all the time (he was even writing her in the hangar while we were sitting around waiting to go), so who knows? You might see the picture before you even get my letter. He took a couple of me, too, so make sure you get those. Nothing special, just me standing around. Smoking. (Thought I'd tell you before you saw it…I started again, but only because of where I am. It makes no sense not to smoke. I'll quit when I get home. Don't think you can use this as an excuse to smoke, though—I'm at war and you're not, you stealer of reasons to smoke.)

Ah, but you have started smoking again, haven't you? I know it.

Have to go—meeting. More later. Oh, yeah—could you put together a package? We have good meals, but I'd like some snacks. Thanks! (You don't have to include a letter, but maybe a short note?)

March 22

—0445— Oh, yes. It is. And do you know why I'm writing you at o-friggin-dark-forty-five on this…actually, pretty comfortable…morning? Because. As I'm learning happens every morning, there is a noise. A thundering, ear shattering noise that William somehow always manages to sleep through. Now, I've only been here for a couple of days, but the first morning it was a convoy. The second morning it was Blackhawks. This morning, a convoy again. Rumble rumble rumble right through camp. Right by my tent, and the Blackhawks flew not near my tent, but right over it. In fact, I think the pilots just decided to hover on my head for no reason. You know, Mia, the one thing that passes time faster than anything else is sleep. Word is, if you take away sleeping time, we're only gone for six months instead of twelve. Or however long. Just cut the full *length in half. How am I supposed to sleep this deployment away with these pesky morning noises?*

March 24

So, it's day three here, and it may as well be day one. If these past few days are any indication of what's to come, then I can look forward to tomorrow being just like today. And the day after tomorrow being just like yesterday. Routi

March 26

An interesting thing happened yesterday.

So, I was taking a shower and heard this ZIP right by my ear. We have these windows in the shower stalls, so to speak, so I looked outside to see what was going on, then realized, "Hey. That actually kind of sounded like a bullet…" I ducked and crawled out on my hands and knees (after grabbing a towel, of course) to get everyone down and find out what the hell was going on. Never found out, though. It just stopped. People think it might have been a weapons cache exploding. No worries, though! It was more funny than it was scary. Besides, those guys have shitty aim. Their mortars are constantly being shot way over our heads and exploding on the other side of camp. (Um, I don't really mean constantly. I just mean that any time they do fire a mortar, they miss by a mile. That's a good thing.)

I guess I'll tell you why I had to leave so abruptly before. No big deal— just a mission. Came on all of a sudden-like. It was actually pretty cool, because we left early the next morning (when I stopped writing it was to plan), and the mornings here, much as I hate to say it, can be pretty outstanding. Anyway, that morning, two days ago (it's really late at night, now, and I'm so tired I might have to end this pretty soon), I stepped out of the tent and stood on this porch we built with scrap wood. The clouds in the distance were really thin and low, cutting the mountains in half, and the temperature was perfect…cool, but warm, if that makes any sense. The sun was just coming up over the mountaintop, but the sky directly above me was still dark enough so that I could see the stars. I wish you could have been there.

Have to go to sleep, now.

(Next day…)

Feeling kind of sad, so having this chance to write tonight is just what I needed. No reason for the sadness. I mean, no reason that's really unusual or bad. Just miss you. So much. You're everything to me, M, and though I know I'm here for a good reason (my guys) and wouldn't come back early if I could, I dream about coming back just to see you. The days are so long, and I think about you more than you know. That it's been a month since I last saw you is

44

unbelievable for two reasons. In a way, time here has gone so fast that I can't believe four weeks are already in the past, but in another way, time has dragged so slow and I miss your face so much that I can't believe this foreverness only just started. If I were going to be gone three or four months, this would be nothing. But it's different when one month is only the first step on a much longer journey. (I still don't know anything for sure, but six months is looking less and less likely.)

March 27

Sorry it's taking me so long to get this to you, but we've been really busy (nothing much to talk about—going here and there, nothing really dangerous, so don't worry). This probably won't be long, because I have to go somewhere again and I'd like to get this out to you so you don't think I'm not writing. You hear a lot of guys out here saying that they get letters from their wives and girlfriends who complain that they don't get enough mail. I don't know what it is they think we're doing out here, but I can say from experience that if we're not writing, it's probably because we're damn busy. Not to be a dick, but we have more important things to do than write letters. (You know what I mean. But, while we're on the subject, I hope you know I write whenever I can.)

I don't know why, but I thought today about the earrings I gave you for Christmas. Did you really like them? I never saw them on you again after New Year's. I was afraid you'd be disappointed because I know you wanted something else. We've talked about it so much I almost don't want to bring it up again because that horse has been pulverized, but it's so important that you understand. M, it just didn't seem right. Before we found out about the deployment, we weren't even talking about it. Remember? Because we knew it felt too soon. And then after we found out, it would have been like we were getting married because of the deployment. And that's just not a good reason. I only want to get married when it's because it's what we want. You have to try to believe me. Okay?

I'm not looking forward to this next mission. Not because it's more risky than any of the others (which it's not), but be

Mia. This is William. Jake asked me to write that he's okay and he loves you. He had to go on a mission and he wanted me to get this mailed for him. Tell Denise hi for me. -William

45

APRIL 9, WEDNESDAY

HE FELL. Right in the middle of everything, he fell. Torn down, toppled and dragged by a rope. The same scene plays over, over, over, and my cheeks hurt and I'm wearing the earrings, and I'm dizzy-drunk from celebrating and waiting for my phone call.

APRIL 14, MONDAY

"…MUCH OF THE city taken. Meanwhile, the administration applying pressure to stop supporting enemy…"

Major operations over, they say, but still no phone call.

Cleanup and advancing might be all that's left. Air Force planes have been sent off, away, home, and someone, somewhere, was captured. Someone big and important, they said. Or was the someone killed?

I wonder if Jake has killed anyone. *Killed* anyone, Jake, *killed*, and wonder if I would think it sexy or sad.

I pull up the blankets and try to sleep.

Chancey, snoring, wakes me and I'm strangled by sheets. I try to return to a dream I feel more than remember—swinging, gliding, and there was water below.

The floor is cold on my feet when I get out of bed.

Chancey follows me to the kitchen.

Shellie sounds less than happy to hear from me and reminds me that this is the third day I've called in. One more and Lionel will fire me. "It's been busy," she says.

I tighten my throat to sound sick and promise her I'll be there in the morning.

Probably another hour, or so, before the sun comes up. Another eight hours until the mail comes. Three in the afternoon, Jake's time. I dump the rest of my coffee in the sink and go to the bedroom and climb under the blankets, watch the shadows on the wall misshape and dissolve as the sun comes up.

"Denise. It's Mia."

"Mia?"

"I—I wanted to ask about the party."

"Are you excited?"

"I am. And, I just wanted—It's on the…When is it, again?"

"It's at the end of April."

"End of April. The last weekend?"

"Yes. We tried for Wednesday, but no one was going for it."

"Okay, then. I'll write it down."

"Mia, I was joking."

"What?"

"About Wednesday."

"Oh."

Denise is quiet, then says, "Was that all?"

"M-hm. And, you know, I just wanted to see how you are. See how William is."

"I'm fine. Mia, are you okay?"

"You've heard from him, then?"

"From William?"

"Yes."

"Not recently, no."

"Oh."

"'Oh' what?"

"It's nothing."

"Mia, it's something. You don't call me."

"I call you."

"You have never once called me."

"Haven't I?"

"What is it?"

"It's just—it's been two weeks since some, I don't know, mission or something, and—I don't know."

"They're probably very busy."

"No, I know. I know."

"Please tell me you're not sitting around and thinking."

"Everything's fine. I just wanted to make sure, you know, just see if you heard from William."

"I'm sorry. I haven't."

"Okay, then. All right. Thanks."

"Oh, Mia—before you go, what are you doing tonight?"

"I think—what day is today?—I think his mother is supposed to call," I lie. "We have this once-a-week update thing we do."

"You're a better woman than I."

"Thanks again, Denise. I'm off to work, so…"

The popcorn bubbles on the ceiling are uncountable.

I reach two thousand and lose my spot, start over.

The downstairs door slams and I run to the window, watch the blue sack wedged between the door and the frame until it and mailman squeeze out and round the lilac bushes. Downstairs, I tug open the sticking metal door to nothing, no word.

Olivia would have called if he were dead.

The phone lies buttons-up on the couch and its light is red. I run over to pick it up. "Hello?" Air. After pushing the on/off button twice, I get a dial tone. "Chancey!"

Dead.

Dead, dead, dead.

So final, the word, but at the same time, meaningless. Incomprehensible, even.

Dead. Deceased. Passed away.

"Dead" is best. Less clinical than "deceased," less voluntary than "passed away."

How is Jake, Mia?

Jake's dead.

Oh, I'm sorry to hear he passed away.

No. He didn't pass away. He's dead.

Would his casket be open or closed? Olivia would decide, because Jake never wrote a will, never specified, and his mother is his next of kin. "But you get all the money," he said and smiled. "The death benefits."

"Oh, goodie," I said.

Benefits.

Some thousands of dollars, more than I've ever had. What does someone do with thousands and thousands of dollars all at once?

Open or closed will also depend on how he died. There's only so much reconstruction anyone, even the best, can do. How would Olivia have it, given the choice?

Open. Jake's blind eyes staring at thread-sewn lids.

I've never been to a funeral, but I've heard it said that the people in caskets end up looking like doll-painted wax: pink cheeks, red lips, a "lifelike" skin tone. I must tell Olivia they can't do that to

Jake, can't give his light lips a dark pink finish, can't blush his cheeks because he doesn't blush.

And what then, afterward? After the wake, after Arlington, because that's where he wants to be buried. Heroes are buried there, and non-heroes, too, flat under headstones as identical as their uniforms and lined up in perfect formation. What then, after "Taps," after Olivia takes the flag and Jake is lowered into a hole? An empty apartment, a fatherless cat, Jake's clothes in the closet and his car parked out front and his files on the computer. I'll wonder if it was a mistake, if the man in the casket was a stranger, one who just happened to look like Jake. And I'll wait for him to come through the door, wait for weeks, months, because I won't believe he won't be back to eat his breakfast bars in the cupboard next to the cereal, or the nuts he hides behind the flour so he doesn't have to share.

He looks out from the shelves, smiling in a T-shirt and shorts, holding a liter beer from a German Hofbräuhaus. I get up and flip each picture facedown. Bad luck, *badluckbadluck* to imagine him alive and three-dimensional because that means he could also not be.

The alarm is going off or there's a siren or—

—the phone. I crawl to the desk and pick up the receiver. "Hello! Hello!"

Olivia says, "How are you, hon," and I can't answer because I can't breathe because mucus stuffs my sinuses and I'm gulping and tears adhere my lips like wet glue. I gasp that it wasn't worth it, or something that sounds like it, anyway, that nothing is worth it, that *I loved him and thank you, thank you for having him so I had the chance to love him*—

"Mia, what on earth…? Are you okay, sweetheart?"

I say, "Jake."

"That's why I'm calling you, hon. I just got off the phone with him. He's doing very well. And you have some mail coming. Isn't that exciting?"

I wipe my nose and my mouth on my sleeve. "He called you?"

"Oh, I'm sure he'll—well, Mia, you have to—I *am* his mother. I'm positive he'll call you soon."

FORTY-EIGHT MAPLE. Rainwater pours from a gutter onto a slant of driveway that funnels it into a flooding patch of soil. Donny jogs to the cab with a newspaper held over his head and climbs in. Glinting raindrops cling to the ends of his hair.

"Where've you been?" He drops the paper on the floor, sets his muddy feet on top.

"Sick," I say. "Same place?"

"It is if you're talkin' about the construction site."

I pull away from his house and see him staring. "What."

"Nothin'. 'What.' I can't look? Damn, girl, you're in a bad mood again? It's been almost a week since I saw you. You said you was sick, and I was just seein' if you looked sick."

I don't know why it matters—it shouldn't—but I say, anyway, "Do I?"

"Naw. Uh, uh. I ain't sayin'. If I say no, I'm callin' you a liar. If I say yes, well—I ain't even goin' to—"

"Never mind. Forget it."

A mile and a half of silence, and then a long red light. I say, "How's your wife?"

"What do you mean, how's my wife? Why're you askin' about my wife? You know her?"

Too early. It's too early for this, and I'm too tired. "I was just being polite. Fuck it."

He laughs. "'Fuck it'!" He slaps his thigh and his laughter goes on for a quarter mile. "Girl, you're all right. 'Fuck it.'" He lights a cigarette and drops the lighter between his feet, picks it up. "I ain't havin' such a good day, m'self."

"What's the matter?"

He shrugs and looks out the window.

"Will you please open the—?"

"Sorry," he says and opens it, blows his smoke outside. "Ever since the anniversary… I don't know."

I give it a minute, keep from asking what happened, but soon he sighs and shakes his head, so I ask.

"Don't know," he says. "Somethin's just—She changed, she's different." He taps the window. "She's leavin', she says. Wants a separation. From me. From Donny. I'll give it to her, y'know, if she wants it, but she…four years. That's it?"

"Why?"

"I told you. Don't like me goin' out. Wants me home all the time when she's home, and when I'm not home she thinks I'm cheatin', that there's a girl at the bar, or somethin'. But, goddamn, because—see, now, I don't even think that's it. Control. It's got to be. She's mad if I'm out and she's mad if I'm home. I come home sometimes—sure, I was out a few hours, okay—and when I walk in, she's on the couch wrapped in that blanket, from her neck to her toes like she's in some damn cocoon. Can't get her out of there. And she won't talk to me. Just stares at the TV like she can't hear me, can't see me. Know what, though…If she stays out 'til eleven, I'm supposed to be okay with that."

"Is there a girl at the bar?"

"Hell, tons of girls! Beautiful ones, too." He looks at me. "But I don't want 'em. What, you think I'm cheatin', too? I don't cheat. I don't do that. Why would you ask somethin' like that?"

"I just—"

"You just drive the car and watch the road. Thinkin' things like that. You…What kind of a person just thinks that about another person?" He flicks the butt outside and says, "Don't even know me, and you—now, what's the matter? Are you cryin'?"

"I'm fine," I say, but the windshield is a blur of black and white. I wipe my eyes.

"Hell, I didn't mean to make you cry. I'm sorry. Here." He fumbles in his pocket for his soft pack and holds it between me and the steering wheel.

"No, thanks."

He waits, then takes one out and lights it for himself. "Yeah, somethin's botherin' you. I can tell. You want to tell me what it is?"

"I'm fine, really," I say, but now I want one for later, when I can stop and smoke it alone. "Can I—Well, do you mind if I take that cigarette, after all?"

"Thought you didn't want it."

"Never mind."

He shakes the pack until a filter slides up and then pulls it out and hands it to me. "Want me to light it for you, too?"

"I'm going to save it for later."

"You're takin' my cigarette and you won't even smoke it?"

"I'll smoke it, but later, if it's okay."

He plucks it from my fingers and wedges it back into the box. "If I ain't good enough for you to smoke with me, then—"

"All right. Okay? I'll smoke it."

"Now, why do you want to talk to me that way when I'm givin' you a present?" He takes it out again and lights it, a steady flame held just short of the tip and his lips tightening to puff, puff, sending small bursts of smoke into car space. He holds it in the air, just over the center console. I reach for it and he jerks it away. "You goin' to tell me what's the matter?"

"Nothing's the matter."

"Doctor Donaldson. That's me. You need help. I can—I can! Come on, now."

"I don't need—"

"You're goin' through somethin', and don't say you ain't."

"Everyone goes through something."

"But here, I'm givin' you the chance to talk about it. Not everyone gets that. Some people don't have people to talk to. Look here, I'm gettin' out of the car in, what, five minutes? Then you'll be rid of me for good, if you want, but don't you think you'd feel better if you just said? Please," he says. "Now, I don't say please very—I *want* to help, see?"

"Okay."

He hands me the cigarette and I tell him about Jake. He listens, no interruptions, and when I finish he says, "That's right up my— look who you're talkin' to. Donny Donaldson, doctor. Airborne! I was in the Army," he says.

"I know."

"Naw, you don't. You don't know. You only know what you think you know, but you don't. Understan'?"

"Sure."

"Yeah, you'll be upset like you are. Nothin' you can do about it 'til you agree he's right. Bad idea to get married 'cause of a war."

"So I keep hearing."

"Least you're both on the same side! Right? He against us bein'—? Well, he can't say. Shouldn't say."

"We're on the same side." A minivan cuts in front of me and I ride its bumper for a block. "It's really nothing. You're right. I just want him to come home."

Donny pats my thigh and I tense, but he's already pulled his hand away. "You think you're goin' to get hit today by a truck?"

"What?"

"Drivin'. Think you'll get hit?"

"Well, no. Unless some minivan—"

"Y'see? He don't think he'll get killed, neither. But he might be worried about you. But you, you know you're a good driver. Sometimes, anyway. Last intersection you missed that light, and—"

I ask for another cigarette and he tosses the pack on my lap.

"Yeah, now's a good time to be smokin'," he says. "No better time than when your country's at war. I tell you what, though, and I say this sincerely. I mean it. You payin' attention?"

I say yes, yes, I'm listening.

"I hope your boyfriend gets a better homecomin' than what they gave me." He squeezes flat the filter, separating the paper from the fibers. "You just hope. And you tell him you love him, and when he comes home, you do somethin' nice for him. Give him a cake."

"I will."

"You give him that cake and you tell him you love him and that he did good. You hear me? You give him a goddamn cake."

"Cake." I cluck my tongue. "Got it."

Donny rips the cigarette from my lips and flicks it out the window. "Let me out."

"We're a mile from the site."

"If I want to get out, you let me out." He digs in his pocket. "Don't worry. I'm givin' you the full thirteen. I ain't a thief." He pulls out a crumpled ball of bills and weeds out two fives and three ones, says, "Here," and drops them in my lap. "I shouldn't even give it to you. Now stop the damn car."

No tip, today. "I didn't mean anything—"

"Don't matter what you meant. Now stop the goddamn car and let me out."

By the time I pull over, the turnoff to the construction zone is in sight. He gets out and smacks the hood on his way across the street. "Go on," he shouts, and waves me off.

"Shellie."

"Yes, dear."

"Thirteen dollars."

"Does he want you back tonight?"

"He didn't say."

"All righty. Head to Grocery World."

Lunchtime, which doesn't come until things slow down at three, I creep past the coffee shop to check on the painting, but I can't see through the thick and tinted specials-painted windows. I park the cab and go inside and there it is, still hanging. The one that used to hang beside it is gone. That one, if I remember, had a seven-hundred-dollar price tag. I check *Emily's* tag—maybe the price has dropped?—but no, and so I think, think, how to get twelve hundred dollars, but even a straight seven-day work week wouldn't do it soon enough, and neither would being extra nice to fares. Or being nice, period. No one tips.

I order a sandwich and a coffee and sit on the couch where the sun shines through the window. On the table in front of me, a half-played chess game. Brown is winning.

The girl behind the counter opens a jar of mayonnaise and I hear the knife stabbing around inside. "Excuse me," I say. "Is there any chance, maybe, that the price on that painting—the one of the hou—the one with the snow—would go down, some?"

She shrugs and brings me my order, sweeping aside the chess game for space. "I'll ask if he comes in, but I haven't seen him since he dropped it off."

I would put it in the living room, over the desk.

Or in the bedroom, where morning light would hit it from the same angle as the painted sunrise.

But mornings are dark when I leave, and I spend so little time in the bedroom, anyway. The kitchen, then, because it gets the best evening light on the wall, an orange slant just above the back of the chair, and when summer comes in full and daylight stays long, I'll be home in time to catch it.

"Mia," Shellie says.

It's ten minutes before six and I'm almost there, almost free for the day, and I'd thought maybe I would close my eyes for a minute or two before gassing up. Water splashes between rocks on the riverbank and crickets chirp from their hiding spots in the grass. When Jake took me here, he'd brought along his woobie—a camouflage poncho-liner we used as a blanket—and some gas-station fried chicken packed in a paper-towel-lined shoebox. "You said you've never been on a picnic," he said, shooing off a cricket that had landed close to the box. "Which I don't believe, anyway. You're twenty-five and you never had a picnic?" He pulled out two beers in cans, labels hidden by cozies, and handed me a cold, soggy drumstick.

"Mia."

"Yes?"

"Where you at?"

Tap. Taptap. Rain. Again. "The river."

"Donny wants you back where you dropped him off."

The clock says it's five minutes before six. "He asked for me specifically?"

"He surely did. I hope he's not scarin' you, is he?"

"No, everything's okay."

"All righty. He's a little funny sometimes, but that's just 'cause of the war, you know. He's a good man, though. A decent man."

In the background Paula says, "He didn't go to no Vietnay-um," and Lenny says, "Now, you don't know that. Don't go questionin' a man's serv—"

"Construction site, then gas up." Shellie releases her button.

Traffic is thick and rain-frantic until I reach the black, lampless two-lane that takes me out of town and into the suburbs. Reflected raccoon eyes pop up, then disappear over the shoulder, waiting in the guardrail ditch. No headlights in my rearview mirror, and after I pass I will the raccoons to *go, go now!*

The site's clay lot is muddy. I park and stare through thumping wipers at the trailer window until my eyes burn, until the clock reads five after six and I should be on my way home. My legs are numb and I'm tired. I pound the horn, meaning only to pound something, anything, but someone has fixed it and it blares, *hooooonk!* The door to the trailer opens and Donny sticks out his head and yells, "It's my angel, my angel of mercy, comin' to carry me home. Just a sec—I'll be right out."

"Come in with me."

"That's okay. But thanks."

"Come on. For a minute."

"I can't. I have to get the cab back."

"Well, then, drop it off and come on back."

"I have to go home," I say.

"Why? Your husband ain't there."

"He's not my husband."

"Husband, boyfriend." He gestures and spills beer on his thigh. "Goddamn it." He wipes at it and forgets it. "Nothin's goin' to happen. Just a drink."

"Really, I—"

"Look. I ain't goin' to hurt you. Did I ever touch you, or say somethin' to you that made you think different?"

"No."

"No," he says. He slides the beer can on his thigh, back and forth. "And besides, my wife left me."

"But this morning—"

"This mornin', what? I didn't want to tell you this mornin'. I'm tellin' you now. She left me and now there's no one. Says she's only stayin' gone 'til I move out. A week is all I get. She's at a man's house. What do you think 'bout that?"

"That's—I'm sorry. Really."

"She's gone, and I'm alone. I got nobody."

"It's just—I have to feed my cat."

He starts to say something, then stops. He pulls at the tab on the top of his can, click, click, click. "You said you got to feed your cat? That's why you can't come over?"

"I have to feed him," I say, and now I wonder if I'm not lying. I don't remember leaving food or water this morning. Or yesterday. Poor baby, poor Chancey.

Shellie calculates my fare sheet and I sit curled in the corner of the couch with her dog tucked in the space between my stomach and thighs.

"Not bad today," she says.

"It's 'cause she kept the car all damn night," Lenny says, pointing at me. "I missed two runs 'cause of her."

"It's only six forty," I say.

"Forty minutes could be a twenty-dollar fare."

The dog's fur is soft, its skin warm in the shed over-cooled by window-tucked air conditioners. I say, "Did you miss a twenty dollar fare?"

"That ain't the point."

Paula puts out a cigarette. "Quit givin' her a hard time, you damn hypocrite. I remember one time you didn't bring the car back to me 'til noon."

"That was six years ago. It don't even count. I'm sick and tired of everyone givin' her special treatment. I know you got shit goin' on, Mia, but you come in here every mornin' lookin' all pissed off, you take days off, and you don't gas up right. Now, maybe this job ain't for you. Me, I'm done. You can't take it? Quit." He twists the cap on his head so that the bill shades the back of his neck. "And Paula, you got to stop jumpin' in on everyone's business and take care of your own. Ain't your kid goin' to court for child support, now? I hear the daddy ain't goin' to pay 'til he gets another test done. Wouldn't need it if your kid didn't bed down with everyone in the projects."

Shellie's dog fidgets, restless, and climbs over my legs and jumps off the couch. Shellie says, "C'mere, Puddin'," and picks him up, sets him on her lap.

"She only slept with the one guy," Paula says. "He's lyin' to get out of payin', is all. We knew it would happen." She tiredly brushes her thin, white hair away from her eyes. "You're one to talk about sleepin' around. Ain't you keepin' all the whores in crack, all by yourself?"

"You best shut your mouth, woman."

"Why? You goin' to hit me with that infected dick of yours? Hell, we *all* need to be careful of that, make sure it stays quarantined." Charlie, who has been watching TV from the torn leather recliner in front of the window, laughs. Paula lights another cigarette.

"Now, now." Shellie hands me the sheet, and I give her too much of my money. "What's the matter, girl?" she says.

I tell her she's been lovely, which she has, and that I'm quitting.

Lights are on inside the house at 48 Maple, and a mud-crusted blue Jeep sits in front of the house on the lawn. Past the sheers, faint gray shadows. I keep the car running with the window open—the rain stopped sometime while I was handing over my money—and smoke the cigarette Paula gave me on my way out. "Good luck," she said, and Shellie said, "Come back and see us."

It's possible there is no wife. I should have asked Shellie. I never saw a wife when I dropped him off, never saw one when I picked him up, and he's never used her name.

I should go home, should roll down the road toward the river, take a right on River Road and get a coffee at the drive-through. The boy behind the window knows what I like and gives me extra whipped cream topped with a chocolate-coated espresso bean. But if I drive through tonight, it will officially be the end of my day. I'll have quit, officially, and with no plans—official or otherwise—for the future. For tomorrow.

Jobless, living on Jake's income the way Denise lives on William's.

"Is that my angel?"

I barely hear him over the engine. Donny wears shorts and a T-shirt and stands in his open doorway, glass in hand. "Get in here," he says. "And hurry up. They're talkin' about a tornado."

APRIL 16, WEDNESDAY (EVENING)

HIS WALKWAY SLANTS and buckles, and lukewarm puddles I can't see in the dark cover my shoes and soak through to my socks. Somewhere far off—over my apartment, maybe, and Chancey doesn't do well in storms—thunder murmurs.

"You finally came over." Donny's bare toes spread flat on a traffic-stained carpet. I take in what I can with quick looks past his narrow figure in the doorway. A couch, plain gray. An end table and a worn, old chair. Against the wall, a towering hutch with clean-lined wood and glass doors, the bare shelves inside spot-lit under recessed bulbs.

Normal, but I'm not sure what I expected.

"Just a few minutes," I say, "and then I should get home."

"Yeah, I know. You got to feed the cat." He steps aside for me. "Take your shoes off. It ain't me—I think carpet's there to be walked on—but the wife…"

I take off my shoes and tuck them under a heating register by the door, but, of course, it's not on. My socks squish on the floor.

"Drink?"

"Oh—no. No, thanks."

"I wanted to say—listen, now—that I'm sorry for before. In the car. I want to say what I should've at the time. Now, there's reason to worry, don't get me wrong. No one ought to tell you not to. But, he'll make it back, is what I should've said to you."

"Thanks."

"All right. Good. Well. Well! Have a drink with me. You came all the way out."

"It's on my way."

"One drink. One! You're in my house. Let Donny be hospitable."

"A small one."

He finishes what's in his glass on his way to the kitchen and tells me to make myself comfortable.

I notice, now that I'm inside, that there is no dining room table in what would be the dining room, but instead a tripod easel standing on a paint-stained drop cloth and propping a stretched, bare canvas.

"Does your wife paint?" The bare walls bounce my voice.

"Nope. Me." He comes out of the kitchen and hands me something gold-brown with a single, rounded ice cube. "I'm an artist. Ar-*teest*." He laughs. Deep crow's feet branch to his temples. "Surprised? Didn't think I had a creative thought in me, huh? How do you think I knew you had somethin' troublin' you? I knew before you said a word. What you got here is a lethal combination. Doctor? Artist? I got it covered! Both sides of the brain, and most people can't make 'em work together. I see the world—naw, I look inside, is what. I look inside you, and I can't even help it. It's a gift. Now, don't get all scared. All I'm sayin' is, I read things, read people. Because I watch, and I sense. *Sense* things."

"Mm. Do you have Coke, or something, to mix with this?"

"Sure, I got Coke." He takes my glass. "This is bourbon, though. Good bourbon."

"Yeah, it's—it's good, but I'd like Coke in there, too, if you don't mind."

He takes it away.

The only thing in the hutch, aside from circles in dust hinting at the recent presence—and removal—of dishes, probably china, is a picture lying flat on the top shelf, its brass frame spotted green. An adolescent Donny, seventeen or maybe eighteen, sits cross-legged in tall grass, elbows resting on his knees and hair hanging past bare, bony shoulders. A new cigarette burns between his fingers. Twisted into the ground in the shadow of his knee is a beer bottle, and his mouth is half-open in a laugh or a smile.

"You want more ice, or was it good?" he says from the kitchen.

"Yes, please. More."

I move in deeper, past the hutch and into the living space where he and his wife—maybe—watched television or fought or drank. A magazine lies open on the coffee table, warped and puckered, the pages a coaster. The old chair is canvas and wood, a hand-crafted piece of a different time I've only read about, when flowers were symbols painted on Volkswagen Beetles. The canvas-back is rubbed and faded from wear, the arms scuffed to pulp at the edges.

Throw pillows with perfect center dents sit at straight diagonals in couch corners, and the end-table lamp shade, nicotine-beige, drops a dim circle of light on a half-full coffee mug. Ghosts of pictures, maybe his paintings, hang on the walls, smoke and time marking their edges.

"For you, my angel."

I take the glass. Close up, he looks older. And shorter. I can see over his head, but just barely. Coarse hairs grow from deep pores in his cheeks and chin and his skin is oily and loose. That this is what came to be of the boy in the picture, that hiding under the hanging skin and somewhat conventional hair and age-inspired glasses is the life-squelched and smothered spirit of the boy in the grass… Maybe it was the war, maybe the drinking, maybe the wife. Maybe all of it, everything. I wonder what he was like back then, when his hair was long and he smiled, and I have a feeling I might have found Donny-the-boy irresistible, would have chased him and played with his hair, sipped from his beer bottle and rolled with him in the grass. The missing shirt would be missing because I'd taken it, wrestled it from him until our knees and elbows were grass-stained, and pulled it on over my own.

"Drink," he says, then disappears into a back room. I sit in the old chair, set the glass on the wide, wood arm and wait.

All the lights are on: living room overhead, end table lamp, kitchen light, dining room chandelier. Light falling on everything, getting in my eyes, and I'm so very visible, awkward in the room like streaks on just-cleaned glass. I look around for signs of the wife, something stronger than the dust evidence in the hutch, but there's not a plastic or dried flower, a collectible cow, a doily, a doll. No left-behind high-heeled shoes on the vent under the window, no frilled umbrella drying upside-down on batwing arms. No blanket for her cocoon. That was probably the first thing she packed.

Donny returns in a sweater and jeans and socks stained gray at the edges. "Like it?" He points at my glass on his way to the couch and sits down, sets his drink on the magazine.

"It's good," I say.

"You ain't even…Aw, c'mon."

"I had a little."

"You said you'd have a drink with me."

I take a short sip, tasting it in my throat before it even touches my lips. "Mm," I say, and hold back a cough.

He nods and drinks from his own glass, makes half of it disappear, pauses for a breath, then finishes the rest and stands. "Another?"

"No, thanks."

"Didn't know you was goin' to be such a little girl," he says on his way to the kitchen, and from around the corner, "You afraid of me? Think I'm tryin' to get you drunk and take advantage, or somethin'?"

"Of course not. No."

"Well, drink up, then."

He comes out refreshed and turns off all the lights but the end table lamp. "All that light—gives me a damn headache." He falls into his spot on the couch and smiles. "You're really here!"

"I am." I make a show of swallowing a heavy sip and then ask for a cigarette. I'd like to take off my socks.

He pulls one from his pocket and tosses it to me, then a lighter. "You can have as many as you want, can have anythin' you ask for. My cigarettes, your cigarettes; my liquor, your liquor. You can even stay over. Now, don't look at me like that. You know I don't mean nothin' by it. I mean on the couch, if you can't drive. It pulls out and it's comfortable. Slept a lot of nights out here, let me tell you." He laughs. "Naw, I'm just kiddin'. But it is comfortable. Em and me, we got it for a weddin' present. Her daddy's rich. Owns the car dealership on the corner, down there by Kelly's Burger. Know the place?"

I do. I nod. "Em? You call her Em?"

"Em, Emily, Emmy. Depends on her mood. When she's bein' a bitch I don't call her nothin'." He shakes his hair out of his eyes, says, "Naw. I'm lyin'. That's when I kiss her ass, call her my darlin' Emiline," smiles. "You know. Like Clementine?"

"You have a painting at the—downtown, in the coffee shop?"

He holds up his glass. "Good girl."

"*Emily's at Dawn*. Yours?"

"Course it's mine."

"I only ask because of the initials on the—on that thing, the tag. The label."

"For 'God damn, I love that woman.'" He looks at me. "That's right. God *damn*. That's what it stands for." He leans back into the couch, puts his feet on the table and stares at the wall. "Yep. That was one of my better ones."

For minutes, I don't know how many, we both sit and stare, saying nothing, until he says, "It's Gary. First name's Gary. Donald's the middle."

His phone rings, then, and he gets up fast and jog-walks to the kitchen with his drink held steady. I fantasize that Jake has somehow found out I'm here and is calling because he simply has to talk to me. I fantasize—for the twentieth, hundredth, millionth time—that two days ago didn't happen, that he did not call his mother before calling me.

The receiver slams down hard enough to ring the base. Donny comes back out with a refilled glass and sits on the couch and lights a cigarette.

"Are you—"

"None of your goddamn business."

I pull my feet under me, used to the dampness, now, and hold my drink and wait for him to finish his cigarette before asking about the painting. "To sell it after such a long time is…I don't know. Why are you?"

"It ain't old. Painted it…I think it was about two years ago. You talkin' about the date? That's part of the title, not the year I painted it. That's her house back in eighty-one. She sold it, I don't know, ten years ago, maybe more. It was her first, her fixer-upper, you know. Did a good job on it. Made some money. But, she didn't like it. Didn't want to mess with the contractors and didn't like dust and paint, so the next house she bought, she kept. This one."

"It's nice," I say, but it's a standard ranch.

"Yeah, it's all right. I'm goin' to miss it while I'm gone, but I'll be back."

"You aren't getting a divorce?"

"Divorce? Hell, no. She ain't goin' to leave me. Not for good. She needs me. Can't get through a month without the doctor. That's me." He points his thumb at his chest. "She could die. She's sick. Understan'? I help her make it through the days, medicate. She don't know how to self-medicate like I do. Always goes too far, won't practice *moderation*." He finishes another glass. "More?"

"I'm fine."

"You ain't had more than three sips. What's the matter? You don't want to drink with me? Donny ain't good enough for you? I thought…y'know, friends."

"I drink slow."

"No one drinks that slow. Come on. Drink up. Do it for me. For Donny. My wife left me."

"I'll have to be able to drive home, and everything, and there are police all over the place."

"One little drink ain't goin' to get you drunk. You think I want you drunk? What would I want that for? You're havin' tough times and I just want you to relax, that's all. Nothin' more. What, you think—? What could be in your head? Ain't you learned nothin' about me, yet?"

When he's angry, his lips spread thin and his cheeks tighten to narrow his eyes. When he is angry, I've finally learned, there is nothing good to say; there is only waiting for it to pass.

"You think I'd take advantage of you when your man is off at war? There ain't nothin'—*nothin'*—worse than that. I have respect! Respect, that's what, and you want to know how I can respect a man I don't know, but you wouldn't—he's my brother." He punches his chest. "You hear? Brothers. Donny Donaldson. Sergeant Donaldson. Airborne Infantry. Eighty-second. Airborne!" He slams his drink on the magazine and it splashes out onto the table, his hand. He wipes the back of his hand on his jeans and says, "What's his name?"

"Jake."

"Jake. Jake what."

"Just Jake."

"Tell me his last name."

"Why?"

He shakes his head. "All right. Whatever. What's he do?"

"I told you already."

"When?"

"In the car."

"Well, I don't remember. Tell me again."

"He flies Apaches."

"That's right. I remember. I remember, now." He tosses his hands in the air. "Y'see!" he says. "Airborne. Brothers! But, I know, I know. You don't see because you can't. Never will. You're a woman—Naw, now, I know there's women in the war, so don't get all…What I meant to say is you're a civilian, don't know shit. It's in here." He holds his hand over his heart. "I'd be the worst kind of man to come after the girl of a brother at war. You—You're like my sister. If I ever—now, you listen—if I ever come after you, you kill me. You hear? I have a gun. You use it on me. Hell, I'll kill myself."

"I'm not going to kill you," I say. "And I'm sorry. I didn't really think that, but you never know."

"Naw. Don't be sorry. Just don't think it. Can you do that? Could you trust me and not think I'd do that?"

"I—sure. Yeah."

"You're lyin'."

"I'm not. I am not lying."

"Full of shit."

"I just told you. I don't know what else you want me to do."

"You can drink what's in that glass, for starters."

"Getting drunk will—"

"Did I ask you to get drunk? No. What'd I say? I said drink what's in the glass. It's one little glass and it's mostly cola, anyway."

I take a few swallows and try not to gag.

The buzz comes abruptly.

"That ain't all of it.—Now, there you go. Mia, you're a beautiful angel. You know that? What d'you think your boyfriend would say 'bout you bein' here?"

I hold up my glass. "I don't really care. If he doesn't, why should I?"

"Have I told you I love you?"

"Do you?"

"What's that?"

"Nothing."

"Ain't nothin' but a kid." He narrows his eyes at me. "If I was younger, though…Boy, if I was younger. Don't mean I don't love you, though. Love ain't got to be about that."

I don't want to talk about it anymore. My head is spinny.

Love.

Me.

What he loves, and who—not *me* me, of course, because he doesn't even know me—and…but…*why* does he? Love. *Love.* Sounds like 'lub' in my head so I think the word over and over, and whatever it means, I shouldn't like it, not from him. He loves me. *I love you.* I rub my finger on the glass and go, "Mm."

"It don't mean nothin'. Don't—look, I love people. People get me here, in my heart. It's the spirit I love. Artistic love, it's different. Deep. Like it—it transcends, y'see, what most people think love is. Superficial. Not mine. Theirs."

"You don't know me."

"You're goin' to argue with me 'bout this? I damn well—I know what I know, and I love what I know. You can't tell me who I love and you can't tell me who I don't. Listen, no man anywhere—or woman, all right? or woman—can say what's right to feel. If I say I love you, you just sit there and take it. All right?"

"Okay."

"I love you."

"Okay, Donny."

"You hear me?"

"Both times."

"Well, all right."

It's not bad, the drink, even if it burns my throat a little. Bourbon spreads delightfully warmer than vodka. Yes. Delightful, like I've just swallowed a vial of Anbesol and have been numbed stomach to chest. And he loves me, he says, which may or may not be true, and I am beautiful, he says, and safe, he says, and love is love, real or imagined.

"Ready for another?"

"I am."

While I wait alone, the rain returns and pats the windows, then pelts harder with heavy winds. He comes out of the kitchen and something's changed. His head bows and I know the expression, now, know the face, the mood. Quiet time, but I'm bourbon-filled and brazen, and when he passes by I slap his leg and say, "What's the matter with you, all of a sudden?" I am him: "What a goddamn baby," and laugh and look up at him. He hands me my drink and sits down.

"What d'you mean, 'What's wrong?' Nothin's wrong. What's the matter with you? Why you sittin' like that, all curled up? What, I scare you?"

I tell him no, of course not, that I'm just a little cold. "Lighten the hell up, will you?"

"Now, what the hell's gotten into you?" He watches me.

But no, not *me*, and when it goes on for too long I say, "What?"

He slides along the couch toward me and reaches for the lamp and nudges it to one side, to the other, and then tilts the shade to shift the light. "Sit there just like that. Don't you move."

No more wind, no more rain, no more storm. The tornado missed, touched down somewhere else about three miles south, they say on the radio. Donny turns it off, then, and says, "Damn weathermen. I like a storm. You like a storm?" I say yes, I like a storm, and maybe next time.

My chair has been turned to face the dining room and my hair is loose from the ponytail, pulled forward—by him—to hang down the sides of my face. I haven't been able to look at my watch—"Quit movin'!"—but the last time I checked, it was midnight. Soon after, he started filling my glass with plain soda.

"Quit it, now. You was sittin' straighter before."

Painting has sobered him—impossible, it would seem, since he's gone through at least six rim-full drinks—and what I think is number seven sits on the floor against the baseboard where he won't kick it over. He moves around the canvas like a hummingbird, stepping aside to add some shading, aside to fix the curve of my left nostril, and I wait, fingers tight around my glass, for him to fall, to trip over the easel or a toe-trap in the drop cloth, but he never does. Wrinkles are anticipated and he smoothes them with his feet without looking, and when he is so close to the easel that the legs might get in his way, he steps around them, dances with them, dips for his drink while staring at his work and then swiftly replaces it, his charcoal pencil fast returning to the face staring out from the corner. A hair gets in my eye and I blink. It won't go. I shake my head, but just a little because it's so heavy.

"Naw, naw," he says, and he kneels in front of me and touches my cheeks with warm hands, turns my head to the left, brushes down my bangs so they hang in my eyes. His fingertips are gentle and his breath is pleasantly strong and I am taking it, making it mine, noticing his long, curled lashes and falling forward just a little bit. I start to put out my hands—a hug, just a hug, a touch, a body—and he stands again and steps back to the easel, to the face that looks nothing like my own.

Her eyes are deep and dark, not plain and light like mine, and her nose is narrow, low, elongating the face. My cheeks are round, but hers are sharp—pointed, even—and with dark hollows underneath. Her jaw is weak, the mouth thin with a down-turned upper lip. I check the eyes again. The bottom lids are missing, just upper lashes and irises and whites that pour into the face.

"Almost there." He draws the hair in straight, quick lines criss-crossing over my forehead, uses scribbles to cover my ears and shoulders, then drops his pencil on the floor and picks up his drink and steps backward until he is standing beside me. "Beautiful," he says.

I tell him thank you, but that it looks nothing like me, though—slowly—I'm starting to see it.

"It's you, all right." He sits on the couch.

I turn the chair back to the living room and tuck my feet, but I can't get comfortable.

He closes his eyes and swoops his fingers in front of his face, drawing closed an invisible curtain. "I see," he says. "What I see with my eyes closed is what you see there." He points at the canvas, opens his eyes. "Artist. Capital 'A'." He squints at me. "Doctor." He laughs. "Donny Donaldson. Doctor. Artist." He lights a cigarette. "Doctist."

"Actor," I say. It's too bright because he turned on all the lights again, said the one lamp wasn't enough to 'reveal' me. "Where's the light switch?"

"There by the door."

I hold steady both ways with a hand on the back of the couch.

"What do you mean, 'actor'? You think I lie, or—damn, just like my wife," he says. "Do somethin' for her and two minutes later she's kickin' you in the head. Don't like me doin' nothin' for others, neither. Got mad 'cause I helped out a friend—so what if it's a woman?—and took everythin', went to her mother's."

I try to remember. He said she was somewhere else, that she left to stay with someone, but not her mother. "I thought you said she was at a man's house."

"Now, why would I say that?"

"I don't know. But you did. I remember."

"You think I'd be sittin' here with you if my wife was with some other man? What kind of a man would I be to let that happen? You think I'm some piece of shit, candy-ass that'd let someone get on his wife?"

"But you said—"

"Naw. I thought you had somethin' beautiful and kind and decent inside, but then you go and say what you did."

"Donny."

"Don't you know me? I ain't goin' to lie to you. Not you. You're my angel. I love you." He slides off the couch and hobbles over to me on his knees, stopping at my legs. "I know you don't mean what you say, and sometimes what comes out of you is 'cause you're upset about things. Let me do my—let me fix it for you."

"I don't need you to fix—"

"Doctor Donaldson! I want to help."

He is close enough for kissing, his eyes shining and brown and two inches from mine, but he doesn't waver, doesn't fall in. His hands wrap tight around the chair arms. I close my eyes and he is Donny-in-the-picture, peacenik hippie. The before image.

"Donny." I open my eyes and reach out for him and he pushes off to stand. My drink falls in my lap and bleeds through, cold, to my thighs.

"You know Judy?—Naw, you don't know Judy. I'm the only one that knows her, 'cause she's like me. Artist, but she's better. Genius. You should see what she—me and her, no one else gets her, you hear what I'm sayin'? I tried to tell Emily—no, not sex, not lust, not with me and Judy. We don't live in the world of sex and lust and—Sex! Sex! She's always makin' something real into somethin' else. Y'see? We, me and Judy, we *are* the—the earth, or—the veins, like blood. The love and the shit of it, all of it, and you can't talk about it, can't tell someone about it. That's why, art. You…people like you…you take good bourbon and you mix it with Coke 'cause you can't take it, got to make the hot go away." He bends to grab my hands and closes them in his, kneels again in front of me. "Artist," he says. "Understan'?"

"I guess I don't."

He leans forward until our shoulders touch and holds me and whatever he said is already gone, lost in settling bourbon-heat. I am in someone's arms, snug, not tight, and breath falls on my neck just under my earlobe. I hug him back and his hair brushes my eyelashes and I hug him back and feel a pulse that isn't mine and I hug him back until he stops and pulls away, telling me again that he loves me, that I am an angel. He stands again and asks if I'm ready, now, for another bourbon. "You ain't drivin' tonight," he says. He smoothes my hair off my forehead. "But don't worry. I got clean sheets for the pullout."

APRIL 17, THURSDAY

BEFORE-MORNING DARKNESS. I can feel it without opening my eyes, recognize the shape of my chair and the fold my body forms to fit. Chancey purrs on my hip. A commercial jingle plays. I feel around for the remote control and find it under my arm, press the power button, try to remember how I got home. Not my car. Lionel. He charged full price and accepted the tip. I might have begged him for my job back while we waited for my burger and shake at the drive-through, and he might have said to ask again later, when I'm sober.

My head throbs and I'm thirsty.

I close my eyes.

Scratching, rapid and insistent. The corner of my chair is sleep-breath rancid and my back and shoulders ache when I stand.

Chancey's bowls are empty. I fill the water dish. Pour in food. Chancey doesn't come, but instead guards the front door, meowing. Through the peephole I spot the rear end of one of the downstairs cats, the gray one, and across the hall a couple of newspapers in yellow cellophane on the neighbor's straw welcome mat. I push Chancey aside and go out to the hallway, carry the gray cat down the stairs and drop it in apartment three's open doorway. Back upstairs I check the wrapped papers, find today's, and bring it in. I open it to the classifieds and fix a drink.

Secretary. Secretary. Medical technician. Truck driver. Factory worker. Factory worker. I crumple the page, my fingertips ink-sticky and black, and toss it in the living room for the cat.

Blue sky outside and green-studded, slender branches on the oak. The woman from downstairs—I try to remember her name…Safia?—stands out on the sidewalk, looks up at her first floor window and waves, then turns her back to the wind and exhales, the smoke immediately whipped away from her cigarette. She is barefoot with colored toenails, and the frayed hem of her peasant skirt blows around her ankles. Sitting nearby in the grass, her black cat. I open the window.

"Safia," I call down—hoping it is, in fact, her name—and mime smoking. "Can I have one?"

"Of course!" she says. She points, jabbing over my head, and nods.

I'd meant to meet her, to take it and smoke it alone, but she's already picking up her cat and carrying it to the stoop. "Come on up," I shout just before the main door slams.

Smoke spirals stretch and unwind over the table. Safia drinks black coffee, brought along in a bright yellow mug. Three in the afternoon seems late for coffee. Maybe she thinks three in the afternoon seems early for my alcohol breath.

She looks around, eyes pausing on wall hangings, the clock, the open bottle on the counter, me. I smile and say, "Thank you. Again. And I'm really sorry. I'm buying some today, and—so, I mean, I'll pay you back."

She shakes her head, waves me off. "I have never seen any of the other apartments in the building. It is hard to believe the same floor plan can look so different."

There is a wedge of an accent I hadn't noticed before. I nod, say, "Mm," and, "I thought so, too. Isn't it strange?" The only one I've seen, aside from a small part of her kitchen, is my own.

"Safia!" Her name comes loud, suddenly, from somewhere.

"One moment," she says to me. "Yes?" She leans under the raised window, her nose pressing against the screen.

"I'm going. Do you need anything?"

"Fish oil," she says, and her husband, standing curbside, writes it in the air before leaving. We watch out the window, listen for the starting engine, and smile fast at one another when we make eye contact. She waves at their car when it passes.

I say, "Have you been married long?"

"Not long, no. Nearly one year."

Nothing to say, again, so I ask how long they'd known each other before marrying.

She shrugs and takes a sip from the yellow mug, then sets it down and looks out the window. "Not long."

Her skin is dark, lotion-smooth, and her hair has, since the last time I saw her, been dyed a sort of bronze, an attempt at blonde, maybe, and strikingly 'American.' She turns her face to the heavy breeze and closes her eyes.

I have a feeling I could disappear right now, and when I did she would hum or sigh, finish her coffee, and glide out of my apartment, never even here.

Pulse-circles vibrate in our glasses under the low pass of a Chinook. They've been flying often, lately, following the pattern, crossing west to east over the roof.

"Chinook," I say and watch it disappear.

"They are so loud," Safia says. "So late, sometimes—*thump thump thump thump thump*—and I wake up and cannot go back to sleep. I wish they would *all* go away. Go to Iraq. Go to the moon. Let them go anywhere, but let them be quiet."

I put out my cigarette, then chase burning tobacco bits and flatten them to ash. I take—without asking—another one from the pack she's left on the table and light it. "Not Iraq, maybe."

"No? But, the faster they go, the more that go, the quicker it is over. It is a stupid war," she says.

"Mm."

She tilts her head. "Mm?"

"I'm just sur—A lot of people don't talk about—well, they won't say that. Not that."

"Say what?"

"That it's a stupid war. I mean, I know people think it, but—well, you know. It's just not popular to go around saying it."

"But I can say I like the war, and no problems?"

"You can say anything you want. It's just—well, because people are getting killed, and everything. Not agreeing with it isn't—it won't make you popular."

"Yes. I know. Your husband is there?"

"He's not my—Yes."

"I am sorry."

"It's okay."

"I did not mean I want them to go *there*. I do not hate *them*. It is not their fault. I only meant to say, please, that I want peace at night. Only that."

I hear something tapping, bouncing. Her foot, maybe. She looks inside her coffee mug and then out the window.

I say, "Let's not talk about it. Okay? There's enough unpleasantness as there is, don't you think?" *There is enough unpleasantness, don't you think?*

Olivia would say that.

"Oh, no. Not *so* much. The war is only one thing, and there is much beauty." She rests her chin on her hand and her hair falls forward in waves. Her appearance is almost threatening. Brown, such brown, eyes, and a small circle of a mouth. Perfect, barely-pointed chin. I tuck my own hair behind my ears and, oily, it stays put. I'm glad there is no Jake here today to witness this, this contrast. Gentle, flowing spirit-woman and awkward, gawky waif. If not for the cigarettes, I might suddenly have something else to do, might have to ask her to leave, but here she is after having come up the stairs to give me something.

"Are you hungry?" I say. "I'm—I haven't eaten, yet, and I'm about to have a late lunch. Or early dinner."

"Oh! Lunch? Well…" She looks—startled? trapped?—at the clock, then out the window again, and says, "I—eh—"

"It's no trouble. And I owe you."

"Oh, no, no. It is only cigarettes! I have manymanymany."

"Please. Let me just make you a sandwich, or something. You didn't say you already ate, so I have you there. It's too late, now."

"If not now, it will be later?"

"Yes."

She shrugs and smiles, tucks her hair behind her ear. "Yes. Lunch."

I open the cabinets to a rolled, half-bag of chips and a can of sliced mushrooms. It's been a long time since I last shopped. In the refrigerator is enough meat and cheese—none of it really rotten-smelling—for two thin sandwiches, and there's bread in the freezer. I show her what I have and she nods, "Yes, that is good, thank you," and while I tear lettuce and separate meat slices, she bounces her heels.

"When does he return?" she says.

"I don't know."

"No?"

"Six months. More." An unusual odor comes from the open jar of mayonnaise.

"No good?" she says.

I hand it to her and she smells it, hands it back. "I would like some. It is fine. Are you ill?"

"No. I don't think so. It's probably just because…with orange juice, maybe…"

"Dairy and citrus. And vodka." She makes a face. "No good."

I make my sandwich dry and set them both on the table.

"It must be very romantic," she says, chewing. "It is nice to miss a person, sometimes."

"I hadn't thought of it that way."

We look outside when a car honks. Paul.

"I love to think of the day when the missing is over," she says. "What a wonderful day. What is more romantic than a war? The best movies are about war's sad and happy times, and love, and…and correspondence! I like to write with my hand, on paper, so personal. And to receive is like a look at his soul, inside thoughts, and no talk, talk, talk." She *yap-yaps* with her thumb and fingers. "It all means so much nothing. I fall in love with a letter."

"Does Paul write you? Notes, or…?" My glass is empty and I can't refill it, not with her here. Watching.

She wipes her mouth with her hand, laughs a little. "Paul does not like to write. Oh, notes, yes. 'I am at the store. Love Paul.' No," she sighs. "It is the idea, maybe. I *would* fall in love with them, I meant to say. Paul and me, we are together all of the time."

"Try to enjoy it," I say. "It's better than—"

Three raps pound the door and Safia cringes. "He is always so loud," she says. "I want to hit him in the head."

"Come in," I say.

Paul opens the door and steps in, but barely. "Hello, ladies." He nods at me. "Hi. Eating lunch?"

"Hello!" she says. "You are done, already?"

"Oh, yeah. No lines. This is always the best time. Anyway, I don't want to bug you, or anything, just wanted to see where you were. I got you a *pressss-ennnnt.*"

"A present?" She claps. "I will be there in a moment." Paul waves and backs out and closes the door. Safia eats the last bite of her sandwich, smiles, and plays with her mug.

"Don't you want to know what the present is?"

"Oh, it will be there."

"I wouldn't be able to wait, if I were you."

"Well, I cannot eat and leave. We will have a cigarette."

"No, no. I can't smoke any more. Go. You must be dying to know what he got you."

"I am! Thank you, again. This was a good lunch, and not necessary. I am sorry to go so fast," she says. "Are you—?"

"Oh, no. Go. I understand. Really. Don't worry. I have to do something, anyway."

"Yes? Okay, then. I hope I did not keep you!"

"I invited you."

She laughs. "Well, please. Come down to see me."

She grabs her cigarettes and hurries out, leaving her mug on the table. I wash it and set it upside down on a paper towel and make another drink, then pick up the phone and dial L.D.'s number. Shellie answers, and I hang up.

THE PHONE RINGS, and it's Denise. She says as much. But then she just breathes into the phone. "Yeah? Hello?" I stare at the ceiling.

"Hi!" Her voice is sudden, sugary, sweet. "I'm calling to remind you about next weekend, and to tell you that I can't go to the mall tomorrow. I'm sorry! I won't be around."

"Okay… Thanks for letting me know."

More quiet.

I wait.

She says, "And we'll—I mean, *I'll*—Either way, seven-thirty on Saturday. Be ready, all right?"

"Okay. Thanks. See you—"

"Mia?"

"Yes?"

"What have *you* heard about leave?"

"What leave?"

"You know, they get two weeks. Fourteen days. Not now, but sometime in the middle, William said. Has Jake said anything? Such as when it will be, specifically? Or, more specifically than 'sometime in the middle'? How are we supposed to know when the middle is?"

"I don't know. I don't know anything."

She laughs.

"What's funny?"

"Nothing. Nothing is funny. That's—That's just great."

"Well, okay. Is that all?"

I hear something clicking rhythmically on the other end. "He didn't tell you anything? Really? Could he have said something about it before he left, maybe? Such as, if it *were* to happen, exactly or approximately when that might be?"

"All I remember him saying is that it would be a possibility, and only if they were gone a long time. I guess…I guess if William said they'll be getting leave, that means they'll be gone a long time." I think about this for a minute.

"I guess. Mmm…" Something's in her mouth when she says, "Will you ask about it next time you talk?"

"Can't you ask William?"

"I already talked to him, and he would only say so mu—he just said he didn't know for sure. I'd appreciate it if you asked."

"Isn't it good enough that there might be leave? Does it really matter whe—"

"Yes. It does matter."

"Maybe he'll surprise you."

"Spare a quarter…!" She laughs.

"Sorry?"

"Oh, nothing, nothing. I suppose I don't like surprises very much, is all." That noise again. A nail being bitten? "Well," she says. "I have to go, but if you hear anything will you give me a call?"

"I will."

"Thank you."

She hangs up. I toss the phone on the bed and turn to one side, then the other, in front of the mirror before getting dressed for the grocery store. There is still cab-money left, a stuffed-down pile in a Mason jar, enough for some quick meals, maybe. Enough to last until my next job, if I get another job in the next three days.

"Mia. I wish—man, I can't believe I missed you. I was sure I'd catch you after work…What time is it there? Six-thirty, right? Where are you?…What I'd give to hear your voice. I mean, not the voice on the machine, but in real life…Well, I guess—I mean—Hell, Mia. There was so much I wanted to say, and it's really not that much—it's not anything important—but I wanted to say it to you in person. Don't feel bad, though, for not being there. I'm not mad, I just…I miss you…I, uh, hope you're doing okay, and I hope you know that I'm doing okay…I'll call again as soon as I can. You have letters coming. And I got yours! About two weeks ago, and it smelled like you…I'm so happy you wrote, you don't even know…Anyway, uh—I guess I'll try again when I can…Love you, M…Bye."

"Mia, hon, it's Olivia. Are you there?… Hello-oo…Well, I received a phone call from Jakey just a little bit ago and he said he tried to reach you, but that you weren't there…Where are you? Are you all right?. . .We're just worried and want to make sure you're safe, so give me a call, if you will, when you get in. If I don't hear from you by this evening—well—I suppose I'll drive out…It's a very long trip, of course, but we have to know you're okay, because if you're not, as Jake's mother, I can get a Red Cross message to him if I need to…He wouldn't be able to come home, of course, if something's happened to you—sorry, dear, they just don't do that for girlfriends, and I think they should, really—but at least he wouldn't be uninformed…Not that I think anything's happened to you. Heaven forbid…But—Oh, this is silly. I'm sure you're fine. Please call me when you get this? Our Jake is so worried about you—oh, and he said he forgot to ask you to please send him a care package. Unless you've already sent one, of course, but if you haven't, we ask that you please do it soon. He said you know what he wants…If you're too busy, hon, I can certainly put one together and get it out for him tomorrow…Okay, dear. I hope to hear from you later."

THE SETTING SUN falls bright and warm on my face and Chancey meows from the floor. I turn my back to the window and cover my head with the pillow, try to remember whether I fed him before going to sleep but after shopping, after coming home and listening to Jake's message the fourth, fifth, or sixth time. After checking the number he called from and then dialing it, knowing it wouldn't work. Clicks and fuzz.

Sharp pain in my heel. Chancey, his claws plucking my sock. "Sorry." I slide out of bed and follow him to the kitchen, pressing play on the machine on the way. "Mia. I wish—man, I can't believe I missed you. I was sure I'd catch you after work…What time is it there? Six-thirty, right? …"

When his food bowl is filled I sit beside him on the floor and stroke his tail and watch him jam his snout into the kibble. "I'm the worst cat mother, I know. I promise I'll take better care of—"

"Mia?" Her knocks come brief and rapid.

On the other side of the front door, the sound of shifting feet, swipes on gritty linoleum. How many hours since she called yesterday? How many times today did I open my eyes, a second at the most, to gauge how high on the wall the day-shadows climbed? I was going to call her. I'd meant to call her. The microwave says it's eight o'clock.

"Mia?"

I sit stone-still and breathe shallow, open-mouthed, and wait for her to leave. Chancey twitches his whiskers at me, round black eyes watching, watching, and then he is meowing, and I cover his nose and his mouth until he squirms free and runs out, into the bedroom. I think, *Sorry*.

She didn't wait a full day. Here to confirm I'm no good and that anyone but me would be better for Jake. He must have told her when they talked that he's only received one letter. One, compared to how many written by people like Denise? How many letters and stamp-collaged boxes clutter William's side of the tent? I wonder if Jake pretends to be happy for him while making excuses for me. "She's not much of a writer," he might say. "She's not good at putting her feelings into words, you know, but I know she's thinking of me." And William would say that was odd, for an ex-English instructor, and nice try, Jake.

Any other woman, a better woman, would send weekly packages and write letters every other day, would be home when he called. No wife material here, Olivia will tell him. At home at her table she'll write a long letter all about me, hint not too subtly that I'm an unlikely candidate for marriage.

I believe that's how she would phrase it, anyway.

"Mia." She knocks again. "Hon, are you in there? Are you okay?"

I stay quiet. Chancey pads in, his toes lightly *pat-pat-pat*ting on the floor, and eats his last piece of food, sniffs the water.

"I heard you talking before, Mia. Please answer the door."

Damn the cat, anyway.

The sink shines, empty, but the side counters are sloppy-stacked with dirty dishes, plates speckled with stuck food bits and glass-bottoms crusted with dried milk and orange juice.

"Mia?"

Dust devils hug cabinet edges and the final wedge of setting sun falls in orange highlights, as if making a concerted effort to magnify the cat hair and litter on the floor.

She knocks again.

"Just a minute." I get up and rush to the living room—two pictures, there, to turn face-up—and the bedroom—one—and back to the kitchen for the picture on top of the refrigerator, her voice carrying on meanwhile.

"Oh! Mia, I'm just glad to hear your voice. Jakey was so worried. We both were. That's why I couldn't—well, I'll just wait until. . ." She trails off.

I wish there were time to do something with the dishes, the litter box, the stovetop. A cheesed noodle clings to the edge of a burner, and circles of…something brown…spot the white porcelain top. But, no time. I straighten my sweatshirt, check my jeans for dirt and stains, and wipe anything off my eyes. I open the door and downstairs spices mingle with—is it rose? some strong flower—perfume. A yellow ribbon pin clings to the spot over Olivia's heart, and at her feet stands a square bag on wheels with an extended, extendable handle.

"I'm so glad you're home." Her hands clasp in the tight space between her breasts. "I wasn't sure until I heard you. I saw your lights on, and I thought it was your car out front, but…well, you took so long to answer, and you never know. I know how young women like to go out on the town on weekends, and sometimes they can't get home, so they take cabs every—"

"Well, here I am." I ask if she'd like to come in. She picks up her bag, small enough for less than three days' clothes.

"I hope you don't mind," she says, "but it's a long drive, so I brought some things. I thought maybe you and I could shop for care package items for Jakey. Unless you've already sent one, of course. Look at me, talking without even thinking. Did you, hon?"

"I tried and tried, but there's just—I've been working so many hours, and everything. I was going to do it tonight."

"Oh. Okay. Well, that's fine, then. But, let's not go tonight. Let's go in the morning, together, all right?" She moves past me into the kitchen and stands there in the middle, then pulls a ribbon-magnet from her purse and hands it to me. "Here you go, hon."

"Thanks."

She sets her purse on the counter and I stick the magnet to the oven door.

"I'm just so glad to be here. I know how alone you must be. Jakey said you don't have many friends, and going through something like this by yourself can be—well—it can be difficult."

Jakey. "Yes," I say. "I'm glad you came, too. I was dying for some company." More and more, her voice comes easier to me.

"Oh, good!"

I start a pot of coffee and line glasses in the sink, spray water in each, and wipe off the counters while she sets up in the guest room. It's the one room I don't use, so it's clean, at least. By the time she finishes and joins me in the kitchen, the pot's filled halfway.

"That smells wonderful." Her eyes pass over the sink and she says, "Do you have a clean mug?" She sits at the table and folds her hands in front of her and yawns.

There are no clean mugs, so I wash one and wait for the coffee to finish brewing. She looks again at the sink and then at me, starts to say something, stops, then says, "You're not eating, hon."

"I am."

"Have you looked in a mirror?"

"I'm just tired," I say. "The shifts are long. And they start early. I have to be there at six, you know, so I—I mean, it's…I'd have to get up too early if I wanted breakfast."

"You looked just beautiful at Christmas, and you had the same job, then."

I wipe off the outside of the pot, where dust has layered. Jake and I never think to wash the whole pot. We only swish water inside.

"Mia," she says, "you're a stick. And what is all that?" She flips a hand at the mess on the counter.

"Dishes."

"Those aren't dishes, hon." She slides out from the table and goes to the counter and picks up a sauce pan. "And this?"

"A lot comes in a box."

"Sweetie, I've made pounds of macaroni and cheese in my time. Jake's favorite side—when it's not homemade—and I know how much comes in a box. It's this much," she says, pointing inside the pot, "plus about a half cup." She picks up a short stack of black, plastic microwave trays with serving dividers. "What they put in these could hardly feed a child."

Coffee's on, so I fill a mug and set it on the table. She sits in front of it. "You really should eat more."

"I eat just fine," I say. "I was eating too much before, is all. I'm on a sort of diet."

"Well, I don't know what for. Jakey never liked his girls very skinny."

I scratch my forehead to hide my eyes when I check the clock. Olivia has been here ten minutes and I can't see past another ten, can't see the inside of an hour, or a whole evening. Five in the morning, Jake's time, and that he's probably waking up right now brings a little comfort, stirs something in my stomach. I think, *G'morning*, and say, "How's your coffee?"

"Perfect. Thank you, hon. I need it after that drive. I'd have been here sooner, but the weather was just awful."

"Really? How long ago did you leave? I got your message just a little bit ago, and I was calling you back when you knocked."

"Well, I left that quite a while ago, and I suppose I thought, why not? You need somebody, I need somebody. I'm just thankful the weather didn't get any worse." She looks out the window. "It's fine here."

"I wish you hadn't put yourself through that," I say. "It wasn't necessary. I—really, I was just about to call you."

"Don't be silly." She waves me off. "Anything for Jake. And you. You know that."

I pour my own mug and the hot coffee melts the rubbery ring of a different day's coffee circling the inside. I join her at the table.

"It was awful," she says. "It got so bad I couldn't even see and had to watch the taillights in front of me just to stay on the road. And even then, you never can tell. They might pull off to the side to wait out the weather, and then what? I'd run right into them and be stranded." She lifts her mug, sips, sets it down. "But I kept going, anyway. If you stay far enough behind, you have time to react to anything, and it was just fog and rain, after all. Though, we did end up standing still for about five minutes when we came across a tractor-trailer jackknifed in the median. Horrible," she says. "I don't know if the driver died. There was an ambulance, so I suppose he could have died. It's dangerous out there today. Any other time I'd have stayed home. Dear, I so hope you're careful. You are careful, aren't you?"

"I try to be, yes."

"Well. Because when you look at what it was like today, it just seems there are times when no one has any business being on the road."

"You're a saint to have made the drive," I say.

"Oh, now," she says. "Not a saint. Just a mother. It's the least I could do. Jakey would do the same for me, for you, for anybody. He'd give you the shirt off his back."

Not laughing outright means holding my breath. Two, three winters ago, Jake and I rented a cabin in the woods in Georgia, a two-bedroom, two-story house in the hills, cheap because it was off-season. The forecast had called for spring-like temperatures in the low to mid-fifties, so I left my coat on its hanger and packed light sweaters and sweatshirts. Our first morning there, Jake and I left the cabin with full travel mugs and slid down a rocky slope to a narrow, leaf-padded trail.

The first ten minutes had been lovely, had passed as advertised: a brochure morning of bird calls, twigs snapping in echoes, and a tree-silhouetted, bright orange sunrise over the mountain on the opposite side of the valley. The air smelled like fresh bark and we stopped for a minute to breathe it.

We walked half a mile before the crisp, refreshing breeze turned into a slicing, burning wind. I pulled my hair over my cheeks and said, "It's freezing."

"Yeah," Jake said and closed his jacket tighter.

I tucked my hands in my sleeves, looping a cold finger around the travel-mug handle. The other hand I alternated from ear to ear, warming each for a few seconds before switching. "The forecast said at least fifty."

"I know," he said. "They also said a ten percent chance of snow." He looked up at the sky. "Too bad you didn't bring your jacket."

"What's funny?" Olivia says.

"I was just remem—"

"It's true," she says. "I would do anything for you and Jake. I hope you know that."

"I do." My tongue feels like jerky. I get up for a glass of water and drink it fast. Some of it spills down the sides of my chin and I try to wipe it away without her seeing.

"Water," she breathes. "That must be how tired I am! It hadn't even occurred to me, and I'm absolutely parched. May I have a glass?"

The glass I used was the last clean one. I wash it, fill it with water, drop in an ice cube and put it in front of her.

She drinks half of it. "He sounded wonderful, by the way. Oh, I'm so sorry you didn't get to talk to him."

"That's twice you've talked to him…?"

"Three times, I think. Let me see…once when he first got there, the second time I told you about, and then this time. So, yes. Three. I've been very lucky." She dips a finger in her coffee and gets up to put it in the microwave. "I hope you don't mind me telling you this. I know you haven't had a chance to talk to him yet, but I think the important thing is that he's safe. And, well, he did try to call you yesterday, after all, but I guess you weren't home."

"No."

The microwave stops and she pulls out her mug. "Well, like I said—and I know you agree, hon—all that matters is that he's okay. I listen to the news every day, you know, and not a day goes by that I don't hear about someone being killed one way or another. Did you hear about the crash?"

"No."

"Well, when I hear or see things like that I just think, 'At least it's not Jake.' I feel so horribly—

(*Horrible*, I think)

—for those poor, other mothers—"

"When was it?"

"I'm sorry?"

"The crash. When was it? What kind of helicopter?"

"Don't worry, hon. It wasn't him. It was a Blackhawk, thank God."

"Is *that* all?" I wait, but the sarcasm is lost on her. "Were there survivors?"

"Oh, no, I don't think so. There rarely are, you know. But you and me, and all of them, we have to stay strong. Have to believe in our President, and believe in the work they do over there and know that they wouldn't be there if it weren't for a good reason. You just have to trust that, and know that no matter how many die, it's for a reason. Even if it's a hundred. Four hundred! You'll see. We'll visit the memorial tomorrow, and you'll see. And it's not too bad, you know. The number. Fifteen, maybe? No—I believe it was…eighteen?" She rolls her eyes. "I can't remember. Can you believe it? And I just saw it on the news this morning."

She watches me over her coffee. "It's hard. I know." Her hand slides toward mine on the table, just to the center, and her fingers, the skin shiny like wet dough, beckon. I let her grip mine loosely. "You just have to have faith that he'll be okay," she says. "That's what I do. I feel so badly that other mothers are losing their children to this war every day, I do, but I'm also so blessed that Jake has made it this far, because you never know. You just never know when and if it will be him."

No good response for this, so I say, "He's a good pilot."

"I know he is, I know," she says. "But sometimes, it just doesn't matter. They have those little guys shooting them right out of the sky."

Coffee. I take a long drink to dilute the acid in my mouth. "What were you saying earlier? Something about a memorial?"

"You know it," she says. "The one they're building just off the bypass."

I shake my head, no.

"I came that way on purpose because I read they were going to build something for the boys—and girls—from this post who don't make it back. It's lovely. A beautiful thought. They deserve something like that, a testament to their honor, a show of belief in their cause. I know our Jakey will have thought it was worth it if he doesn't come back."

"Yes." I wish I had a cigarette. "A memorial. Well worth it."

"Yes. Well." Olivia pushes her coffee aside and stretches and asks if there's anything stronger, "Something with a bit of a bite, maybe?"

She only sips at her wine on holidays, rarely finishing even half of what she gives herself. "I have—we have vodka. Left over, that is, from New Year's Eve."

"That would be just fine."

I wash another glass and pour her drink, but she waves it off as too strong. I add orange juice.

"Don't you want a drink, dear?"

"No, thanks…we really only keep that stuff around for special occasions."

We move into the living room. She pauses at the Christmas tree and I wait for her to say something, but she doesn't. Too tired, maybe, or at a loss. What's there to say? It's just a tree, an old tree, and people forget to drag out their Christmas trees all the time. But then she touches a branch, and needles fall. She takes a sip of her drink and sighs, then sits and slips off her shoes and stretches out on the couch with her feet propped on the arm, her glass where she can reach it on the coffee table. I bring my coffee to the chair and wait for one of us to talk. She looks around the room.

"You have nice pictures of him," she says. "I'd like copies, if you can."

"I'll send them to you this week." But I doubt I will. Jake and I put all of our negatives together in a shoebox, unlabeled, unorganized. It would take time, and I need to find a job, clean the house, get rid of the tree. Take Chancey to the vet. A notice that came last week—or was it two weeks ago?—said he's overdue.

"The most recent picture I have of him is from high school," she says. "He never sends me any of the pictures they take of them in their uniforms. 'The man in those pictures is only part of me,' he always says. I think he just doesn't like the way they turn out. But, oh, how handsome he is in uniform, isn't he?"

He is. "Yes," I say. "And no, he doesn't really like them, the pictures." Something about the way his mouth sets when he's not smiling. He brought one home for me to see, said, "Get a good look," then tore it in half and dropped it in the trash.

"I'll be right back."

In the bedroom is a years-old picture of Jake in his BDUs embracing his car when it was new, the first morning he took it to work. Chrome glints in flashes here and there and the roof reflects his face from the chin up. That was two years before I moved in, when he had the other girlfriend. I unfasten the back and peel out the picture and bring it to Olivia. She smiles and presses it in her palms.

"He wasn't my first, of course you know."

"Your first?"

She sits up and drinks from her glass like it's straight orange juice. "I was eighteen when I had her, and she died seven months later. Seven months. Shelbi." She died in her sleep, Olivia says, and she knew right away, woke straight up from a dream. She's buried in a cemetery in Granby, Colorado, plot 87. Just her name, Shelbi Lakeland, but no dates, Olivia says. "A soul is ageless, timeless, don't you think? And to tell her age, well, that would just make people stop and think, 'Oh, how young, how sad,' but no one would remember her name."

I don't remember ever having heard about a sister.

Olivia's husband is buried beside his daughter in a family plot with a Rocky Mountain view. Olivia and Jake will end up there, too, she says. When the time comes. I don't tell her about his Arlington plan. She'll be long gone by the time his turn comes around, and if it makes her happy to believe he'll be buried in Granby, so be it.

"Jake did tell you about Shelbi," she says.

"Of course, yes. Very sad."

"You looked surprised, is all."

"Oh, no. No, I just—it's just a fresh feeling of sadness every time I hear it."

Olivia says I can't imagine the pain of losing a child. I agree. She says I can't imagine what it's like to worry she'll lose another. I nod. "Jake is all I have," she says, both hands circling the glass. "Someday, hon, you'll know. If he makes it back and you two have kids of your own." She sighs. "Jake would make a wonderful father."

"Yes," I say.

"You would have to see him with his young cousins to know, dear, but he really—well, you'll learn, in time. What's it been, just a couple of years?"

"Three."

"And you want children, of course."

Not sure what to say, I smile at her.

She waits, looking at me. "Well." She rubs her hands on her pants. "If you'll excuse me. Sometimes I think I'm nothing but a funnel!" She jostles the table when she stands and her drink splashes over the rim.

"I'll take care of it. You go ahead."

I wipe up the spill and avoid thinking about children, the one I don't plan to have, the ones she'll never get from Shelbi. When she returns she says "Yes, thank you" to a refill. She stirs it with the spoon I left in the glass. "Jake tells me he's only received one of your letters," she says. "Have you sent many?" She sets her spoon on a piece of paper towel left on the table.

"Two or three."

"Oh?"

"I think it takes a long time for mine to get to him."

"That could be."

"It would have to be."

"He's received all of mine," she says. "I think I've sent him…let me see, now." She mouths the numbers while counting on her fingers. "Eight. I know it's not many, but I'm so busy at work and taking care of things around the house, and…well. I write when I can."

My coffee is cold, now, but I drink it anyway. The living room falls quiet minus ticking from the helicopter clock on the shelf. A gift from Olivia for Christmas, crystal and brass. Not Jake's taste, and not an Apache. "It's a Huey," Jake said, looking at it with half a smile, "but to her, a helicopter is a helicopter."

"When did you say you mailed your last one?" she says.

"Excuse me." I get up. "I guess it's contagious."

I lift the lid so that it taps the tank in case she's listening from the living room and sit on the floor.

The phone rings. I haven't been in long enough to go back out there naturally, so I wait for the machine. It's most likely Denise.

If it is Jake, Olivia will pick up, and I'll still get to talk to him.

"Mia, hon, your phone is ringing."

"The machine will get it." The bathtub presses hard on my back, but the throw rug is soft and I am alone, the bathroom a vault, a cave, a haven. I reach up to turn off the light and a low moon shines through the window.

"What if it's Jake?" she calls.

"Please answer, if it is."

The phone stops ringing and the machine answers, plays my recording, beeps, and a voice says, "Mia," and now it's too late. To run out would look suspicious, especially now, so I wait it out and run through a list of explanations while he talks.

"Hey…You there? You workin'?—Course you're not. Charlie drove me this mornin'—hey, when did you leave? He said you quit…I'm goin' to miss my mornin' angel. You think I like lookin' at that bearded bastard every day? Come over. You left your picture…Or don't. Free *TV Guide*. Bye. Donny."

THE GROCERY STORE is, at six in the morning, empty and fluorescent-bright. Generic easy-listening tunes play soft through the overheads. No cashiers stand guard behind the only two open registers; rather, they roam the aisles, re-shelving expensive items discarded at last minute and replacing products carried aisles over before becoming second-thought castoffs. Olivia walks in front of the cart with two fingers curled in the corner grating and pulls it behind her. I rest my hands on the guide bar and tap the plastic with the rhythm of the squeaking wheel.

"He likes these," she says, pulling a box of chocolate-covered wafers from the shelf.

"I know," I say, but I don't remember having seen them in our cabinets.

She slides the wafers between a can of soup and a box of dog-shaped crackers. She drops in a bag of candy. "He went just crazy for these when he was ten," she says.

She doesn't look at me, hasn't since last night when the argument about Donny ended without resolution. Afterward, Olivia stared out the window, the way Jake does when he's angry, and then spent close to an hour in the bathroom. Sleep tempted while I waited, but coffee without sugar or cream, hot and pouring fast, kept me awake. When she came out, she stood by the door and wiped at her nose and said, "Good night," and "I'll be leaving tomorrow, in the morning. I'd like to get the shopping done early. If you'll still be sending him a package, that is."

Olivia winds around an end-of-aisle sugar cone display and I follow. Her heels tap loud, and sharp waves of yesterday's perfume, heavy on her skin, make me nauseous. I breathe in through my mouth, out through my nose, and pull a can of spreadable cheese from the shelf and drop it in the cart.

"Oh, Jake doesn't like that kind, hon." She puts it back on the shelf and replaces it with a milder flavor.

"He does," I say. "He tried it and said he liked it more."

"But it's so rich," she says. "He doesn't like rich foods."

"He likes that one."

She looks at the cheese on the shelf, the cheese in the cart, me.

"Help you find something?" The stockboy is eighteen, maybe, and wears a red apron.

"We're fine," she says. "Thank you."

Olivia watches his back until he is gone, then watches me exchange the cheeses. When I start to push the cart forward, she lays her fingers on the metal. "Was that your type?"

"Pardon?"

"That boy. Was he your type?"

"Jake is my type."

"But you looked at him. He was attractive—even I could see that. Would you date someone who looked like that?"

"I wouldn't date anyone who looked like anyone but Jake. And I didn't look at him. He asked us a question."

She moves the cheese to a different spot in the cart. "And six months from now? Will he still be attractive?"

"Who? Jake?"

"Jake. Or the boy—either one, I suppose."

"Jake will. I already forget what the…boy…looked like."

"Do you?"

"Mostly."

"So, you did notice him," she says.

"He stood right there."

"You noticed him and you were attracted to him."

"No," I say, "I was not."

"Jake could die," she says. "He could die right this minute and you're noticing a boy in a grocery store." Wet mascara dots the skin under her eyebrows when she blinks.

"I noticed no one. Please believe me."

"You're staying at men's houses, flirting with stockboys—"

"For—! Olivia, I told you I didn't stay at his house. And I didn't flirt with the stockboy."

She wipes her face, pulling a streak of black from her eye to her temple. "Will you be faithful to my son?"

"Of course I will."

"Will you write him more often? One letter is simply not acceptable, and—"

"Yes. I'll write more."

"Send him more packages?"

"I'll send one every day."

"Don't be ridiculous." She shakes her hair and sniffs. "You'll grow tired of missing him, you know."

"I am already."

"You're a woman. You're human. You'll eventually want companionship. And when you do, what will you do? He loves you so much," she says. "He would die if you hurt him."

"I won't hurt him."

"It could be an accident."

"Accidents do happen."

"What if you decide you want someone like that cute boy to keep you company?"

"I didn't even notice the boy."

His eyes were green, not like olives but like leaves, and there were two freckles on his cheek in a direct line from the corner of his mouth his earlobe. He wore a loose hemp bracelet that fell low on his hand and he was tall, taller than I am by at least six inches—shorter than Jake, but not by much—and if he were to have held me, my head would have fit comfortably into the curve of his neck, just under his chin.

"Oh, hon, are you sure? Are you positive?"

"I promise. Six months or six years, I'm waiting just for him."

"And that man, the one on the machine. Since you quit your job, I don't suppose you'll have any reason to stop by his house again."

"No. I don't suppose I will."

"Good, that's good."

She turns and continues down the aisle and I hang a few steps behind. "Olivia?"

"Mm?"

"Has Jake said anything to you about leave?"

"About—what? Leave? What do you mean?"

"A friend of mine said her husband said they might be getting leave. Midtour leave."

She bites her lip and picks up a can and reads it. "I'm sure, no. No, he hasn't said anything like that, hon." She sets the can in the cart and pulls it along, past the fruit cups, which he likes. Peach squares, the ones in the jellied sauce.

With Olivia gone, the apartment is twice as quiet, twice as empty. Chancey scratches the litter box and I hear it through the walls, nails-on-chalkboard scraping, and it goes on and goes on until I scream his name and he runs past me, into the living room and under the coffee table, where he stays.

Nine in the morning is too early to have already finished half a normal day's activities, too early for it to feel like noon but without the benefit of those three hours having truly passed. I'd thought of asking Olivia to stay. Not for me and not for her, but because that's what people do, they encourage visitors to stay. She stood in the doorway the same way she'd come in, hands clasped between her breasts, and—words stuck to my tongue—I opened my mouth to force out the words, but she said, "Well. I really should start heading back, because I have an appointment I'd forgotten about entirely."

I read, again, the card she wrote and sealed and asked me to include in the box. On the front is a picture of one polar bear beside the dotted-line tracing of another. The inside reads, in comic handwriting and signed with a cartoon pawprint, "Something's missing. I think it's you." Olivia's note is written below it:

Dear Jake,
I do miss you. It feels like you have been gone for so very long. I hope you are well, because everything here is fine. I am taking care of Mia as you asked, so please don't worry. She is working hard and she loves and misses you very much, as I do. I hope you like the food, as Mia and I picked it out together. Take care of yourself, and please stay safe. I love you—Mom.

I throw away the envelope and toss the card into the box and spend the next three hours packing and unpacking it, arranging and rearranging, stopping to watch the news, and then starting over from the beginning when one pack of cigarettes or one candy bar doesn't fit, until every last thing is in, even if it's smashed. Except for the sucker-dart gun. That stays.

On the way back from the post office, I stop at the liquor store.

Jakey,
That's what she calls you, and it makes me sick.

I miss you. You can't know how much, because I can't tell you. It's like guilt, in a way. The way it just sits there.

She told me about Shelby/Shelbi/Shelbey (however you spell it), your mother did. I never knew you had a sister.

Why? Why didn't I know about her? Jake, I'm getting so confused. First it was just one thing, and now I find out about your sister, and I feel so far away from you in so many ways. Maybe it's nothing to you, your baby sister dying. Maybe it was so long ago that it ended up being just some thing that happened, but how could you not have told me? What does that make me, to you?

Olivia still thinks you want to be buried in that place in Colorado. Yes, she talked about that, too. I wish you would be, because then I could be buried beside you, unlike at Arlington where I'd have to pass the wife test to get in.

I never told you I can't stand her, did I? I never said anything because I know how much you love her, but I can't not tell you now. You know how alcohol makes you honest? I've only had a couple of glasses—enough to be honest!—but not so much I can't type. Unfortunately(?)

Anyway. (I stole that segue from you.)

Your mother is manipulative and depressing.

There!

I understand, now, why you try so hard to make her happy. Why you let her come to the hangar and why you've called her so often. I love you, you are my life, I'm crazy sick with worry and fear and have this…this rolling, moving pain—(last week when I was driving, I sped, Jake, so fast that I even scared myself, and I thought, just for a split second and in a not-real way, what if I pull the brake and turn hard? wouldn't it be easier?)—and she is the one you called. Olivia. Your goddamn mother.

She'll tell you this eventually, but I'll tell you first: I stayed the night with a man. The one I wrote you about, Donny (did I write you about him?). But I didn't even stay, and that's the thing! I was there a long time, and I think I fell asleep for about an hour before I woke up to call a cab. You can call Lionel the next time you're near a phone. Don't call me, call Lionel, and he'll tell you I didn't stay the night. Do you remember the number? 7465, if you don't. Please call him. He'll tell you.

But I did stay a while, and we did drink together, and he drew me. It's the most beautiful drawing, Jake. Not because it's of me, obviously, but because of the way he did it. If you saw it you would think so, too. But he has this horribly pained soul, is the thing, and it came out in his drawing, I think. I am pained, in the picture. I think I am him. Or he thinks so. I don't even know. You have to see it, Jake. It's beautiful.

Did I already say that?

Olivia doesn't know anything. You have to believe me. I told her all about it—because, yes, he called—but she didn't believe me, and I don't think she ever will. She doesn't like me. She doesn't like me with you, but I don't care. I like me with you. And I wish you would call and I wish you had told me about your dead sister and I wish I could be buried beside you and I wish we had gotten married before you left. Will you marry me, Jake? Will you do it through the mail? No. That's stupid. Forget I asked. I don't know what I want.

You. That's what I want. And I want your mother to explode.

Not really. But I would like it.

Jake.

I'm drunk, now. But look! No typos! That must mean I need more. I'm drunk a lot, though I probably shouldn't tell you that. Don't worry, okay? 'A lot' still isn't very much if you compare me to the blonde woman.

But you don't know the blonde woman.

I still love you.

Mia

Safia—wasn't it?—said something about writing by hand. More personal, she said, so I try. I try to write *Jake* but it won't come, looks like *Yuri* then *fuze*, and then I remember the letter I wrote earlier and put downstairs for tomorrow. Sealed and stamped—the front twice-kissed with lipstick—and I can't send it, not that one. My chair skips, groans rough when I slide it back, and the table isn't heavy enough, pulls toward me when I try to stabilize myself with it, and three inches off the chair makes me dizzy. *Fall soft,* my father said when I was little and liked falling, *fall soft, sideways, and bend your legs.* I try it now, and yes, it is softer that way. Still fun.

"…candles and wine? Come…one year anniversary. Don't you want…me and you?"

"I…but—"

"But what?"

"If…woods, we have a tent, and…when…pictures, they…better."

"Than what?" he says.

Safia is not so easy to hear, even with my head pressed flat to the floor. "Speak up!" I say and shift and slide, looking for ear-suction. I stick my finger in my other ear.

"…if we are just sitting at our table…can take…sitting… means nothing…that movie?"

"What are you saying?"

"…thing."

"Safia."

"Nothing, I…Okay?. . .not be an asshole."

Chancey's nose tickles my hair when he sniffs it and I laugh. They stop talking. I hold my breath, listen, but there is nothing for several minutes, and soon I forget I'm listening and their voices, up again, scatter like words tossed around in a crowd of foreigners, and I wish he were here to hold onto.

APRIL 21, MONDAY

THE SOUND OF their door slamming through the floor wakes me, face flattened and head spinning, and her laughter and his cheery "Of course, doll!" has me following them down the stairs, in my mind, to the bottom landing, the door. To the mailboxes and my letter. My head is in a sunspot, hot, hair wet around my face, and I know, I know it's too late, that it must be four, at least, and that he must have already come, but maybe once, maybe today, he is not on time. I crawl to standing and wipe my face and take the two flights down to the boxes, some of them—not mine—stuffed so full with envelopes they're not latched, and the outgoing bin is empty.

I run outside, across the lot and to the neighbor's porch where he's slipping letters into boxes and I beg him, on my knees, even, *please*, but he says "Sorry, no. I can't."

APRIL 23, WEDNESDAY

LATE APRIL, and already July's humidity saddles the spring heat. I wipe at a moisture ring with my sleeve cuff, back, forth, back, forth on the table with the wall clock's tick tick. Later, maybe, the batteries will have to come out.

The sheet of paper in front of me says, "I'm sorry sorry sorry so so sorry."

I crumple it, tear it, and throw the pieces on the floor.

From as far away as the kitchen, the gun from the grocery store's junk aisle—"What's that for, hon?" Olivia said—loses a lot of accuracy. I miss the Vice President's head entirely, and instead cover the current time with the rubber suction cup.

One in the morning, there, which means he is sleeping.

I wonder if he's called Olivia again.

She would have called me. Maybe.

It's lonelier when he sleeps. Four more hours, or so, until his alarm goes off, if he does indeed wake up at five. Five sounds right, sounds good. He wrote in his letter that he was up for sunrise, but maybe he was awake before that, since he was already drinking coffee at the time.

Jake (*tick*)

Jake (*tick*)

Jake (*tick*)

Jake (*tick*)

Not his face, not memories, but the name, repeating and repeating like a compulsive twitch, a skipping lyric. I whisper—to the air that just might someday reach him—"Sick, sick, sick of you."

I use my last dart when the anchor's head fills the screen, but miss and hit the blurry space beside his ear.

APRIL 24, THURSDAY

THE LOBBY IS blue. Gray-blue, rain, the same as the cubicles beyond the reception desk. Five minutes ago it was "Just another minute" and there are no magazines on the coffee table, or on the spill-spotted counter with the cups and coffee pot, or on the end tables with the dust-covered, plastic plants on skid-proof mats. Behind the receptionist speaking into a shiny black phone, a man and a woman stand just outside the entrance to a cube. He holds a small Styrofoam cup and curls a hand over the top of a wall. She stands with one leg bent, one skirted hip thrust, a one-sided smile working.

My résumé starts to wrinkle between my thumb and finger, so I smooth it, set it on the chair beside me.

There is a buzz and the receptionist says, "Oh, will you hold on? Just a minute," then presses a button. "Yes, sir…yes…okay." She presses something again. "I'll call you back." Her finger beckons and I get up and stand at a counter as tall as my chest, a small child's big-people table. "He's very sorry," she says. "He thought he would be able to meet with you, but something's come up. You can leave your résumé…" She raises a beauty-queen palm over the counter and takes my resume and glances at it, then sets it somewhere underneath, where I can't see. "Thank you. We'll be in touch."

"Before I go," I say, "what—just so I know—exactly would my duties be?"

"Basic administrative."

"Which is…?"

"Data entry. Answering phones. Filing. Printing. Copying. Appointments. Collating. Envelope stuffing."

"I see."

"It's work," she says, and more quietly and with a look around, "Work is work, right?"

"I guess it is."

Today, there is a letter. Thin, the envelope containing not my real name, but his play on it, "Mi Amore." I smell it, and it smells like sweat and mud. Against my cheek it is soft with fine grit. Too short to read now, because as soon as I open it, it will be over, so I sit down, first, to write my apology.

April 24

Jake,

Please, please, please ignore my last letter. I didn't mean to send it. Or to write it. Too much to drink—it's not a good excuse, but it's mine. I honestly don't remember much of…I'm lying. I do remember. All of it. I'm so sorry. She's really a perfectly lovely person, and…well, you're not going to believe that, either. But I am grateful to her for driving down to see me! Jake, if I could write "I'm sorry" as many times as I want to, this letter would reach from me to you. I'm sorry I'm sorry I'm sorry!!! There's really nothing worse than having that letter out there floating around between us on top of everything else. It's killing me. You're mad at me about something new and you don't even know it, yet!

What does an ulcer feel like?

Don't hate me. Read my mind! Read it right now and call me! Call me today. Call me tomorrow. Any time before that letter gets there.

I have to talk about something else, now.

So! The weather has been beautiful. A little too warm—you can't kick me from there, ha!—but beautiful, anyway, and not at all humid today, for once. You should be glad you have a dry heat.

One season down, Jake!

I miss you!

Oh! Denise said you might be coming home sometime for leave. Is that right? You must have forgotten to tell me on the message you left. I asked your mom about it (leave), and she seemed not to know anything. In fact, she said she hadn't heard anything about it at all. Maybe you'll actually tell me something first. (Just kidding! Ha!) Anyway, Denise really wants to know if you have any idea when you—or William—will get to come home. I do, too, of course. I'm just trying not to get excited until I hear something from you.

This letter won't be very long. My head won't stay straight, today… I'm in such a wonderful mood. The windows are open and the curtains are swaying and everything feels like spring, SPRING! I want to go for a walk, or go for a drive, or something. You know how it is when you just can't stay inside, anymore?

(I hope this doesn't make you think I'm not still sorry. The whole letter shouldn't be about that, though.)

101

I might finally take down the tree (even if I have grown used to its bulk in the room, and the brown color is really kind of nice and nature-y, in an autumnal way).

I still read the note you gave me in the hangar, sometimes. And I'm trying not to care so much, Jake. I'm really trying not to take it personally. I want you to know that.

Love,
Mia

P.S. Did I tell you I quit driving? I did. I almost had an interview today, but I didn't. I didn't make an appointment, or anything, but just walked in, so I was lucky they even took my resume. They said they'll call.

When the letter is addressed, stamped, and left downstairs for pickup, I read Jake's.

Mia,

You know I don't want to pressure you or anything, but it wouldn't be the worst thing if you wrote again. I miss you, M. I'm starting to think I made you up. If I did, I'm surprised I haven't gotten awards for my superior original design. Specifically in the breast area. (I miss your breasts. I could write about them for pages.)

Seriously, though. It's not about wanting letters or keeping up with William's six letters a week from Denise. It's really about wanting to know what you're up to and how you're doing and getting your thoughts. I tried to call after I got here, but the line was busy. From now on I'll try to write more often, too. I could probably do more of it than I do, seeing that I seem to have enough time to stare at the pages of this book I've been trying to read. I've been on page 97 for twelve days.

Today is April 16th. Late. Did the news cover the capture of the guy they're calling "the third in command"? It happened this morning. William and I were part of it and we're still so pumped I doubt we'll sleep tonight. We've been on plenty of missions since we've been here, but when it's something like this and something that'll be in history books as a huge point for our side…he was bad, M, so I don't feel wrong for having killed him. Or for having helped kill him. I don't know if I did it or if someone else did, but if it was me, it was me. And if it wasn't, maybe I kind of hope it was. Fuck him. He deserved it. He deserved worse. I know I was against all this before, but I don't know anymore. It's starting to feel different.

Hey! Now April 16th is a day to remember for two reasons. You remember the 16th, don't you? I remember your skin against those black sheets of yours. The best first time, have I told you? It took years, but it was worth the wait, I tell you. Well worth it.

Sometimes there's so much time to think that all I do is remember, and it's like taking a vacation and coming home for just a few minutes. (Before William comes in and knocks something over, or just makes loud noises in general. He has this picture of Denise in a heavy as shit frame, and he knocks it over every day. I'm not kidding. Every single day. I'm starting to wonder if maybe he does know about that guy from last year, because how many times can someone accidentally knock over the same thing? But it hasn't cracked yet).

Anyway, those few minutes with you refresh me like you wouldn't believe.

Speaking of William, he just came in and now we have something to do in a few minutes. Meeting, he said. Surprise, surprise. More later.

-J

OUT. GOING OUT, getting out, doing something new, and giddiness—foreign, now—pinkens my skin; no need for lipstick-rouged cheeks. Just the lips, full and soft-looking, the stick labeled kidney-bean red.

Fifteen minutes until Denise is due. I slip in another quick drink and it spills, some, down the front of my dress when I try not to ruin the lipstick. A blow dryer takes care of most of it; the stain is hardly noticeable.

In the mirror, makeup is good. Breasts are successfully lifted to crescent shadows. I covered dark eye-circles with a skin-colored stick, and though the dress bunches differently now that it's home, it still works and is still, as Denise said, stunning.

I put the glass on the counter, pet Chancey, and go downstairs to wait behind the door.

"You're so fucking skinny!" she says through her open passenger window. "How are you keeping that thing on?"

Her date smiles from the driver's seat and then looks away, puts the car into gear.

Denise grips the pewter flask in her lap. "You'd look so much better if you had a flower to tuck in your hair. Remember I said—? Don't you think so, Brian? Or…I don't know. Is that a stain? What happened?"

I wait for one of them to unlock the back door.

Cheap, wrinkled velvet curtains the same bright red as my tree skirt hang from rods draped with uneven light strings across tall living room windows. Good furniture has been carried away to make room for white plastic patio chairs edging the walls like school-dance benches, and the dance floor is a bamboo area rug. A man and a woman Denise introduced using names I've forgotten are the only two bouncing to reggae; the rest mill at the edges.

Before the reggae it was country and synchronized line-dance stomps, Denise stumbling over Brian and Brian curling her to him, guiding, spinning her when the step called for women to be spun. She looked over once, over his shoulder, and smiled and winked and mouthed to me, *Just a friend*, laughing when his hand moved from the small of her back to the satiny lump of her behind. I laughed back and raised my drink, and now they're I don't know where.

"…needed something like this," says the girl to my right. She is nineteen, maybe twenty, with yellow hair and blue eyes. "I just got so sick of being at home all the time, you know? He called, like, once, and that was about a month ago." She shrugs and closes her lips over a narrow straw, sucks some punch, then pushes the straw away with the tip of her tongue. "I love him and all, but whatever. If he's not going to write… You know?" She is not addressing any one person, but our two-man, three-woman cluster, most of us preferring a punch bowl and the crackers-and-nuts platter to dancing. The third woman, who introduced herself as "Dick's Fiancée," wobbles in her heels and wrings the ends of her silk wrap while searching the room for something. Not Dick, because he's gone with the rest of them— "Convoys 'round the clock, the way he puts it," she said—but something, constantly something.

"You've already defended yourself ad nauseam, Charlene," Dick's Fiancée says. "No one is judging you, okay?"

"Of course they are," she says. "And they're judging you. What do you think this whole thing is for if not to see who's doing it?"

"If that's what you think," Dick's Fiancée says, "then why did you come?"

"Well, obviously, I was curious."

The man standing next to Charlene says, "I'm glad you're here, baby."

"Oh, shut up, Rick." She stirs her drink. "I just wanted to get out of the house."

"And there's nothing wrong with that."

"Thanks, but I wasn't looking for permission, or anything."

"Of course you were," says the other man. Mick, or Marc.

New song, now, this one a dance craze, and bodies crowd the space in a wave of claps and twirls.

Dick's Fiancée fills a plastic cup with punch and says, adjusting her wrap, "Country and reggae. I'd go out there if they would play something I can dance to."

"Anyway," Charlene says, "I don't think you should talk to me like that while my husband is deployed. What are you, anyway, a Judy?"

"A what?" Rick laughs.

The other man says, "I think you mean 'Jody.'"

"Judy. Jody. Whatever. Either way, I just want to have some fun. I'm not here for bad reasons."

"Neither am I," Rick says. "As soon as my shoulder heals, I'm off again to fight for your right to turn me down. But, since I'm here now, how about a dance?"

I fill my glass, which seems to be emptying quickly. The punch is tasty, not too sweet.

"I'll find someone else, thanks." She stands on her toes, looks around, then comes back down and stirs the ice cubes in her drink. "It's just, everyone expects me to, like, sit by the phone for a year, and be this…this…I don't know what. But he has his life over there, and I have my life over here. That's all I know. And it took me long enough to figure it out."

"Yes," says the other man, his eyes dull. "He can't be expected to have all the fun, can he?"

"Marc," she says to him, "Will you dance with me?"

"I think Rick has—"

"I don't want to dance with Rick. Besides, he can't be trusted."

"What makes you think I can?"

"Please?"

"Sorry, Char. My knee."

Rick waits, attention shifting, then reaches past me for a cracker and says, "Dance?"

"No, thanks."

Charlene says, "I'll be gentle."

Marc nods at the dance floor, smiles thin, says, "I can't keep up."

"Oh, come on," she says. "I promise you won't get hurt."

"Charlene." Marc shifts on his bad leg. "You're almost irresistible."

She slumps, sagging in her strapless top, and grabs Dick's Fiancé by the hand. "Come on." She drags her through a cloud of poker-game smoke.

Rick salutes Marc. "Thanks for tryin', buddy." He scoops two punches from the bowl, crosses the floor, and hands a glass to a girl in a blue dress. Only Marc and I are left staring out at the bodies randomly bonding and separating.

My glass is empty again, so I refill it, then tug Marc's shirt sleeve. "What happened?" I say. "To your knee."

"Explosion," he says, like *flat tire.*

"So. It really happens, then." They—casualties—are real people, after all.

"As far as I know. It felt real enough."

"You must be happy to be home."

The dance ends and quiet falls under laughter and dragging feet and somebody screams for a DJ—"Who the hell is in control of the music, here?"—to play something, anything, or everyone'll go somewhere else.

"Not especially happy, no," he says.

"Are you going back?"

"If I can."

"What are your chances? Of going back, I mean."

"They don't know, yet." He looks at his watch.

"Well, do you think they're pretty good?"

"Do you want a refill?"

"I mean, how serious did your injury have to be for them to send you home?"

"Refill, or no?"

"Yes, please." The cup he hands me is punch sticky. "Sloppy, but thank you. What were we talking about?"

"We were talking about you."

"Nope," I say. "We weren't."

"Are you having a good time?"

"That's not what—"

"I'm asking it now."

Where is Denise? Somewhere. "I'm having a great time." Marc's aftershave smells like citrus. "Delicious."

"Excuse me?"

"You smell good. It doesn't mean anything."

"Thank you."

"You're welcome."

He looks at his watch.

"Going somewhere?"

"I don't know," he says. "I'm not sure."

"How can you not be sure?"

"Plenty of ways."

"Tell me."

"I'd rather—"

"You're standing right next to me and looking at your watch. What is that, if not an invitation to me to...*for* me to?...*to* me to...ask what you're doing?"

He says nothing.

"Are you meeting someone?"

"No."

"You like this. Don't you? You're playing a game, right? You're making me ask you questions in some backward flirting thing."

"No." He looks down at me. "Do you know your dress doesn't fit you very well?"

"What?"

"First thing I noticed. It's tight."

The punch is lovely and sweet and poor Marc has hurt his leg. "It's fucking stunning," I tell him.

"Maybe. On someone."

"I don't. . ." I refill my cup. "Why would you say that?"

He swirls his drink and looks down into it. "I just thought you should know. In case another party like this comes along and you consider wearing it again."

I slide my hands over the material on my breasts and smooth the small wrinkles crossing my hips and know he is wrong, the dress is wonderful, and I am wonderful in it. "You're an as—"

"Don't bother. Listen, I'm only standing here because this is where the food is. If you don't want to be bothered by me, there are plenty of other places for you to stand."

"I like it here."

"Fine."

"I like your wedding ring, too. Where's your wife?"

He sighs and looks at his watch again.

"Why don't you leave?"

"Because," he says. "She won't be asleep, yet."

"Don't want to wake up your daughter?"

"I don't have kids."

"Jesus. Never mind."

And there is Denise, and there is Brian, both of them coming in from outside.

"Look," he says. "If you had a husband, and he stayed out until after you went to bed, would you think he were having fun?"

"Depends on when I go to bed."

"Eleven, usually."

"When he comes home, is he rumpled and smelling like another woman?"

"Rumpled, sure. I can do that. And alcohol instead of another woman."

"Then, yes. I would think he had *oodles* of fun. D'you like that word, 'oodles'?"

Denise and Brian push through the bodies on the floor and disappear down a hallway. I empty my glass and fill my glass and drink from my glass and twirl until my gown fans like a yellow umbrella.

"You're going to make yourself sick," he says.

"Worry about her, not me," I say, and my shoes, the heels high, spin like ice skates and heads blur by in a steady speckled stream and I've no control, anymore, because my arms pull me around and around and I'm one with—

He catches my hand and stops me, holds me up, says, "I don't want you to throw up on my clothes," then waits until I can stand on my own before releasing me. "Don't mean to ruin your fun," he says, "but trust me, you'll have a better time without the spinning."

I throw my drink at him, thrilled because I've never thrown a drink at anyone, and a pastel stain spreads on his white shirt and the hairs on his neck spring up as the punch drips down his chest. "Sorry," I say. "Not your job."

He holds his shirt away from his skin and walks away toward the bathroom.

I move through the house. Hallway wall sconces, floating wax discs in shallow bathtub water, tea lights in holders on the windowsills and light strings nailed around doorframes. No one else is in the kitchen when I find it, and the clomping of my heels is lost in thudding techno. Multicolored liquor bottles line the counter like a bar display.

I check the refrigerator for orange juice and find only beer and water and a single orange with a spot of green mold. I mix something else, blue and clear and red and soda, colorful and tasty and strong in a red plastic cup, and take it back out to the living room.

Couples of one kind or another fill the floor and hands slide over hips and pelvises glide. Open mouths, almost kissing, fingers breast-stroking blankets of air, all in dim light like afterglow, and they all know each other, or seem to, laughing, touching shoulders. I inch around the room with a smile, always a smile, alone without Denise or Charlene or Dick's Fiancé or Marc, until a plastic chair bumps the backs of my knees and I sit, back straight, smile stuck on so I look alone on purpose. A rest from all the dancing. My glass empties fast and I skirt the floor to mix another, thinking I hear someone say, "Who is *she?*" and remembering I look like a movie star—a goddamn movie star—tonight, if nothing else.

I don't dance, but I am, and Denise is, too, monster with a red mouth and matching body all beautiful and vaginal—she would love to be called vaginal, so I shout it over the music, "You look vaginal!" and she shouts back, "Damn straight!"—and in that instant we connect because we *get* one another and we move closer and dance the way girls dance in movies, part-time lesbians for show, her arms coming around me from behind and her hands sliding down my waist and over my hips and we're laughing and watching the men watch us and she puts her mouth to my ear and yells, "This'll be good," and runs her splayed fingers over my pelvis, not touching me but almost—they think she's touching me, you can tell by their eyes—and we laugh and separate and move on our own, in our own heads, until a man grabs her and a voice says in my ear, "You're something." For a moment he is behind me and we're dancing the way Denise and I were dancing and then he touches me and I spin and Marc is smiling and smelling faintly of punch and watching his hips close the distance to mine.

I pull away. "Thirsty," I say, and he takes my hand and says, "It's just dancing."

"I'm done dancing."

"But you do it so well."

My heels are too high, so I take them off and carry them to the kitchen and lean against the counter. He follows me, just close enough, and stands between me and the doorway with his arms crossed. "I didn't mean to scare you."

"You don't scare me."

"And I'm sorry about—all that, what happened earlier."

He says something else, about his wife, about how she's been strange since he came back injured, "Broken, she said," and in the middle of his kiss I tell him to stop, get off, and he does, but his hands still touch my back. I yank free to find Denise because it's time to leave, it's been fun but it's time to go. She and Brian stand across the bamboo and her lips touch his neck. When I reach her, I yell, "Let's go."

Her hair has fallen out of its clip and hangs in loose strands and her lipstick has faded to a sick pink stain.

"What are you doing?" She pulls my hand away from her hair.

"Time to go.'

Her head dips and her eyes blink slow. "No."

"Yes."

Brian strokes Denise's shoulder and she twists away.

I say, "I don't feel well."

"The bathroom is down the hall."

My head spins and I reach for her arm. "We have to go," I say, and she says, "Mia, let go."

Brian says, "Throw up. Then see how you feel." He looks at Denise, but she does not look at him. She tugs at a loose piece of hair and steps away from him and it's true, what people said. She was with someone the whole time.

"I thought you loved William."

"You're drunk," she says. "There's nothing happening, here."

Denise's fingers twist into a white braid on her lap.

Brian smokes a thin cigar and blows his smoke into the wind. "Hell of a night."

"Too windy back there?" Denise says.

"I'm fine."

"Are you sure?"

"I'm sure."

"Because he can put it out."

"No," he says. "I can't."

"Brian."

"Denise."

"I just don't want her to be uncomfortable."

"She said she's not. What's the matter with you?"

"Nothing."

He laughs.

"Is something funny?" she says.

"You are."

"No, I'm not."

"No," he says. "You're not."

I rest my head on the window, good and cool.

"What do you mean, I'm not?" she says.

"You said it first." Brian taps in the ashtray and turns up the radio.

"You said it differently."

"Well."

She sighs and looks out the window.

"This is it," he says.

Denise slides the stone of her wedding ring around her finger.

"Did you hear me?" he says.

"Not now."

"Yes," he says. "Now. This time." He looks at me in the rearview mirror. "How you doing?"

"Fine," I say.

"You're not going to throw up again?"

"I don't think so."

"Denise?" He pushes into a higher gear. "How are you doing, baby?"

She shakes her head.

"What was that? I didn't hear you."

"Fine."

"Everyone is fine," he says. "Wonderful."

Somewhere on me is the smell of Marc's aftershave.

 I rub my fingers over my skin and smell them until I find the spot, the back of my shoulder near Jake's favorite mole.

Denise stares straight ahead when I get out of the car. Her nose is red in the light from the open door.

In the dark and in my head I am with him, with Marc in my bed and his arms are around me and his stranger's mouth is kissing me the way he kissed me in the kitchen, the way I saw Brian kiss Denise before they disappeared down the hall, after Denise said she wanted to stay a little longer and after they thought I was locked away in the bathroom. I imagine them together and then I think of him, of Brian, and then of Marc and of Jake, all of them touching invisible me and I pretend I am Denise, not me, and spread my legs and arch my back the way I think she would.

DENISE CALLS WHILE while I'm sleeping and says she's coming over with coffee from the café downtown, the one with "that awful girl." I ask her to find out whether the house painting has been sold.

"Oh, that thing? Now I want to know, too. Could you imagine someone buying it?"

"It was gone," she says in the doorway, each hand holding a capped foam cup. Her eyes are red, swollen, and a loose band holds back her hair. She pushes past me, muttering that anyone would have to be crazy to pay more than ten dollars "for that stupid picture of a house" and hands me a cup, drops her bag on the floor by the couch, and falls into the cushions. "I swear, this summer is going to be oppressive. Have you been outside?"

"No, not yet." I wonder who could have bought the painting and if the coffee girl might give me the name, not that I would know what to do with it if she did.

Denise complains some more, looking at me and looking away, touching her hair and taking short, quick sips from the hole in the plastic top.

"So," she says. "You must have questions."

"About what?"

She shakes her head and reaches into her bag and pulls out an envelope. "These are for you."

I'd forgotten about the pictures. I snatch them from her and she waits while I sift through them.

Jake standing in front of an Apache.

Jake sitting on a pile of sandbags.

Jake posing beside the painting of an Apache and pointing at the sun hanging low under a dusty sky.

Jake with a cigarette, the pack tucked in his shirt sleeve.

"Which one?"

"Hm?"

"You're smiling. Which one?"

I show her.

"He looks good, doesn't he?"

"Different." In miniature, as part of the matte-finished grain, he's beautiful—painfully—in his way. Bronze-brown skin, tanned and dirt-stained, and the expression on his face—new, to me—is one of certainty and of confidence and of correctness in time and place and purpose. The pictures I already have, ones we've taken over the years in front of statues or lakes or rivers or famous buildings, are of a different person. Jake of this country, all-American boy who rarely traveled outside of his state. Light, clean, and basic. Unlike this new Jake, flat in my hands, who—just an image, yes, but—leaves me feeling like the girl with a crush on the boy she hardly knows and wonders if she'll ever have.

"Thanks," I say.

"They're yours."

I stack them—there must be ten or eleven—and set them on the table and straighten the edges. Denise gets up and smoothes her pants and walks around the room, pretending to study wall hangings and knickknacks. She squints at pictures she turns right-side-up on the shelves—"Oh, you've been there? William and I were there last year," and, to another, "That's one of the places he wants to visit when he gets back."—and when she runs out of things to pick up or point at, she sits back down. "Your tree is dead."

"I know."

"Why is it still up?"

"I've been busy."

"Do you want me to help you?"

"No. Thanks. Chancey likes it."

She drinks more coffee, her eyes on the ceiling, and then fumbles in her bag for a cigarette. "Want one?"

"Please."

Cigarettes lit, we sit smoking with no breeze coming in through the open windows. The cloud hangs in the middle of the room.

She bites her nails.

I look at the clock. Eight o'clock, Jake's.

The remote control sits on the arm of the chair. For three days, I've been disciplined, have watched only half an hour before going to bed, much of it replayed footage from the first days of the war. Explosions, explosions, gas masks and bunkers, *Just over a month since the official start of the conflict, Janie and Tom.* The killing of the third in command must not have been important to the media. The story was brief, buried, gone in two days. They're onto something bigger, now: war protestors spray-painting an Ohio recruitment office, then burning a Mercedes belonging to a high ranking marine.

"Why were the pictures upside down?"

"Sorry?"

"Your pictures on the shelves. They were upside down."

"It's nothing. Sometimes Jake will write things on the backs of pictures for me to find later."

"And?"

"And what?"

"Did you find any secret messages?"

"No." I tip my cup for the last few drops of coffee. "I think I want more. Do you want some?"

"Sure."

I bring the ashtray with me to the kitchen and fill the pot, dump grains in the filter, and stand there while it brews. Denise comes in to flick her ashes and leans against the counter. "Thanks for having me over. William's mother is coming, so I've been cleaning like crazy. I had to get out."

"When will she be here?"

"Tomorrow."

I take a long drag, exhale over her head. "William's mother must be so happy to know he has a wife who loves him the way you do."

She laughs, then coughs. Smoke-puffs the shape of mushroom clouds shoot out with bright, sunlit drops of spittle. "I've been waiting for you to say something."

"It's none of my business."

We put out our cigarettes.

"No, it isn't, but still…I think I know what you think. I think you think we're just having fun, doing a little something on the side. You can tell me."

"I don't think anything."

"Where are your coffee mugs?"

I point to a cabinet, and she pushes through the moderate collection until she finds one she likes. She chooses one that reads, in large, comic letters, I LOVE COFFEE.

She says, "I have to ask you to not write Jake about him. What you do is up to you, of course, but I would appreciate it."

"I don't keep secrets from Jake. But, if it makes you feel any better, it hadn't occurred to me to write him about—about this." I'd probably tell him about it if he were here, but putting it in a letter borders on malicious. Writing is…*intentional.*

"Well, whatever. Anyway, Mia, this is between William and me. If you do write Jake, he'll tell William, so…"

"No, he won't."

"Then William would find the letter."

"I'd tell Jake to burn it."

"Quit smiling. This isn't funny." She chews her lip and taps her mug. "You don't understand."

"What don't I understand?"

"This. The whole thing."

I wait, listen to the clock. I never took out the batteries.

The coffee finishes and I pour some for each of us and we go back out to the living room.

I think of Denise and William, of Denise and Brian. What she can mean when she says I don't understand.

She's probably right. I don't understand. Not really. But when I imagine the two of them together, I think of Marc and that stock boy and I want to know how Brian does it—if it's different from what William does, and in what ways. Does he smell like citrus? Does he grip her side instead of her back? Does he bite her ear and whisper strange, private things about the way her skin feels, maybe, or the shape of her shoulder? I want to know, What's it *like* to be with someone else, with someone new?

I put my feet on the table and my toe touches Jake's pictures and I look at his face and someone could have killed him *at that moment*, that single second of innocent fantasy, and it starts a panic, a strange sort of fluttering in my throat, so I think *In real life never, I promise*, and I imagine the painting and the timelessness and endlessness of the love in that old house in the snow. It's Jake and me, I know it is, it is it is it is it is it *is*—

—and I *need* it, the painting. Need it the way the religious—and maybe (or especially) the not-so-religious—need their crosses over the dining room table, their Mary statues gazing down from the fireplace mantle.

Denise wipes her eyes and dries her fingers on her pants. Her face would be a mess if she were wearing makeup, but as it is, there's charm in her red eyes and puffed mouth. Maybe it's that I've never seen her like this. Or maybe her pain gives me pleasure for no good reason. Whatever the case, her swollen, splotchy face is strangely beautiful in a way she couldn't duplicate with all of her foundation and blush.

"I love him."

I rub my eyes, dry and tired. "Does he love you?"

"Yes."

"What about William?"

"What about William," she says. "That's the problem, isn't it? What to do about William."

"Does he know?"

She bites a nail, looks at it, folds her hands on her lap. "It was some time last year, winter I think, when someone, some…nosy bastard…told William he saw me with another man—who was, yes, Brian—at the shopette. We weren't doing anything *unseemly*. We were holding hands while looking for donut holes. He prefers the chocolate ones, and I like glazed, but all we could find were powdered." She pulls her sleeves down to cover her fingers, then pushes them back up to her elbows. "That was the only time William ever said anything. He told me someone had seen me in the store with a man, and he asked who the man was. It wasn't serious yet, so I told him I didn't know, that it wasn't even me. He let it go. But now," she says and puts another nail in her mouth, "he must know *something* is off. We don't kiss anymore. Not unless we're…well." She shakes her head. "Isn't that funny? I can say it when I'm talking about Brian. 'I sleep with Brian.' 'I have sex with Brian.' I can't say it about William. Anyway, that's when we kiss. Or, that's when he kisses me and I let him. You would think he'd feel that, or that he could tell. How can anyone be that oblivious? Anyway, time passes—months, sometimes—in between, and it's not like we hate each other. We're adults, after all, and fairly sexual people. But we don't hug. Or touch, or laugh. He has to have an idea. He can't be that obtuse."

When I realize she's waiting for an answer, I say, "I don't know."

"If he's not, and if he does know what's going on—or even that *something* is happening, whatever it is—he's never brought it up again. And," she shrugs, "if he doesn't say anything and I don't say anything, it isn't really happening, is it?"

"No," I say, "I mean yes." I set down my mug, wipe my face, sticky and cold. A week, maybe two, before he left, Jake was quiet. Where we usually kissed or groped one another in passing in our narrow hallway, he walked right by. And he worked late. "We're loading up, so I'll be busy," he said. He could have someone, someone he knew here and who has gone with him, someone he laughs with at night after flying, before going to his tent, someone whose hair he touches when they have a moment alone, someone he tells stories and wants to kiss, someone he smiles at over the table at lunch. She, that woman, could be his reason for not wanting to get married, but I don't—won't ever—know, and for a moment—small, less than a second—I wish he were dead.

"Are you going to tell William?" I say.

"What other choice is there?" She says this while pulling the band out of her hair and shaking her head, raking her fingers over her scalp. "If I don't, we'll just end up throwing away more time. So, yeah, I'll tell him I don't love him anymore. But I won't tell him about Brian, because Brian has nothing to do with any of this." She flips her hair behind her shoulders.

"Doesn't Brian—I mean, it sounds like he has everything to do with it."

"I would still want to leave, with or without him. William's not right for me, period. In any case, I doubt Brian will still be around when William gets back. He—Brian—said that if I loved him, I would have already left William. He doesn't trust me, anymore." She laughs. "Maybe he shouldn't. I didn't leave, did I? It's been a year and a half, and I'm still married. He has no reason to think anything will change."

"He should have left in the beginning."

"William or Brian?"

"Brian. Or William."

"You say that because this is all so simple, to you. Black and white."

"Sorry."

"Mia, what you think about all of this—how you're judging me right now—doesn't matter. I know you think I'm a…that I'm an *adulteress*. Don't you love that word? These women—the ones who get in their groups and talk about other women, other wives—they love that word because it sounds so scandalous." She laughs again, and there's little fun in it. "Check their scrapbooking rooms and I bet you a million dollars you'll find little stacks of red velvet in their fabric drawers. Anyway, you probably think I'm rotten, the worst person you've ever known, because I'm cheating on my husband—my husband who's at war, no less—and I understand. But—and don't take this the wrong way, okay?—I don't care. I don't care what you think, I don't care what they think, and I doubt when I finally tell William whatever I tell him that I'll care what he thinks. What he feels, yes. What he thinks," she lights a cigarette, "no." Smoke curls in wide loops from her nostrils. "But if you feel like you have to write Jake about this, at least include the most crucial piece of truth: I never meant to fall in love with Brian. Ever. He was…he was someone to talk to, is all. I never meant for it to get past a passing friendship, and I certainly never meant for it to last this long."

Who, I wonder, is Jake talking to? What if he does have a woman friend, a woman he doesn't mean to turn into more than a friend?

"And by 'it'," she continues, "I actually mean my marriage. If I weren't still married, there'd be no affair to have. I meant to leave William a while ago because I wasn't happy, and then again, later, because I felt things for Brian I've never felt for anyone before. And because this is my life. My happiness has to come first. It just does."

"Why didn't you leave him, then?"

She throws up her arms. "Because he's always deployed!"

"Well."

"Oh, Mia, don't—are you okay? Here, let me…" She digs through her purse and pulls out a pack of travel tissues and hands it to me. "You know, don't you, that this isn't about you and Jake, and that what's happening with me and William has been happening for years? It has nothing to do with him being deployed. You know that, right?"

I don't know. I don't know anything. I tell her, "I know."

"If you feel sorry for him, just know he's not perfect. We had problems before I met Brian."

"Why is Brian always here, anyway? Why isn't he deployed with the rest of them?" I sound and feel like a child.

"Oh, he isn't always here. He's been to Korea, and now he's getting ready to PCS to Alaska, which is why he's not deployed. Timing."

"If it was has hard as you say—can I have another cigarette?—you couldn't have held it in for so long."

She tosses one over the coffee table, then kicks a silver lighter across the floor. "It seemed easier than breaking things off with someone who's at war. How do you tell someone when they finally get home to the life they've been dreaming about that the life they've been dreaming about doesn't exist?" Denise yawns. "I'm starting to understand why some women pack up and leave while their husbands are gone."

"That's awful."

"I know. I don't mean it," she says. "But when no time is right, what do you do?"

"You wait."

She gets up to stand at the window and looks outside, taps her ash between the ledge and the screen. "You're right," she says. "Of course I'll wait. For the next goddamn year, I'll confine myself to a life I haven't wanted since I fell out of love with him almost two years ago. I'll do it because William is in the Army, and because William's decisions have sent him to war twice. I'll keep suffering—silently, the way 'good' wives are supposed to—for his choices and put my life and my needs on indefinite hold so his aren't disturbed. Brian will leave me—I'm sure of it—and I'll just have to deal with that, too, so my dear husband doesn't suffer any inconveniences or undue pressure. Can't trouble the boys while they're at war. The world must revolve around them and around maintaining the illusion of a happy home-life—like a protective bubble—even though they're grown men, trained professionals, who should be able to handle…"

She trails off and shakes her head and covers her eyes. "That was wrong. Selfish." She sighs. "I'm just—I'm just so tired of his life being more important than mine."

"But, I've gone on and on about me," she says. "How are you?"

"I'm fine."

"I know you have to miss him."

"I do, but. You know. It's gotten better. I'm pretty busy."

"Oh? Driving?"

"Yes. No. I'm looking."

Denise studies her nails, bites one she hasn't bitten. "Having any luck?"

"Not yet."

"Mall this weekend?"

"Um…I don't—no. I don't think so."

"Why not?"

"I have a job interview."

"On a weekend?"

"Yes."

"You're lying," she says.

"I'm not."

"A job interview won't take all weekend. Is it because of Brian?"

"Why would this have anything to do with Brian?"

"I think you're upset."

"Denise, I'm not."

But, I am.

She's worthless to me, now.

She is one of them, one of the others. The man she cares about is here, safe with her. She can't understand about dusk, the sun's evil teasing. The time of evening too far from sleep and an 'x' across another day, but too close to darkness and the hollow air of no conversation that amplifies the TV sounds of over-acted dialogue and rehearsed applause. Denise doesn't know the taunting, subtle fade that cues the lighting of yellow windows, the drawing of curtains to hide people living normal lives, eating dinner, yelling top floor to bottom about who wants milk and where are the scissors. She would have little to say about time spent staring out the window at shapeless clouds and cracked sidewalks and meticulously trimmed shrubs, all of it so cheerful and commonplace while over the rooftops and trees and a plane-ride away, "everyday" is mission-planning and mortar fire and grass is something they might find tucked in the fold of a letter.

"It's not Brian," I say. "It's that you seem to want to find a way to—I don't know, legitimize?—the sex you're having. None of what you said was about anything but you and Brian and your 'relationship,' and it's just so fucking trivial. You know? People are dying and the…the…your husband is over there, and he's doing stuff, and you're here upset because you want to fuck your boyfriend. And quit making that face whenever I say 'fuck,' because I know you've heard it before." My mouth is dry. I swallow. "What about the state of the world, the global implications of the war?"

She laughs. Long and hard, she laughs. When she catches her breath, she says, "You're kidding, right? First, Mia, I never knew you were so naïve! It's actually kind of cute. But listen: sex is the only thing we have control over. Nothing is *reduced* to being all about sex. And my relationship with Brian is far more complex than a simple sexual…what have you." She leans forward. "And second, you don't think about any of that—the 'global implications' of the war—any more than I do. If you do, I'm impressed. Seriously. But I don't think you do. Admit it—it's not our concern. We live in our small American neighborhood in our small American town. All we worry about is ourselves and how this war will affect us and the people we love." She returns to the couch and lets her head fall back. She looks at me through slitted eyes. "When Jake is home, you'll see. You'll care less about the war." She shrugs. "It's callous, but it's true. You'll care less because the soldier blown up by an IED won't represent Jake, and the woman crying on TV won't represent you."

I don't know when she put out her last cigarette, but she lights another, and I don't know when I put mine out, so I ask her for one. For the next few minutes no one says anything, and then Denise leans forward and picks up her bag, slings it over her shoulder. "I'm meeting Brian. Wow, that feels good to say. You know how it is when you have something finally out in the open…? Anyway. You don't believe me, what I said before, because you can't," she says. "But when it happens—because it will—try not to feel bad, and know you're not the only one. It helps to know that."

When the door is closed behind her, I look for Donny's number and call it.

No answer. No answering machine.

I pick up some cigarettes on the way to his house and park on the street. The blue Jeep has been moved to the curb and is clean, sparkling. Loud music comes from his living room's open windows. He must be in a good mood.

I knock on the door with a cigarette pulled and ready for him. When it opens, she—his wife?—stands there in an oversized T-shirt and jeans, brown hair hanging long and straight, thin and frizzed at the ends. She holds a beer.

"Hi, darlin'," she says. "Help you?"

"I'm—I was—" I slide the cigarette back in the pack. "I'm Mia," I say. "Donny has this painting, and—I wanted to ask about it."

"Naw, he took all that with him. Been gone two days, now. Livin' on Crossland in the Duncan Motel. You want to see him? Let me get the room number. Hold on right there."

I look inside, notice china in the cabinet. The easel is gone.

She comes back and hands me a piece of paper. "Here you go." Room ten, and the phone number. "You be careful, all right, sweetie?" She closes the door.

I park in front of room ten and the window shades to rooms nine and eleven slide open, then close. A door opens a few rooms down and a man with a shirt hanging open around his ball-shaped stomach smokes…something…on the walkway. I knock on Donny's door, listen for sounds—snoring or a TV. I knock again.

"Hey," the man with the stomach says. "Who you lookin' for?"

"Donny Donaldson."

He shrugs. "Don't know no names. What's he look like?"

"Brown hair. Glasses."

"Short fella?"

"Yeah."

"Gone. He was here two nights ago, left this mornin'."

"Do you know where he went?"

"Darlin', why would I know that? Half times, people leave 'cause they can't pay for the room. If he went anywhere, you might check the Y."

I press my face to the window and look inside, just in case, but the bedspread is flat and the pillows covered. "Thanks," I say, and the man nods. In my rearview mirror, I watch him watching me leave.

THE COFFEE SHOP is closed, so I wait with the window rolled down in the shade of a hackberry. Ten minutes until opening, according to the sign, but the girl arrives five minutes early and parks her car next to mine. I bend to see her through my passenger-side window and ask if I can come in.

"Sorry," she says. "We're not open yet."

"Oh, no, I know. I just want to check on something. It'll take two seconds."

"Five minutes," she says, walking toward the building. She unlocks the door and then closes and locks it behind her.

Seven minutes later, she plugs in the neon 'open' sign and waves me in from behind the long window.

"I didn't even notice," she says, looking from behind the counter at the spot on the wall. "It must have gone yesterday or the day before. I have weekends off."

"And there's no way of knowing?"

"Not until I talk to Sherry. She was here."

"Maybe she wrote it down somewhere. You guys don't have a book, or something?"

"We have a book, but Sherry is the owner, and she keeps the books. I can't help you," she says. "If you want to come back later, she might be here."

"Might?"

"She comes and goes."

"You don't know when?"

"No."

"Can you ask her if she knows who bought it?"

"She won't give out that kind of information."

"It's just a painting," I say. "Just a stupid painting of a stupid house. What's the secret?"

"If you want to make an appointment with her, I can give her a call later and set one up for you."

"Forget it. It's not—never mind."

The girl pours a bag of beans into a grinder.

"Are you always alone during the week?" I say.

"Pretty much."

"Are you—is she…Sheryl?"

"Sherry."

"Is Sherry hiring?"

The girl presses the button and the machine, loud, whirs and grinds. "I don't think so, no," she almost shouts.

"MIA. DONNY DONALDSON. I got a—I got beer, and I got—uh—I got—what the…? Bourbon, brand new, fresh in the bottle and never opened…Yet…But we don't got to drink. You can have soda or water…whatever…It's a bad day…I'm out…Outta the house…a week, now? Naw, two weeks…No chance. No chance, she says…I got a place." Laughter. "A real fine place on Riverside. Rooms. A front desk. Bellhop and room service and a spa…This is Doctor Donaldson speaking…Come over. Midtown Motel, room eight…Or call. Four five oh eight."

"Zero," I say from the couch. "Four five *zero* eight."

Water drips from the kitchen faucet. The television is green, night time at war, a few hours from sunrise. Now full color, a shot of the sky where something was before it wasn't.

I've put the clock keeping track of Jake's time next to the computer. I don't need it by the TV, anymore, because their graphics people have designed one for the corner, a cheerful banner that flips through the stateside time zones and, now, war time. It's green and blue and red and the letters—the numbers—are big and white, like grammar-school numbers, and they flip, flip, flip, in a happy soothing rhythm like a…like something that would do that. Doesn't matter, really, what it is, because it's just a happy silly graphic, and it's my time and war time and all the time is war time. A time on a clock. An exciting time, this time in history, all other countries, the rest of the whole wide world, forgotten by the media for this

very exciting time

in history, this progress, this momentous action on the part of the administration that has burped the rest of the planet into oblivion, off the

sip

priority list, and if they would just stop. Cut to a commercial. Cover Japan or Havana so I could blink, sleep dreamless for a minute or two, relax distracted by the world between me and Jake and the something that was there before it wasn't.

Not the TV.
I need that.
The wall.
It's louder than I expected. One of the chunks lands on the shelf and breaks the plate he bought at the Grand Canyon.
Shit. Not *that.*
This!
And this!

Someone knocks at the door, *knock knock knock*, has been for what seems like hours. I reach for my coffee, but it's cold, and when I get up to bring it to the kitchen my head spins. I steady myself on the chair and feel strangely tall, the kitchen is crowded, too small for me. I take a step and Chancey runs underfoot and I kick out, catching his tail. *Knock knock knock.* I close the mug in the microwave and set the time, watch the glass dish spin around and around and—
"Mia."
The microwave dings.
"Let me in."
I pull the mug from the microwave and it is hot on my palm. I set it on the counter, pick it up by the handle and walk to the door, open it. Denise shoves in and closes the door and walks straight to the living room. Her footfalls stop short.
The cup really is very hot. I set it on the counter and open the refrigerator and stare at white grated shelves, white walls, a wrapped slice of cheese, orange against the stark brightness. I push at the door to the butter bin. Empty.
She stands now in the kitchen entry. I lean in to check the date on a half gallon of milk. Bad.
Bile or something like it floods my throat, fights against being swallowed down.
Denise takes my hand and leads me to the living room. "…no word…," they say through the small holes on the side of the TV. Denise asks what this is.
"It's my living room."
"What did you do to it? The shelves are bare."
Yes.

The shelves are bare.

Her nails are rough and scrape into my palm. I pull my hand free and she grabs me again—my wrist, this time—but more gently.

"Is this any way to treat your things?" She smiles, tugs my arm. "Some of them were so beautiful."

Yes. Beautiful. But it can't be owned, beauty, can't be trapped in my lungs and tasted on my breath when I exhale. It's fleeting, like a silk scarf lost to the wind. An abstract, empty indulgence, so I threw—hurled, really—the geodes, but they wouldn't break, or even chip. Edges like painted glass, and inside, a cavern of dazzlingly perfect crystals, so perfect I wanted to eat them, wanted to pluck out the individual shards and push them into my eyes. I read somewhere that people are doing that, having garnets of all colors embedded in the whites of their eyes. Eye jewelry. But then, they can't see it unless they look in a mirror.

And the jade figurine, a bird on a stump with carved flowers—pansies, I think—at its feet. It was heavy. Solid. The petals folded delicately open and the feathers, chiseled so smooth, promised to fan. But what *good?* I took pleasure in all of it, in *decorating*, in placing the bird just so next to the old dictionary. Jake enjoyed it, too, putting things here, putting things there. His things, my things. The apartment was ours because our *things* lived here. The first night, all moved in, we made hot chocolate and sat on the couch and looked at our arrangement of *things*.

Denise picks up the half of the bird she finds partially hidden under the lowest shelf. "Pretty," she says. She drops it on the floor and it dents the wood. I look at her feet. She's standing in rubble. She nudges our things with her toes. Pieces of a painted gourd Jake picked up at an import store. Gray rocks from my Zen garden. Shards of baked clay from the matching pottery jugs we bought at a street fair from a man with red cheeks and blue wool mittens.

Stereo cords coil under the mess and the speakers are on separate sides of the room, one of them upside down, the other facing the wall. The stereo lies face-down in the middle of the room with a split spreading across the case.

She asks where my broom is. My dustpan.

"Why?"

"I'll find it," she says, and she does. What's not broken, she sets on a shelf. What is broken, she sweeps into a pile and dumps in a paper bag. She asks where the cat food is and I tell her I fed him an hour ago—or several hours? today, anyway—and that his water is fresh. "Just checking," she says, but she shakes the bag of food anyway, calling, "C'mere, kitty." He doesn't, which is unusual, because even when he's not hungry, he usually does. I ask her if it's possible he sneaked out when she came in.

"I would have noticed," she says.

We search the apartment until we find him behind my hamper in the bedroom closet.

"Maybe you scared him."

I ask her how.

She picks up the bag of broken things and puts it outside the front door. "I wonder, Mia."

Quarter after eight in the evening, Jake's. Denise has been here an hour and a half.

We've done nothing. Watched the news. News and more news. We turned our attention to the machine when Olivia called and left a message—"I don't think it's him, hon, but if it is, you'll be okay. We'll just have to help each other through it."—and then went back to waiting.

"Why haven't you been answering your phone?" she says. "I left messages. Didn't you get them?"

"I wanted to keep the line open."

"Not just today. It's been over a week." She runs through the channels again, ending on the original station. The screen has cut from night vision to the news desk. No new information, they say. No names because they're "awaiting an investigation and family notification before revealing specific details."

"I've been out trying to find a job."

She says, "Your car is in the same place it was the last time I left. Exactly."

"It's a good spot."

She sighs.

I ask her if she wouldn't rather be at home.

"No."

"Are you sure?"

"Yes. Now stop."

The phone rings. We look at it. On the machine, I suggest the caller leave a message at the beep. *Beep.* Olivia says, "Mia, are you there? Pick up if you are, hon."

Denise looks at me, whispers, "What if it's something?"

I shake my head.

Olivia chews gum into the phone. "I'm just so worried about you," she says. "You know Jakey would want you to be strong at a time like this."

Denise says, "Are you sure you don't want to answer?"

I shake my head.

"Well, okay." Olivia exhales. "No one has called me yet, or come over, heaven forbid, but as soon as they—oh, will you listen to me? Of course I mean *if*—if anyone does, I'll call you right away… I'm so sorry you have to rely on me to do it. Sometimes I wish you two were married, hon, because I think I'd much rather hear the news from you…Anyway, call me when you get this and we'll muddle through together."

Denise waits until Olivia hangs up and says, "Encouraging."

The news takes a commercial break. A woman wearing a shapeless pink collar shirt and equally shapeless khaki pants dances with a dust mop, her uninspired hair swinging neatly against the base of her neck.

"Yeah," Denise says. "Dusting's a blast." She picks at the seam of her jeans. "I need a drink."

"So do I."

"What do you have?"

"It's only noon, though."

"What do you have?"

She pours two glasses and we lean against opposite counters. The television is loud enough to hear from the kitchen.

"Strong." She coughs and clears her throat.

Behind me, the faucet drips.

"I really don't think it was them," she says. She takes two cigarettes from the pack she set on the counter and lights them both with that shiny lighter, hands me one.

I hold it between my fingers and watch the tip turn to gray ash. I want it, but my stomach is unsettled. Jake would say that probably means I should put it out.

Two days ago, I stopped thinking about him while waiting in line at a drive-through window. It was sunny, warm, and I was hungry and the chicken smelled good. A minivan stuffed with children idled at the ordering box, their small heads bouncing up and down, front seat and back again, changing orders, adding sides. I turned the radio up loud and sang with a song I hated. I thought only of the lines, wondered how I somehow knew every word, and then I thought about the food I would bring home, and how much longer it would take for that minivan to pull out, and how loud and messy kids are.

Then another song played, a favorite of Jake's.

How long had it been? Minutes? An hour? Forever. *That* could have been the moment he died, his absence from my thoughts a sign, a goodbye.

I open the kitchen window and pull up the blinds to let out the smoke.

"I can feel it," she says. "About William and Jake. Sometimes you just know."

"How can you feel that? How can you be sure?"

Drip.

Drip.

"Your faucet is dripping."

"Is it?"

Denise crosses to the sink and turns the handle tight and stands beside me. "I haven't heard from him in days," she says. Heavy powder—too heavy—shines in flecks under her eyes and her hair, up close, looks stringy. Normally so put-together, so well maintained.

"You will," I say.

"It must mean something."

"He was probably busy."

"I don't know. It's not like him. Even if he's busy, he usually finds a way to contact me."

"I'd be more worried about him being alive."

"Oh, he's alive, all right," she says. "But, you're right. Sometimes I wish he were dead. It would make all of this a hell of a lot easier. Not *really*, of course. But, have you ever—"

"Jesus Christ, Denise. You know they fly together a lot."

"What are you talking about?" she says, and, "Oh, no. Oh…Mia, I was—" She runs water over her cigarette and drops it in the disposal. I almost don't hear her say, "I wasn't talking about William."

I understand, then, why she's so sure of their safety. It's the confidence of someone with nothing at stake.

"Mia…Are you there…? Pick up if you're there."

"What are you doing?" Denise mutes the television and stares at me. "Aren't you going to pick it up?"

"Damn it. I just can't seem to catch you at home. . .You don't know how bad I want to hear your voice…The machine isn't enough…If I could hear you laugh, then—"

"Mia," Denise says, "if you don't pick it up, I'm going to."

"—everything, this whole day, would be just a little better…Something happened … don't want to talk about it, sorry, but—well, maybe it's on the news—but I just want you to know—"

I can't breathe, but she is right. I have to pick up the phone.

"You have to pick it up, Mia. You can't just—"

There is a knock at the door. I wait for more from Jake. Wants me to know—wants me to know what?

Can't just breathe, and it should be easy.

"—that I love you."

Denise sets her glass on the desk. "I'll get the door. You talk to Jake."

"I love you so much…and I kind of hoped I'd be able to use this time to ask you about your last letter…You sounded so angry, M…and that you would write to me and accuse me—"

There's a pause, a wait, and I rush to the desk and pick up the phone. "Jake?"

"Talk to him!" she screams from the hallway.

"I am," I say, and Jake says nothing. "Jake?" Still nothing. I blow into the phone and hollow air comes back, then two, three clicks, like connecting to something that won't connect. I slam down the receiver, and then I slam it down again, again, again, and squeeze and twist it in my hands.

Denise stands in the doorway, her arms and body limp, heaping forward. I hang up the phone, pick it up to check for a working dial tone, then hang it up again.

Denise says, her eyes not quite focused on mine, "It was a shorter speech than I thought it would be."

She fixes drink after drink, not saying a word, and smokes cigarette after cigarette. Her fingers shake.

Jake hadn't wanted to talk about it.

But Jake is okay. Jake is safe. Jake is alive.

William is not.

It could have been Jake.

But it wasn't.

I don't feel like smiling—there's nothing to smile about—but I have to fight not to.

I can't look at her. When I do, my lips, my cheeks, all of it tugs toward a grin.

Jesus. I don't want to laugh. I don't feel like laughing.

If Jake died, would I be this way at his funeral?

When I feel her looking at me, I pretend I have an itch on my upper lip so my hand covers my mouth. My eyes water and I look down. There is a hole in the toe of my sock.

Denise says, "Are you smiling?"

She stares out the window and smokes. "Green-suiters," she says. "That's what they call them. Did you know that?"

I tell her I didn't.

"Captain James Collins. That was his name, the one who talked." Her ash falls on the floor. "It's funny—I think he looked at me after a few words like I was going to stop him. But I wanted to hear the whole thing."

"The Secretary of the Army expressed his regret," she says. She laughs and wipes her eyes. "I don't even know who the Secretary of the Army is, and I'm pretty sure he doesn't know me. Or William. So what's he have to be so fucking regretful about?"

"James—Captain James Collins—asked if I was Denise White. I almost said no. I could have been you, if I'd wanted. Could have sent him away. Anyone could have left your address on my door. I can't believe he actually came, you know? I didn't think they'd actually come." She slides her glass around on the table. "But then he asked if I was the wife of Chief Warrant Officer William H. White." She picks at her finger until a line of blood spreads around the base of her nail.

"I can't leave," she says. "I just can't. I don't know where I'll go. Or do I? What if I know exactly where I'll go?"

"You can stay," I tell her. I bring out a pillow.

"I didn't want it to happen, Mia. Do you believe me?"

"I believe you."

"He wasn't shot down," she says. "Somehow, that's worse, isn't it? Or is it better? I don't know."

I ask her what happened.

"That was the only thing I asked them. How did it happen?" She brings her empty glass to the kitchen and says, "Wires. They said he hit some wires." She comes back out. "He always said he was such a good pilot. Do you think maybe they made a mistake? Maybe it wasn't even him."

I shouldn't say it, but I do. I say, "Maybe."

"He was so sweet," she says, and grimaces on 'sweet.' "It's a dumb word, but you know what I mean. He didn't deserve it." She crushes her fifteenth cigarette in the ashtray. "I didn't deserve him." She brushes her hair off her face, gently at first, absently, but then with harsh yanks.

I say, "I'm sure you were a wonderful wife."

She looks at me while lighting another cigarette. She's smoked them so constantly that imagining the taste of yet another pull on a filter almost makes me gag.

"I mean, as far as he knows. And that's what's important."

"Shut up, Mia. Okay?"

"William was good to me. He was a good husband. A good—a great—friend."

"He knew you loved him," I say.

"Maybe," she says. "But what if he didn't?"

Denise cries. She says, "It happened at midnight, his time. Do you know what I was doing at three o'clock yesterday?"

I don't ask.

She doesn't say.

I sit beside her with my hand on top of hers.

"I'm going to hell," she says.

Strands of hair cling to her cheek. I pull the blanket to her shoulders even though it's not cold, and I start to pick up Chancey from behind her legs. She makes a noise, then mumbles without opening her eyes, "Leave him," and tucks her fingers under his chin.

I watch her from the chair, watch the moon's shadows roll over her face.

"I'LL BE LEAVING soon," Denise says, "but when I come back we'll do something, okay?"

I turn up the volume on the phone. "Are you all right?"

"I'm okay," she says. "You know." She pauses and takes a breath. A moment passes. I watch a cat outside tug at a low-hanging pair of pants on the clothesline. She says, "I just wanted you to know I'd be gone so you wouldn't worry if you called and didn't get an answer."

"I'm sorry I haven't called," I say. "I just thought you'd have so much going on, you know. And I didn't want to—I didn't know what to say, and I thought—"

"It's okay."

"Take care of yourself," I say. "And tell his mom—tell her that Jake is sorry. Or something."

"I will."

I didn't know William very well, and so I don't know what to say. He was Jake's friend. "He liked the chicken joke," I say.

"What?"

"The chicken joke. Remember? He told it twice that night, after the ball. He thought no one appreciated the humor, and the second time he told it, we all thought about it. And we all laughed. Remember?"

"I don't know."

"He was funny. Or—Denise, I'm sorry."

"Listen—um—I gave Brian your address because I left my lighter at your house, the silver one with the—"

"I found it." With the initials engraved on the back. W.W.

"So, he'll stop by sometime in the next few days and get it so I can take it with me. I would do it myself, but he lives just a few blocks from you—did you know?—and...anyway. If you have to go somewhere and he hasn't come by, yet, maybe you can just put it in an envelope with his name on it and tape it to your door. His name is spelled with an 'i'. 'B-R-I—"

"I know how to spell Brian."

"Right. I know." She pauses. Takes a breath.

"I'm sorry. That was unnecess—"

"It's over," she says. "So you know."

I say nothing.

"Did you hear me?"

"I heard you. It's none of my—"

"Whatever, Mia. Okay? I'm telling you. It's over. I just wanted you to know."

May 6

Jake,

I'm sorry. About William. Were you there? Did you see it?

Dumb question. How could you have, unless you were there?

Was there a lot of blood, and was it fast? I shouldn't ask these things, I know, but they're what I'm thinking. I hope it was fast.

Poor William.

How could he have been alive last week and be dead this week?

I'm back to watching the news, now. I stopped for a while. Did I tell you? It's never good, so I stopped. But now, maybe it's useful. For something. I have it on, never turn it off. Never again, because what if I miss you?

Please be alive next week. Please be alive, stay alive, do whatever it takes because I can't stand to think of Denise at William's funeral and I wouldn't know what to do with your clothes and your aftershave. But that's not what I mean at all.

Denise was here when they came. Were you not flying with him? Were you with him, but you survived? What happens to a helicopter when it flies into wires? Is it an electrical fire, or is there tangling? I'm sorry. I shouldn't wonder. It doesn't matter what happens except what happens.

I was there when you called, but I missed you. Again, I missed you. But I heard your voice and thank you, thank you for calling. They came when you called. Denise left a note on her door, and they came to our place looking for her. I never thought they would come to our place and they did.

Did you get my letter? The one after the one about your mom and your sister? I'm sorry. For all of it. For what I said about all that.

Don't die. Don't die.

Too much unresolved. Don't die. Denise didn't even see it coming. There was something on the news and she was fine and she said she knew you two were okay. But she was wrong. Do you see? She was wrong, even though she was so sure she was right.

I'm not sure of anything, anymore. I can't be, can I? Not that I ever was. But, sometimes, I would think that if I just knew you'd be okay, you would be. But it's not true.

What do I do now?

No. Don't worry. These are just my thoughts today.

Everything will be fine tomorrow.

I love you I love you I love you. I do.

Mia

Stifling top-floor humidity cools, thins, on the way down the stairs. A thick and steady wind comes through the hallway window high on the wall, and for a moment I stand there, letting the breeze—though warm—chill the sweat and lift the heat from my skin before I move on, down to the ground floor.

My mailbox is empty, but the white corner of an envelope sticks out from behind the brass door of number one's box, the one beside mine. It's been such a long time since there's been a letter for me that there could—there must—be a mistake. The mailman might have accidentally left my letter in the wrong box, for example. Or he might have had a substitute, someone new who didn't care about the route or about the people waiting for important mail and who just wanted to get the day over with.

Unlike the corner of a business envelope, this one, I notice as I tug at it, has none of the black bar code lines near the bottom edge, and nothing on it crinkles the way an address window would crinkle. The paper tears a little with the yanking, snags on some sharp imperfection in the thin brass, but it's out almost far enough for me to see the address and the handwriting. Black is all I'm getting, now, just the bottom curve of an 's' in the town name and the points making up the bottom of 'TN.' I push it back inside the box, bit by bit, holding the smallest wedge of corner so I can slide it up higher, maybe bypass that—

The door opens and I let go, step back and examine my own envelope to make sure the address is correct, the stamp right-side up.

Brian, windblown and sweating, smiles with white, square teeth.

"Good timing," he says.

His loose clothes, khaki pants and white shirt, cling to his sweaty skin. But I don't notice. His attractiveness is obvious. Uninteresting.

I tell him I was just checking the mail.

"Ah. As you were."

I reach up to put my letter in the bin, which is not a bin at all, but a thin, plastic bookend, its flat bracing ledge tucked between the wall and the tops of the mailboxes.

The landing is small, and when I turn, Brian's body blocks the stairway. "Excuse me."

He steps aside. "Denise wants me to pick up her lighter."

"It's upstairs. You can come with me, if you want. Or you can stay down here."

He waits in the kitchen while I lift cushions and rug corners. At the desk, I sit down and move stacks of paper and slide the lamp to the side. It leaves a clean path in the dust.

He bends around the corner. "Find it?"

"Not yet." I spin to face him and cross my legs.

He steps into the room and leans against the door frame and puts his hands in his pockets. "Do you think you might keep looking for it?"

"I will. I'm thinking. I could swear I just saw it, and I'm trying to remember where."

He waits, looks at the muted commercial on the television, and then behind me. "Is that your Christmas tree?"

"So," I say, "do you think it'll be over soon, then?"

"I don't know if you've noticed," he says, "but Christmas has been over for a couple of months, now."

"I mean the war."

"The war?"

"It's almost over, don't you think? News has been good. Considering."

"I don't know." His fingers move in his pockets and there is clicking, clinking.

"You must know something. You're one of them, aren't you? In a way, anyway."

"Like I said, I don't know," he says. "It's pretty hard to change a country, no matter how pretty the pictures they give us. We see what they want us to see."

"But, we're in control, now. We have the control. Maybe it'll be over in a month."

"Maybe," he says. He runs his hand over his head, through hair thick with waves. It hides his fingers. "Don't worry," he says. "He'll be fine."

"William wasn't."

William wasn't. *Wasn't.*

That William is dead…William is *dead*, dead, *dead*…does not seem real, or likely, or probable. They say, yes, on the news, that people are being killed. Every day, almost, they say someone dies, but surely they're not actually being *killed*.

William is not really *dead*.

"True," he says, "but what are the chances of both of them not making it back?"

"That doesn't work."

"I guess it doesn't."

He lifts his chin, looks across the room and out the window. "Still," he says, "you'll get nowhere assuming the worst every day."

I swivel in the chair, side to side, and then spin. "No," I say, "but it's safe," and I spin, pulling my legs to my chest, and spin, using the desk to push me along. I think of Superman, circling the Earth fist forward, around, around, fast enough to reverse the rotation and reverse time and arrive with just moments to save Lois. I close my eyes and try for the second week of February, the day before he came home with the news. We would fill the gas tank and load the cat and drive the scenic routes to Canada or Mexico.

Brian says, "What are you doing?" but I don't answer, just spin, the chair knocking at its base under my unbalanced weight, and it is when the spinning starts to feel like sitting stationary—though I knew it before, of course—that it comes. Future as fact rather than as a possibility with options on top of options.

We would never have made it.

We'd never have gotten out of the state, because (I stop pushing, open my eyes and watch the floor spiral) Jake would never have left with me.

The chair slows, then stops, and I am dizzy and sick. I rest my head on the desk and he asks if I'm okay.

"Don't you think it's a little strange," I say, "that she sent you to pick up something of her dead husband's?"

"Proximity. That's all it is."

Sitting straight helps level my head, but he still sways some where he stands. "Why did you say yes?"

"Pathetically devoted. By the way, I really have to get the lighter to her before she goes tomorrow, so if you—"

"I'll find it. I just have to remember where it is."

"Did I come at a bad time? You seem…troubled."

His hair is too long. Jake has seen hair shorter than that and has bent to whisper in my ear, "That's not regulation." (I feel his breath, thinking of it now.)

"Not a bad time." William's lighter presses against the crease of my upper, inner thigh, through my pocket. I adjust it.

"Well," he says. "I suppose I can wait a bit."

I stand up to look behind the computer monitor, twisting the screen, even. "What did you think? When you heard, I mean." I sit back down.

"About William?"

"What else?"

He sighs and again runs his fingers though his hair, then pulls a brown box from his shirt pocket. "May I?"

"You may."

"I'm quitting when I'm thirty-five," he says. He smiles. "And I don't know why I told you that." He tilts his head while lighting, then slips the matchbook back into his khakis. "I don't mean to be impatient," he says, "but the sooner you find the lighter, the sooner I can go to—I can get it to Denise." The sun has shifted behind the blinds and shines in his eyes. He squints, shields them. "You know how you women are about our things." He turns to the TV and it's dust, dust and sun.

"Especially once you're dead."

"I would imagine, especially then."

I turn up the sound, but there's nothing new, today, just a replay. A reel from early April. Citizens—miles, towns from Jake—push through the square like a water surge and surround the stories-tall fallen statue. A boy, nine, maybe ten, smacks it with a shoe he's taken off and grips tightly in his hand, and his rage—it should be impossible in someone so young—is mirrored in those around him, their cheers filled with triumph, resentment. The anchors smile. It's a good day, still, looting aside. We must remember that, they say.

Brian watches with an eyebrow raised.

I open a drawer and move pens around, pick up a linked string of paperclips and unhook them one by one. "Denise, for example. All she has left of William is whatever he left behind. Imagine having only that to hold onto."

He shrugs. "I—"

"You can't imagine, can you?"

"I can't."

"Of course you can't. You haven't been over at all, yet, have you? I never thought it was possible for one person to have so much luck."

Brian plucks a piece of tobacco from his tongue, looks at it, and takes it into the kitchen. He runs the water, comes back out, and stands where he was before, again shading squinted eyes until he notices the sun has moved. He drops his hand. "You think I've somehow, what, manipulated the system to keep myself out of the war?"

"I didn't say that."

"No. You didn't."

"Is that possible?"

"I'm sure it is, to some degree."

The paperclips unstrung and loose, I return them to the drawer and close it. "And have you?"

He looks at me while see-sawing his cigar between his fingers. "To some degree."

"Well," I say, and it happens so quickly—my getting up, my walking over—that I am surprised by the hot, itching sting of his face on my palm. He yanks my wrist from where it hangs in the air—just beside his cheek, floating—and pushes me away. There should not be tears—this is not a time for tears—but I must have them, because once he seems sure I won't try to hit him again, he goes into the kitchen and comes back with a paper towel and uses it to wipe my face.

"I understand," he says. "Don't be sorry."

"I'm not."

"But I think you might want to take a minute to try to understand me, too. I'm not a deserter."

"You may as well be."

"And? What if I were? If you're so in favor of the war, why aren't you suiting up? What, because you're a woman you're exempt from duty to country? If you're on the side of the war, surely you feel the responsibility to—"

"I never said I was for it."

"No?"

"No."

"And why?"

"I'm just not."

"That doesn't answer the question. Come on." He points at the television. "You saw that as well as I did. The statue fell, the people rejoiced. Did you see? That was the word they used, I think. 'Rejoiced.' How, after something like that, can you offer no support for your opinion one way or the other?"

"Anything I say will sound stupid to you, because I don't involve myself in politics, and I don't—"

"Ah."

"What do you mean, 'ah'?"

"I understand, now."

"What do you understand?"

"You. It's natural, of course, but it's a shame that your involvement….or, rather, your interest…only exists because your boyfriend is there."

"I didn't say that."

"There was no need."

"You're wrong."

"Am I? In that case, I'd be interested to know your views."

"Leave it alone, will you? I watch the news. I know enough, but not enough to discuss it with you like someone who has all—or even one—of the answers. I don't know. I don't know anything about why it happened other than what they told us, but I know it feels wrong. That's enough for me. I'm against it, and that's all."

"Well, good," he says. "That's good. You understand me, then, and you see I've done nothing wrong."

"Nothing wrong?"

"No."

"You joined the Army and you're avoiding the war—"

"War? When did it become a war?"

"The conflict, then. You avoid the conflict, and you see nothing wrong with that?"

"I've done nothing illegal—"

"Adultery. That's illegal in the military, isn't it?"

He sighs. "Nothing illegal, and if they needed me, they would send me."

"They do need you. To replace William."

"It doesn't work quite that way."

"Lucky for you."

"This is not a war I agree with," he says. "I don't even think it was a war William agreed with."

"Should you be talking about him?"

He doesn't answer. He folds the paper towel into a square and slides it in his loose cargo pocket.

"How do you know what he thought, anyway?"

"I am—correction: I *was*—a pretty close friend of a friend." He doesn't make eye contact. His free hand fiddles again in his pocket and coins scrape.

"But he went," I say.

"He did go. Yes. And now? Where is he now?"

He's looking down at his cigar. *Should have been smart, William, like me,* I imagine him thinking. *I was screwing her—did you know?— when you died.*

"You're disgusting," I say, and I swing at him again, wanting to draw blood this time and wishing I had the strength, a man's strength, to leave him crumpled on the floor. He catches my arm—I should have expected it, but didn't—and clenches it, his fingers pressing hard on bone. The pain feels good, like a fight I've been craving.

He says, "If you're trying to knock me across the ocean, you'll have to hit a lot harder than that."

"Let go."

"Promise not to hit me again."

I twist my wrist.

"Do you promise not to hit me again?"

"No."

"Fair enough. Do you promise to *try* not to hit me again?"

"Yes."

He releases me and neither of us looks at the other.

"I'll come back later," he says. "I'll write my number and…just call me when you find it."

"No," I say, for some reason afraid to have him leave. "I'm—it has to be somewhere. I haven't taken it out of the apartment."

Brian says yes to coffee.

He sits at the kitchen table and fingers an orange pepper jutting straight from a branch of deep, smooth leaves. I saw the plant yesterday, last minute. It sat among paired gerbera daisies, faded ivy hanging from plastic pots. Red-striped dracaenas and African violets. I scooped it in my arm and took it—and my dinner, frozen in a box—to the cashier.

Jake likes peppers if they're not yellow.

"Milk or sugar or anything?"

"No, thanks."

I set down our mugs and sit across from him and he pushes the plant, tall between us, against the window and taps his fingers on the table. His hands look soft, his nails professionally manicured.

"So." Brian blinks and a long curl tugs his eyelash. He moves it aside with his thumb. "Thanks for the coffee."

His cigar smoke makes me nauseous. Not a real cigar, but a cheap, dollar cigar from the corner gas station. It smells like raspberry and he smokes it like a cigarette.

I ask him why he joined the Army.

"A few reasons," he says, "and none of them too exciting."

"Security," I say.

"Mostly, yes. You were hoping for patriotism."

"I don't care what your reasons are. How much time do you have left?"

He tells me, one year.

I tell him it's probably a good thing.

"Are you sure you wouldn't rather I come back later?" He looks at me with something like the start of a smile and says, "I get the feeling you don't like me."

Two coffee grounds drift in a slow circle in my mug. The window is open wide, but the breeze blows in, dragging the smoke past us and into the hallway, the living room, my bedroom.

I say, "She says she got rid of you."

"Yes," he says. "She 'got rid of' me."

"And you want to see her again?"

"Very much."

"I'm sorry."

"No, you're not. That's all right. I don't know you or like you well enough to care." He smiles and takes a drink.

"You must have been excited—well, or, you know—at first. Just like that, she was free, open, but then, just like that," I hit the table, "his accident is what's left you sitting here with me, just waiting for this little…thing…you can bring her. Like a ball. Or a dead mouse."

He puts out the cigar, barely smoked. "It was more than that, that did it," he says. "I suppose it started months ago. Disagreements. Nothing too out of the ordinary, or too special, but special to us."

"William would be so relieved."

The way the sun—a wide patch broken only by the tree branches just outside the window—falls on his neck and upper chest, his dog tag chain glints against his skin and a thin shadow-line follows the linked balls over his collarbone, under his shirt.

"Why are you wearing those?"

Brian looks down, his neck wrinkling under his chin, and tugs at the chain. "These? Why?"

"It's just a question."

He laughs.

"What?"

"You're incredibly unremarkable."

"I don't know what you mean."

"How do you continue to find ways to take issue with me, bit by bit?"

"What issue?"

"Outstanding." He laughs. "But, I'll play. What else is there to do while I wait?"

"Sorry. Really—it was just a question. Someone like you—"

"Someone like me. Listen, now." He leans forward and talks fast. "This—the Army—is my job, the same as it's John Smith's job to take the elevator to the seventh floor every Monday through Friday. But, in a curious way, you're so involved in what some of you—and by 'you,' I mean civilians, but more specifically, the respected wives and girlfriends (and, of course, all praise given is due and your job is the hardest job in the military, and all that, as they say)—call the 'military way of life' that you will sit there and question what I wear. For the record, there is no dog tag regulation. Did you know that?"

No. "Yes."

"But, let me get back to your question. Why *am* I wearing my dog tags?" He taps his chin with his finger. "There's no good reason. I forget to take them off, half the time. Now, what if I were to ask you why you're wearing red underwear? You have no boyfriend here to wear them for. What must that mean?—Yes, I saw them. When you were bending over your desk. My point is, you're very eager to enforce rules you don't—as a civilian—have any obligation to live by, but I have a feeling it hasn't occurred to you that it's not any of your business." He picks up his cigar, relights it, takes two short puffs and puts it back down. He looks at me through the smoke. "You get so engrained, some of you. And you're not even married to the military, yet. How is that? How does it happen?"

"I'm not engrained."

"Aren't you?"

"Just because I know things doesn't mean anything," I say. Much of my familiarization happened sporadically and by accident. Jake's salute of a higher ranking officer outdoors came after a simple nod he'd given another higher ranking officer while we were inside, and I'd asked him why, when indoors, he only nodded.

"Because we were inside," he said.

"So?"

"So, you don't salute inside."

"Why not?"

"You just don't."

"But why?"

He sighed. "I don't know, M. Tradition."

Some other time, some other day, on a trip to the commissary, Jake and I drove past a Humvee convoy.

"Are they going to the field?" I said.

"Maybe. I don't know."

"They're wearing helmets."

"You have to wear your Kevlar any time you're in a military vehicle."

"Even if you're just driving from one building to another?"

"Yes."

"Why?"

"I don't know."

"But—"

"Mia. I don't know."

And the language—some of it, at least, bits and pieces—came over time: K-pot, MOLLE, DONSA.

Controlled flight into terrain.

Involuntary loss of life.

"It's a culture," I say. "There are customs. Traditions. You can't help learning them."

"Obviously, to a point," Brian says. "But people like *you* sometimes go too far, and you forget you have your own role in the universe. That his life is not your life."

"I know that."

Brian is right, of course, and Jake would be disappointed, would wonder who I've become, if he knew how much I think about him. His world, his day-to-day.

"I'll be right back," I say. "I think I know where the lighter is."

In the bedroom, I sit on the bed next to yesterday's underwear. I stuff them under the blanket and look outside, at the house across the street, the weeping willow in the front lawn.

I close my eyes and take a breath and immerse myself in a cloud of nothing.

No Jake.

There is no Jake.

Emptiness, this letting go, but at the same time, less hollow. Exciting, but scary—like waking up in a strange man's bedroom in the blind hours after midnight.

Brian calls, "Are these peppers edible?"

A pepper, half white and half purple, floats into my nothingness. "Yeah, sure, have one." The peppers, some are—

"No, thanks," he says. "Just curious."

—yellow, the pretty yellow that comes between early-phase white and end-phase red, and whether Jake likes yellow doesn't matter, now.

I like it. *I* like yellow.

Brian's chair slides, and alone with just him I am suddenly very aware that his attractiveness isn't ordinary, at all.

"Hellooo," Brian says.

My eyes open to the willow, swaying, and to the bedroom I've come to hate, and to his picture taped to the wall beside the bed. I touch his forehead.

When I lean out of the doorway, I see Brian waiting in the living room with his hands in his pockets.

"Tell me," he says, "is there any chance I'll be leaving with that lighter before evening?"

"I just remembered where I put it." I step back into the bedroom and pull the lighter from my pocket. William's initials shine like scratches in the brushed silver. Expensive. Worn. Too precious for war? A gift from Denise, maybe. "What's so special about it?" I look in the mirror, put on just enough lipstick to moisten, but not so much he'll be likely to notice. "The lighter, I mean."

"His father gave it to him. That's what Denise said, anyway," he calls back. "Why?"

I squeeze it, and then I hide it in a bowl of makeup—old lip gloss, old mascara, the lipstick I haven't worn in full force since the party. As I enter the living room, he opens his mouth to say something and someone knocks on the door.

"Just a minute," I say, and, "Come in!"

Safia swings open the door, but stays in the hallway with her black cat draped over an arm. Shoes scrape in the stairwell behind her and Safia takes a step inside when my floor neighbor, long red hair caught under the shoulder strap of an oversized bag, says, "S'cuse me," and drags her feet to her door and struggles with her lock.

Safia smiles over my shoulder at Brian. "Hello." She uses her cat's paw to wave, then invites me ("And you, too, if you would like to come," she says to Brian, who declines) to a Friday dinner. Just a few friends, she says, and plenty of good food. I tell her I'm busy, and I'm sorry, but she insists I stop by when I'm done doing whatever it is I'm doing. "Please," she says. "You made me lunch and I would like you to come."

"Lunch was to pay you back," I say.

"Yes! That is what I said, but it was too much for one cigarette. You must come, and we will be even."

I tell her I'll try to make it.

"Not you?" she looks at Brian

"No, I don't think so," he says. "I'm…busy on the weekends."

"It will be fun! Mia, bring your friend."

"He's not my friend."

"Ohhh," she says, smiling, flipping the paw at me.

"Really," I say.

"Maybe," Brian says. "I'll see if I can get out of—of my engagement."

"Good!" She claps her hands and her cat jiggles on her arm. "I will see you then, and if not you, then you." She points at me. "You for certain."

"For sure."

She waves again, hand and cat paw both, this time, and pulls the door closed.

"You're not going with me," I say.

"It was just an answer she wanted to hear. I never say no to anyone."

"Clearly."

"Give it a rest."

He follows me into the kitchen and leans against the counter. "So, I'll be happy to get out of your way whenever you want to give me that lighter."

"I thought I knew where it was, but—" I spot my mug on the counter behind him. I reach around his waist and he doesn't move. His shirt smells like soap or aftershave or something fresh and light. He watches with little interest while I drink what's left. "Don't worry, though." Coffee clings to my upper lip, so I wipe it off with the back of my hand. "I'll keep looking, and when I find it, I'll call Denise or run it over myself."

He rubs his forehead, like feeling a bruise. "You don't think— maybe I could help you look for it?"

"If I don't know where it is, how could you?"

"Right. You're right, of course."

I tell him while I mix a drink that he should visit her anyway, if he needs to say goodbye, but he says he can't show up without the lighter.

"It's not your fault you don't have it. You should go, anyway. For closure, or…"

He sighs. "That's not what I want."

"What do you want?"

"Her."

"After all that's happened?"

He tucks his hands in his pockets and fiddles with whatever is in there.

"Her husband is dead," I say.

"I know. And—truly—it's awful. You don't want to question how I feel about that," he says, and the way he says it, I don't.

More knocking on my door. When I open it, my red-headed next door neighbor looks inside, around me. "Have you seen my papers?"

"Your what?"

"My newspapers. I go out of town for a few days, and when I come back, there's nothing."

"I don't know." I haven't had a chance to taste my drink, yet, so I taste it, and it's good enough. "No," I say. "I haven't seen your papers."

"Are you sure? Because they leave them right outside my door, right there on the mat." She points at her mat.

"I haven't seen your papers," I say. "But if I do, I'll let you know."

"I was looking forward to them," she says. "I do the crosswords every day."

"I'm sorry. I don't know what to tell you."

"It's only ten dollars to subscribe, you know," she says before I close the door.

Brian says, "Did you?"

"What?"

"Did you steal her papers?"

"I don't even know what she's talking about." And then I say, and I don't know why, "Brian, she never loved you." To hurt him, maybe. To keep him from going to her.

"Yes, she did. She still does." He takes his keys from his pocket and hooks a finger through the ring. "I know, because she's hurting."

"It couldn't be because her husband is dead."

"It's different. Trust me. But, I don't expect you to see it. Denise has said you're a very black and white sort of person, so you'll see what you see. And you won't see what you can't see. And I think there's a very…obvious…reason for your inability to understand what's happening between Denise and myself."

"Denise and me," I say.

"Pardon?"

"Why wouldn't I understand?"

"I believe—I believe you have to have been truly in love to recognize it in someone else."

"I've been in love. I am, I mean."

"I might be wrong." He shrugs. "A few weeks ago—or was it a month? I don't remember—Denise mentioned that William had emailed her to find out why your boyfriend wasn't getting mail from you. He'd hoped she would have some information, something to boost his morale. Denise said there wasn't an explanation she could give him. And I…well, I think there's something to that."

Before I ask him to leave, his answer to, "You mean they have email?" is, "Of course."

Kudzu's wide leaves canopy bushes and hang from high tree branches like dark Spanish moss. "Don't be too impressed," Jake said once. "Most of what's under it dies. It's not a gutted zebra on the animal channel, but it's close. Just on a smaller scale." I don't watch the channel, don't enjoy the bloody throat-tearing, but I am drawn to kudzu's deceptive strength and determination to consume. It flows alongside the guardrail, rising and falling in smooth waves and mounds and spilling over into a corner parking lot, spreading thin on the concrete, its vine-tips reaching out to nothing.

Right turn on Riverside.

The single drink I had while Brian nursed his coffee has made me tired. I need another.

Bourbon, maybe.

The light turns green and I follow a Subaru, rear hatch piled high with shapes wrapped in canvas, until I see the sign for the Midtown Motel and pull up in front of room eight, close to the door. The lot is pocked and potholed under my sandals and pavement cracks sprout weeds. At the sound of my knocking on Donny's door, curtains open in neighboring windows.

"Mind your own goddamn business!" I scream, and all but one curtain closes. From behind the exposed window a woman stares out, mouth tight, her small eyes dead.

I knock again.

"Yeah!" he says. "Who is it?"

"It's Mia."

"Mia!" Something jostles. "Hold on just a second, girl."

I look back at the woman's window, but she is gone, the curtain closed.

Donny opens his door wearing jeans and a pressed, short-sleeved shirt. His hair is wavy, and wet at the base of his neck from sweat or a shower. "You got my message," he says. "I didn't know if I'd ever see you again. What's it been?"

"Not too long," I say. "You look nice." But he doesn't. He looks older, thinner, and more frail, but at the same time, he's hardened.

"What d'you mean?"

"You just—you just do. I don't know."

"What the hell're you—what do I usually look like? What, I look different from any other day?" He touches his buttons.

"No, I—Jesus, Donny, I was just saying something nice."

"Well, c'mon in," he says.

I follow him into the living room. "Do you want your door closed?"

"Naw. Leave it open."

The room is bright, clean minus the full ashtray on the table, and hot. I take one of the chairs by the window and vinyl cools the backs of my knees. A temperature control unit sits silent under the window with its panel door propped open, most of the knobs plucked off dull metal pegs too small to turn with fingers. The switch is flipped to 'on.'

"Broken?"

"Naw. I just like the heat." Donny grabs a half-empty bourbon bottle from the nightstand mounted to the bedside wall. "Course it's broken." He sits down and wipes sweat from under his glasses and fills an expensive-looking tumbler.

"Want some?" he says.

"Sure. Okay."

"Ask, then. Don't sit there starin' at it."

"I wasn't staring."

"You're starin' now."

He leans back in his chair, stretching his legs out in front of him, and crosses his ankles and watches the lot through the open door. A gust blows in, swirling ashes over the ashtray and cooling my hair and flattening Donny's shirt against his stomach and chest. It stays there, bonded by sweat. He closes his eyes and holds up his drink. "Thank *you*."

I say, "May I have a glass?"

"What's the magic word?"

"Please."

"That ain't it. Guess again."

I look around the room. "Light switch."

"What? What the—light switch?"

"I don't know, Donny. Maybe you picked some arbitrary—just—may I?"

He looks at me. "'May I—?' Girl, who d'you think—ask me for a goddamn glass."

"I did."

"Naw. What, we ain't friends? Don't talk to me like I'm a—what, I'm a stranger, now?"

"Never mind."

"What d'you mean, 'never mind'?"

"Forget it."

"Just ask me for a goddamn glass, goddamn it. What the—I'll give it to you, but you got to—"

"Okay. All right? Can I have a glass? Goddamn it?"

"There! Magic word! Now, yes, you *may*. See? What're you bein' all polite, for? It's Donny! Here. Go get one of the ones by the sink, there." He points to the back of the room where a shrink-wrapped plastic cup sits on the counter. "This one," he swirls his glass, "I brought from the house. She can't have my glass. Got almost everything else, but she ain't getting' this. This is mine. Mine. Bought it m'self."

When I sit back down with the unwrapped cup, he fills it. "No ice," he says. "And no Coke, either." He smiles. "No Coke. Straight up."

We sit quiet, then, and stare out at the empty lot and sip our drinks. Sweat builds behind my knees, runs down my calves. "Thanks," I say.

"For what?"

"For letting me come over. For the drink."

"Naw, Mia. Don't thank me! You can always come over, you know. My angel! 'Sides, what the hell else have I got to do? Can't work, 'cause I need to be here for when Archie comes by. Says he's comin' at night, but—Archie, he says one thing, but never sticks to it. He comes by, I got to be here. Has my stuff in his car, in the trunk. Hell, I'm glad you're here. No one else comes. No one visits Donny."

I pull a pack of cigarettes from my pocket and slide it toward him on the table. "I owe you."

He lights two and hands me one and we smoke.

Tenants pass by and nod. Donny nods back and says some of their names once they're gone. "Don't you call 'em by those names, though," he says. "They won't answer. I made 'em up. Clark is for Crackhead Clark, see. Dick for Dope Fiend Dick. Lost. Lost causes, most of 'em." He flips his hand at the door. "Half ain't worth it. But the others…one or two, maybe, they'll do it. They live here. Get that? Not just stayin', like me."

He makes less sense than usual and I wonder what time this morning he started drinking. "For how long?"

"A week, maybe," he slurs. "I'm goin' to give it another day, maybe two, to get 'em used to me, know my name. A couple already know. And then, the Doctor is in. They don't do it right. Moderation. See? A cookie a day—just one, one cookie—won't get you fat." He spreads his arms out in front of him, as if circling them around an inordinately large belly, and laughs. "And you even get the good from the chocolate. Chocolate's got antioxidants. Know that?" As abruptly as it started, his laughter stops and he watches the door. "It's got to be the dark, though."

"I didn't know."

"So, you eat a bit, just a little, every day, or every week, and it's okay. It's all right. Understan'?"

"Yeah."

"Naw, you don't. One cookie, that's—some people eat a bag, but you eat one, and that's moderation. Get it?"

"I'm not stupid, Donny. I know what moderation means."

He wipes again at the sweat under his glasses. "Oh, yeah? You know? Do you know what it means to someone who's self-medicatin'?"

"Well, isn't moderation modera—"

"Don't know shit." He glares at me and shakes his head, turns again to look outside. "They need me. Need the doctor. Doctor Donaldson."

"Do you want me to leave?"

"What? Hell, no, girl. Why would you say that? You just can't talk about what you don't know nothin' 'bout, is all. That's all. Naw, I don't want you to leave. You stay as long as you want." He puts out his cigarette in the dense flower of packed, crumpled butts and gray smoke rises from somewhere underneath. Burning filter. "Aw, hell," he says and covers his nose. He uses a butt to mash it out, then empties the ashtray in a trash can by the dresser. "More?" he says and looks at my glass.

"Okay."

"So. How's that hus—boyfriend of yours?"

"Fine, I guess."

"Fine, you guess. You don't know?"

"We don't get to talk much."

"Alive, though."

"As far as I know."

"Good. That's good. That's what matters. What's his name? Jack?"

"Jake."

"To Jake!" He drinks. "Fightin' the good fight." He drinks again. "I saw on the news the other day some people—in shape, maybe, in form, or…but not in here," he touches his chest, "holdin' signs against the soldiers. What the *fuck's* the matter with people?"

"I don't know." I put out my cigarette and smooth my hair away from my face. Too long, for this heat. My face feels swollen.

"Get a goddamn sniper rifle and shoot 'em all down, one by one. Get far enough away and no one'd know, you know that? *Bam!* from behind a tree across the street. Run run run, duck back behind a Dumpster, an' *bam!* Right in the neck. Motherfuckers."

"Jesus, Donny."

"Easy for them to hold their little painted signs. Wonder how long they spent on 'em. D'you think they made it a family activity, makin' them signs? 'What color paint you want, darlin'?' 'Oh, I think periwinkle, dear.' 'Here you go, pumpkin.' 'My that's purdy.' Where do they think they'd be if people like me—and that Jake of yours, too—sat home like they do on fat, peace-lovin' 'make love not war' asses? Do away with the military, they say. Okay. All right." He smiles. "They'll see some shit, then. See how things run without a military when the rest of the world ain't gettin' rid o' theirs. Goddamn hippies."

"Where were you in Vietnam, anyway?"

He lights another cigarette and exhales the smoke through his nose. "Why? You know the place? You goin' to know where it is if I tell you?"

"No."

"You goin' to say, 'Gee, Donny, I remember that area. I *studied* up on it. Gosh, Donny, I heard a lot of people got shot and blown to bits there. It sure was kind of you to help those poor people with their legs shot off into the bushes before goin' to kill those innocent little babies.' You goin' to say that?"

"No."

"You goin' to tell me why not one person could say somethin' nice to Donny when the tour was over and the plane landed and I was h—back? I almost said 'home.' You hear that?" His eyes are dark behind his glasses. "Almost said 'home.'"

"I don't know anything about that."

"All right, then. I don't want to hear you talk about it."

"Okay. Sorry."

"For what?"

"For—I don't know."

"Don't say it, then."

"I mean, I'm sorry you were treated that way."

"Didn't have nothin' to do with you."

"Still." I touch his hand, just long enough, and pull back. His fingers are rough.

"Screamin' at me. Spittin' on me, too. On my jacket right here." He touches a spot on his shoulder. "Right there. Found it later, 'cause there was so much goin' on that I didn't notice right off."

"People, the ones who know the diff—they're not all bad, I mean. Most of them loved you, or people like you. They did."

"If they did, I never saw a one. But, you're tryin'." He folds his hands in a cup over his heart. "Angel," he says. "Thanks, girl. Thanks for tryin'. It ain't the welcome home I needed at twenty-one—young, ain't it? Twenty-one? I, me, Donny Donaldson, was twenty-one, a kid—but it's sure sweet. Appreciate it."

We finish our drinks at the same time and he pours refills. The bottle is almost empty.

"Got somethin' for you," he says.

"What is it?"

"It ain't here right now, but I got it. Archie, a friend of mine— wait, I told you about him? yeah—he's bringin' my stuff by tonight. She got the car, you know, the one that works, so—art supplies, some of my things. This is it for now." An open suitcase, clothes folded neatly inside, lies on the full-sized bed. A thin nylon strap belts each half. "It's in his trunk. That picture, the one I drew of you. I ain't got a use for it."

I had forgotten about it. I tell him thank you, and I hope his friend doesn't bring it to him. I'm not sure I want it, don't think I'd like that…face…around.

"You'll have to come back. Tomorrow, to pick it up. I can't bring it to you. Ain't got a car."

"I know."

"So you'll be back tomorrow?"

"I don't know. I'll try."

"I just want to give you the—it's a present."

"I'll try."

"You want it, don't you?"

"Of course I do. I loved it."

"Well, you come by tomorrow, then."

"I'll try."

He puts an elbow on the table, rests his chin in his hand. "You're beautiful," he says. "You know that? An angel."

I smile at him and look away, toward the door. *Email.* Heat haze grains the air, softens the lines of the bush growing across the lot. I rub my eyes and take a drink and something rises in my throat. I rub my stomach and swallow, hold it down, take another sip and wish I hadn't, wish there hadn't been the cup before. Too late to drive home, now. I look over at Donny and he smiles, eyes wrinkling behind his glasses. "Glad you came over, girl," he says, and his face is warm and I don't want to go anywhere, anymore. Don't want to be anywhere but here, where nothing is real and where no one knows me or Jake or the sickness inside my stomach.

"Donny," I say.

"Yep?"

I look at the cigarettes. "I think I might be—" I take one. Light it. "I think I might be drunk."

"Aw," he says. "You ain't drunk yet. What, you had two little cups? You ain't even finished that one, so it's more like one and a half. Go on, finish up, have another. Get real drunk, for real. It's Tuesday."

"To Tuesday." I try to drink more, and fast, but can't. Donny pours anyway to make up for the room I left, then taps the rim of his glass on my cup. *Cheers,* I think, and what a wonderful word.

"Cheers," I say.

"Good girl."

Something *tap tap taps,* somewhere, and Donny says, "Yeah!" A woman, maybe Donny's age or maybe younger, with orange-red hair and wearing white shorts that fall to her pink knees, stands in the doorway.

"Judy!" he says. "Judy, darlin', come in. Come in! Have somethin' to drink with us."

"Thanks, no," she says, smiling. She nods at me. "Hi." Her voice is dusty.

"Hi," I say.

"Donny, I just stopped by because…well, actually, I was already out this way. Do you know the flower shop on the corner?"

"I know it."

"Well, it belongs to a friend of mine. Can you believe I didn't even know? She bought it last month, she says, and she has the most beautiful alstroemerias. They have these long, spe—"

"Sure, sure," he says. "I know astr—yeah. How 'bout that? You should paint 'em, sculpt 'em, or somethin'. Mia, this one—she does it all. Paints. Draws. Sculpts. Ain't nothin' she can't do."

"He's exaggerating," she says.

"You goin' to paint 'em?"

"I *am*. I bought three bunches, and I'm on my way home, now, to set them up. But I stopped by to tell you, and I'm so sorry, that my sister won't be leaving until a little later than we thought."

"A long time?"

"No, no," she says. She shifts on her feet and lifts the hair from her neck. "It's hot, isn't it?" She smiles again, a nice smile, and laugh lines wrinkle around bright green eyes. "Maybe another week or two." Donny's eyes go up and down her body, nice for any age. I cross my legs and sit straighter.

"That's all right, Jude. That's fine."

"I'm so sorry. I know we made these plans, and…I feel just awful."

"What're you sorry for? It's your house, and your sister can stay as long as she wants."

"Well, all right," she says. She looks at me, and Donny says, "Judy, this is my little friend, Mia. My surrogate daughter, my new patient. Mia, Judy. Artist extraordinaire."

"Oh, Donny," she says.

"You should see," he says. "I ain't nothin' compared to her."

"Nice to meet you," I say.

"And you, too," she says. "I should go, though, Donny, so— I'll give you a call, or we can meet later, all right?"

"Sure you don't want to stay? Have a drink? C'mon, sit a while."

"No, really, but thank you. I want to get the alstroemerias home before they wilt and sag. Like me!" She actually giggles, and then tucks her hair behind her ears. "Kelly's out shopping, too, and it's the silence of the *heavens* when she's gone."

Donny laughs and Judy laughs and Donny says, "That sister of yours." Their laughter trickles and fades and I say from my chair by the window, "What's funny about your sister?"

"Oh, you would have to meet her," she says. "Anyway, so…"

"Nice to meet you," I say.

"Yes," she says, "you said that." She waves, hand down by her hip. "I'll see you later, then, Donny."

"Sooner," he says, and she is gone. Her car door slams and an engine starts. Someone in the lot hoots and calls, "Where you runnin' off to, mama?"

Donny raises his glass, drinks, and slams it on the table. "That was Judy."

"I guess it was."

"You know Judy?"

"Donny, you just introduced us." I take a drink and the bourbon is smooth, now, not at all like when I first started drinking it, that first time, when it tore at my throat and burned my chest. A few more swallows and the glass is empty and Donny fills it up again. I push it away and try to steady my head.

"Ain't she somethin'? Ain't she beautiful?"

"Beautiful."

"Emily, she—Judy and me, we're—we're artists, the two of us. One mind between us. Our connection, it's spiritual, and no one can understand."

"Beautiful, yes, you're both very deep," I say, and, "Do you miss Emily?"

"Naw," he says. "Naw, I don't want to talk about Emily. Judy—she, well, I ain't nothin' next to her. Brilliant. Genius! You ought to see what she does. Painted a landscape like a dream, like the dream that ain't over. Like the song."

I don't know what song he means, and I don't care. "Landscapes already exist."

"What's that s'posed to mean?"

"Nothing."

"Judy, she takes somethin' like that and makes it new, is what I'm sayin'."

"What was she saying about her sister?"

"The story's none of your business, but she's stayin' for a while, and when she's gone I get the room. Me and Judy'll be roommates.—Just roommates, you know. Nothin' like—now, what's that face? I'm a married man." He smiles. "Naw, but yeah. Just two friends, two artists. We bounce ideas."

"That's good."

"You should come, too. I'll ask. You can live there, too."

"No, thanks."

"Naw?"

"I already live somewhere."

He flips his hand. "Whatever you want. But you should see her art. Beautiful, like her. You want to know an angel? Judy. The truest angel there ever was. Real smart, that one. Real talented. A natural talent."

"Mm."

"Sun's goin' down," he says.

"I think you love her."

"What's that?"

"Judy. I think you love her. But make sure you only get married 'cause of love. No other reason. Not war, not a—not anything."

"What? I got a wife. You talkin' 'bout Judy? Course I love her! Not like that, now. I love—she's—I love her spirit, is what. She's somethin' else. An angel. Kind of like how I love you."

"Right."

"I do."

"Donny, just—I wasn't trying to get you to…just stop."

"Stop what?"

"Stop saying you love me."

"Hey, now. What's the matter with you?"

"Nothing."

"I can't say I love you, now? All the sudden?"

"Say whatever you want. I'm just sitting here."

"Don't just sit there, then. Drink up."

"Can't."

"Hell. Wish she'd stayed, then. Look at you, ready to pass out."

"I want to go home," I say.

"What for?"

"I want to go home."

"Now, don't—it's all right. It'll be all right. I'll get you some water. You just need a breather from it. I know. You listen to me, do what I'm tellin' you, all right? Donny's here."

I close my eyes and hear stumbling and banging, and when I open them the water is in front of me and Donny watches me from across the table.

"Okay?" he says.

The water's coldness makes my throat ache.

"Will you call Lionel for me?" I say.

"What d'you want me to call him for? You're all right. You're okay. You just sit there and wait. Listen to Donny."

Something bangs, scrapes, and I open my eyes and the room is dark, the door closed. Outdoor lamplight bleeds through the window and makes a dim square on the wall, and a broken nylon thread from the bed's polyester comforter scrapes my drool-wet cheek. Too tired to shift, to care, and a dark figure moves toward me, then passes by, and I close my eyes.

Later—minutes or hours or days—fingers in my hair and against my scalp, soft, gentle, stroking, down to my shoulder, my arm. "Everything's goin' to be all right," he murmurs. "Doctor Donaldson says so," and then he is snoring, his hand lying limp on my waist. I pull his arm around me and press my back into his chest and sleep.

MAY 7, WEDNESDAY

BASS POUNDS IN the lot, vibrating the bathroom walls. I finish being sick, flush the toilet, and wait for it to quiet before opening the door. Donny is still asleep in his shirt and jeans and socks. I slip off his glasses and set them on the nightstand before leaving.

"Stanley and Kellerman. How may I direct your call?"

Lowered blinds keep out the bright blue sky and aspirin hasn't reached my headache. It hurts, some, to say, "Hi, Olivia." Behind the blinds the window is closed, but humidity still finds a way in. Under the door, through the walls.

"Well, hi, hon! How can I help—Oh, listen to me, will you? That's what happens when you call me at work!…Anyway, sweetie, what can I do for you?"

My hand sweats around the phone. "I—"

"I can't speak for very long—so busy, today, for a change—but I can call you back at lunch, if you'd like."

"No, I—I just wanted to ask you—"

"Oh, no…You saw the news last night, too? I'll tell you what, hon, if another…"

I hold the phone away from my ear. When I listen again I catch only the end: "…and I can't believe it. Isn't that terrible?"

"It is, it is," I say. "Terrible."

"Tsk," she says.

Brakes squeal outside and I turn the handle on the blinds to open them. A rusted, blue car parks in front of the house across the street and honks.

"Are you there, hon?"

"I'm here," I say. "I'm just—you know—taking a second. Thinking about what happened." The car honks again and a girl steps onto the porch and opens a pink umbrella. "A parasol?"

"What's that, hon?"

"Nothing."

"Well," she says, "I know how you feel. That poor—"

"Actually, Olivia—sorry to interrupt—I'm just…in light of all that…see, I seem to have lost Jake's email address—his new one, I mean—and I'm, well, I'm just frantic to get a hold of him. Do you have it, by any chance?"

"Well, why…? What do those poor children in Oregon have to do with Jake?"

"Children?"

"Yes. The ones that mother was keeping in cages as if they were little more than…"

I wait it out. I'd thought it would be about the war. Her bad news has always been about the war. "Well," I say when she finishes, and, "It's a bad place, the world. Or, I mean, it can be. You know. I guess—I guess I just want to talk to him to reassure myself that there's some good in it all." I switch the phone to my left hand and wipe my palm on my shorts. "You do have it, don't you?" I close my eyes.

"Of course I do."

The pulsing thickens in my head, so I lay my face on the table. "I thought you might." The veneer is cool on my cheek.

"Don't you have it on your computer? Doesn't it save in your address book?"

"My hard drive crashed last week," I say. "I lost everything." When the spinning comes, I raise my head and look out the window. Softer now, the pulse, so maybe the aspirin is working.

The car across the street pulls away from the curb, and a hand pokes through the half-open driver's side window to drop a piece of trash.

"Oh, no. Well, let me just get to my address book…" Rustling. Fingernails clicking on keys. "Here it is," she says and gives it to me. "I'm so happy he's emailing you now. He asked me not to tell you, back when, because he thought it was just another thing that would help along any worrying, but I told him. I said he should—"

"Thank you," I say. I hang up.

The monitor stays blank through seven cigarettes and I am nicotine sick. I get up and mix a strong drink and sit back down and light another cigarette and set it in the ashtray. Smoke drifts past the monitor.

I type, *Jake.*

Today is William's funeral and the lighter lies buried in a bowl.

I wonder if Denise will look, if the casket is open. I wonder if I will look inside Jake's open casket.

Jake sent an email on a Thursday the week before he deployed. It's saved, number one. *Long day, but longer when I think about you and how many hours until I can come home. Can't wait to see you naked! Lather on some peanut butter. —Moi.* When he walked in after work, he had the face. It was not a day for joking about peanut butter, or for the lingerie I felt half sexy, half awkward wearing. I put on my robe while he told me.

When Denise comes back to Tennessee, I'll invite her over, listen to her talk about William and about Brian and we'll drink a bottle of something strong and I'll ask her why she never mentioned email.

We'll have a nice dinner.

But the only food in my cabinet is a box of macaroni and cheese, and I'm out of butter.

I type *Bastard* and delete it.

Surprise.

Delete.

I can't be mad, can I? I don't get to be mad. You're at war, after all. Anything I feel is inconsequential.

Delete.

I could be at your funeral. You could be flat in your casket regretting that we didn't communicate as much as we could have.

"Hypocrite," he would say.

Delete.

Hi, Jake, and nothing more.

Send.

Eight o'clock, his time. I mix another drink and sit back down and wait.

From where my desk sits, the view outside is of trees and rooftops, and all of the street sounds are scattered mysteries. A car door slams and mutterings drone unintelligible and low, the words' possibilities unending. I pretend the slamming door belongs to a taxi and that down on the street, where I can't see, Jake pays the cabbie. The taxi pulls away and Jake shouts at my—our—widow. "M!" he shouts, and I get up and cross the room. I look down. He stands in the lot in all of his gear. The duffel bag hangs on his shoulder. He smiles. He spreads his arms wide, the way he does. Like a boy. And emails don't matter, anymore, because he is here, the secret was kept to protect this surprise, and I slide up the window and yell, "I'm coming down!" and—

The computer speakers chime.

My touch brings back the screen. In bold letters, 'CW2 Jake Lakeland,' Jake's name right there on the screen, just now sent from where he sits at his own computer, linked by—whatever it is that links us—and it's almost—almost—touching, like being across from one another in the same room, immediate, now, talk-typing, and I don't even read his before sending my own, *I'm here I'm on now* and no time to punctuate or sign before sending.

I stare at the screen and breathe, breathe, drink, light a cigarette. Tug back my hair and wipe my face and wait, wait, until the shaking stops and the cigarette is out, but nothing. Nothing comes.

I open his message.

To: msharpe@email.net
7 May / 2034
Subject: Hi, there!
Hi, M. You found me! I'm glad. Sorry I didn't tell you, but my mom probably explained why. I figured Denise would have leaked a long time ago, so she's better than I thought. Can't write much because I'm just on a short break. It was so good to see your name, though. Really - so good. I'm okay and things are fine, considering, and I'm safe and relatively comfortable. I love you, you know. More later, I promise. –J.

"You're going to go bald!" comes through the floor, a muffled yell. I listen for more, but whatever it was is over.

How many times a week, I wonder, does he wait in line for a computer, sit down, and spend the time to write his mother? I wonder who else he emails who isn't me.

Safe and comfortable. Well, good.

To: Jake.Lakeland@army.net
7 May / 11:36
Subject: Re: Hi, there!
I'm glad you're glad I found you. And I'm glad you're fine. Glad glad glad. Thanks, by the way, for asking how I am. So. How long have you had email? Do you have any idea how much better I would have felt to get notes from you letting me know you were okay? How could you not tell me? You call your

mother, you email your mother, you probably send her a scented, handwritten, kiss-ass letter every day. You secretly want to fuck her, don't you? You know what? It's all been about you. You you you. Fuck you, Jake. Don't bother writing back.

Send!

My face heats and I can feel and hear my heart. I click on the 'Outbox' folder, but there's nothing there. The message is already gone, moved to the 'Sent' folder.

Smart would have been to write it on paper, first.

Five more cigarettes burn to the filter while I wait for a response.

To: Jake.Lakeland@army.net
7 May / 12:29
Subject: Sorry
I'm so sorry. I didn't mean it, Jake. I swear. I was just mad. Do you understand? Please write me. I know you just care about me

But, I don't send it. I replace the message with, *I didn't mean 'don't write back.' You know I want to hear from you. Love, M.* and send that, instead.

I follow it with another.

To: Jake.Lakeland@army.net
7 May / 12: 30
Subject: One more
I do care about you and don't really think you don't care about me. –M.

To: Jake.Lakeland@army.net
7 May / 12:31
Subject: Last one, I promise
I'm really, really sorry about what I said about you and your mother. That crossed a line. Please don't hate me.

To: Jake.Lakeland@army.net
7 May / 12:32
Subject: Last and final
But I am mad. Just so you know. Write me as soon as you can. Love, Mia

The glass is empty—already—so I mix another and sit in front of the monitor until my back hurts and I'm drunk and out of cigarettes and there's nothing left to do but lay my head on my arms and pass out.

MAY 8, THURSDAY

I TURN THE speakers high in case I leave the room for something, and check the internet connection every few minutes.

By noon, my back hurts from sitting at the computer. Chancey sleeps behind the keyboard.

By seven, I've written and deleted twenty-three messages and closed out four e-cards mid-creation.

By midnight, he's still sent nothing.

I write *Please know me* and click the send button.

SAFIA'S GNARLED-TWINE mat says 'WELCOME' in black. I knock and start a count to thirty.

Music made of bells and chimes and a twanging string instrument filters into the hallway. I inhale a strong, spicy odor that won't confine itself to her kitchen, and I can't identify it beyond *good*. Laughter—Safia's—follows jumbled muttering, gets louder as she nears the door, and is just ebbing when she opens it wearing an oversized sweatshirt and a pair of jeans, her hair nearly white from over-processing and hanging in two straw-like braids from underneath a backward-facing baseball cap. Over the fitting-strap, a yellow embroidered message reads, "Happy Life."

"You are here!" she says waving me in. Before I reach the dining area, she's handed me a glass of wine.

Tea candles flicker in tinted votive holders and a blue and green bubbled glass chandelier hangs over the table in the eating cove. Paul gets up from his chair and adjusts the dimmer switch until a round of "Better!" and "Good!" gives approval to the turned-down bulb. I count heads—seven—and am glad I decided to have a drink or two (three) beforehand. Dull twinges of anxiety linger, but nothing that won't be killed with the wine in my hand.

"Everyone," Safia says, leading me to the table and making me stand there while she motions for Paul to search for an extra chair, "this is my upstairs neigh—my friend," she nods at me, "Maya."

"Mia," I say. I take a long drink and my nose flares from the bitterness. I've never agreed with red wine.

"Mia," she repeats. "I am so sorry. Mia, this is…" She introduces the table. Names like Neil and Kelly and Nina and Joan and Charles, but not necessarily those names. I won't remember them, so I don't try. They nod and smile and murmur "Mia" and "nice to meet you" and then fall silent while I stand over them with my empty glass. Have I emptied it already? I cover the bottom half with my hand.

"Oh," Safia says and reaches for it. She pours to the rim, then hands it back. "Careful," she says and laughs. Everyone else laughs with her. From a back room, Paul calls to Safia, "Hey, doll? Have you seen that yellow chair?"

"In the closet," she says.

"Nope. Not here."

She touches my shoulder. "He will find it. Don't worry."

"Oh, no problem." My face is hot, red. With luck the light is too dim for them to see it. I look around the table and meet their stares, smile, and wish I'd never come.

"Please," Safia says, opening the oven. "Have something on the table." Inside, almost-golden bread bakes in a tin. On the table: chips and dip and water crackers, and I'm painfully hungry. "No, thanks," I say. "I just ate. But, thank you."

"So, anyway…" A woman with dyed black hair and a green-stone nosering returns to a story she must have almost finished before I came in. Something about a girl and a guy walking across New York state from west to east, but not making it past Buffalo. The girl, she says, broke off when she found out their first stop was to be with her boyfriend's other girlfriend.

"Did she at least have a warm meal ready for them?" says a man sitting on the left side of the table. His face is expressionless, and he wears a red flannel shirt and glasses and is older than the rest of us by what must be twenty years.

The girl with the nosering laughs. "She didn't say."

He shrugs. "At least they didn't have to pay for a hotel."

Nosering sighs her relief at being newly single—"I've slept great since he left."—and asks Flannel about his recent marriage. "Three weeks, already, right?"

"I am blissfully happy," he says. He sips his wine.

Hands snatch crackers and lift glasses and I'm still waiting for a chair. I look with feigned interest at pictures on the walls. Many of the faces in a collage hanging above a wine rack belong to those at the table. Safia is absent from most of them; Paul is the one constant figure. I ask Safia if she needs any help.

"No, thank you. Everything is done."

I study the table with a forced smile to leave no question of pleasantness. Their circle is palpable and frustrating in its inaccessibility to me; I feel like I'm standing just outside the reaches of a fire's warmth.

Jake was the only one I was ever truly comfortable with.

Or am I making it up? I was more at ease with him—this is true—than with anyone else. But, was it like this? Like them? Strange that I can't remember.

"I want to know about Mia," one of the women—Kim or Joni or Christine—says. She sits directly in front of where I stand, so her neck twists awkwardly when she looks at me.

"What do you want to know?" My stomach burns, nauseous, and I scan the bottles on the table. Nothing white.

"Well, anything."

Questions suddenly come at me from the ring around the table, a barrage of shouts and reporter-like inquiries that I'm sure they mean to be playful.

"What do you do?"

"What's your social security number?"

"How long have you lived in the area?"

"Do you like pickles?"

Safia appears beside me with a bottle. "Do you need more wine?" I hold my glass under the stream and swallow half of it, at least, when she pulls away the bottle.

Safia says, "This is *May*—*Mia*," she says. "Remember? The girl upstairs?"

The table falls quiet, again, and the woman in front of me reaches for a cracker. "With the husband fighting in the war," she says. "Right?"

"M-hm," I say, and the word "husband"…*husband*… Saturation is all it is, most likely. One more minute thinking about Jake, missing Jake, being angry with Jake, loving Jake, and I'll either drown in self-absorption or come to fully detest him.

Paul, still in one of the back rooms, calls, "Hey, love? I can't find it," and Safia excuses herself.

"Sorry to hear that," says the woman. "About your husband."

"It's okay." *Husband!*

Flannel laughs. His face reddens to match his shirt and his eyes water behind his glasses, and I think of paintings depicting demons I don't know are demons until I study the look in the eyes or the mark on the skin. I am asking him if I said something funny when Paul and Safia arrive with my chair. The group shifts sideways to make room, and I squeeze uncomfortably into the space.

"'It's okay', you said." He takes a slow drag from a cigarette and exhales a white cloud into the yellow-brown light falling out of the shade. The table is circular, so there is no escaping their eyes, all of which rest on me, waiting. "It was the look on your face that made me laugh. It was clearly not okay."

"It was," I say quietly to her, now sitting next to me, and she whispers that she meant nothing by it.

He still smiles, his eyes shining. He raises his glass to me and I take a drink without returning the toast. He laughs again, his mouth opening wide and his face turning even redder. "She hates me already."

Nosering, whose mashed, chewed cracker clings between her top and bottom teeth, says, "Beth's husband was going to join, remember? Last week, sometime, he said he was thinking about it. Guilt, or some such…" She looks at me. "Or something. But now he thinks this will all be over in no time, and he doesn't want to waste three years of his life for nothing."

"It would be for nothing either way," says someone else. "Things will just go back to the way they were. People can't be forced to change."

Safia bends through shoulders to place a wood cutting board of cheese and bread in the center of the table, then takes a seat next to Nosering.

"I don't know," I say, and they all stare at me, the authority on such things. I hold my glass tighter. "I mean, it seems like maybe they just needed a little help to change." It doesn't even sound genuine to me.

"A boost over the wall, you might say," says Flannel.

"Yes." I ready my glass for tossing. Whatever I might think of the war, I dare any one of them—Flannel Demon or Nosering or anyone—to say something about Jake, the military, their brav—

"You can't believe that," he says, and instead of throwing my wine, I drink it.

The woman sitting to my right says, "I don't know how any of you can think it's almost over. A statue falls and you think the President will withdraw the troops? The government didn't spend all the money to send them over there just to bring them back less than three months later. They'll be there for years. Bet on it."

"And like little toys," says Safia, "they follow mindlessly, the winding knob on their back twisted until it cannot twist more." She walks her fingers on the table, the 'feet' kicking straight up.

"You don't know what you're talking about," I say, but they're laughing and don't hear me. I yell "Shut up!" and Flannel's smile turns kind toward me as the rest of them fall quiet. He says, "Hey, now," and I say, "Never mind," because I'm already back to being too weak to argue for something I don't believe. And Safia might have a point, even though I know—I *know*—she doesn't, not in the way she intends. Nazis, she meant, with her little finger-boots. But then I remember Brian, who didn't follow, didn't go. He found a way out. If being sneaky and cunning isn't successful, there's always Canada or conscientious objection. I once taught an excerpt from a Tim O'Brien novel…the excerpt was anthologized as an essay, and it was too long ago, so the title won't come…about bravery, or at least one understanding of it. Was it bravery that turned his narrator's boat around, away from Canada and back to the States for his trip to Vietnam? Or would he have been brave to continue to Canada as frightened as he was about what his family, his country, would think of his desertion?

"I give it a month," says a man I haven't really noticed until now. He leans back in his chair, stoned-looking, and his hands, covered by the stretched-out cuffs of his long-sleeved shirt, are folded loosely on his stomach. "You'll be out there like monkeys, screaming and pounding your chests, and with or without you, the end is already here."

"Are you going next Thursday?" Waiting for me to answer is a set of bright blue eyes like painted glass set in a pale, porcelain face. A living Pierrot clown with an orange scarf holding back frizzy brown hair, loops and twirls springing out, falling along her cheek to her shoulders.

I ask her what's happening on Thursday.

"Not this Thursday. Next. You don't—? The campus protest. You haven't heard?" She slaps the table and the stoned one turns his head. "See, Safia? I told you no one knows about it."

"She does not leave her apartment," Safia says and smiles apologetically at me. "How is she to know?"

"She lives right upstairs. You could have told her."

"People know. Trust me. Many will come." She tugs at the end of one of her braids and studies the colorless hair flattened between her fingers. "Mia will come." She smiles at me.

The war has become a worn subject. Conversation turns more personal, and the music coming from the living room changes from Middle Eastern to American sixties folk. Flannel has a name— Frank—and he says, when asked about the progress of his new wife's pregnancy, that he can't wait for the baby to be born. The frizzy-haired one—Rose—is in the middle of finishing her master's in art and complains about her unsuccessful formal appeal to change a 'C' to a 'B'. "I can't get a fucking C. But, of course, since he can't be *forced* to change my grade, he won't. The asshole. Now what am I going to do?" Frank suggests—without a hint of humor—that she try sleeping with the professor. "Or are you still waiting for marriage?"

"Oh, Safia, I forgot!" says Nosering, whose name I discover is Jennifer. "You just had your first anniversary. How was it?"

Safia gets up for more cheese, and Paul, smiling at his wife's back, says it couldn't have been better.

I finish my wine—I can barely taste the red in it, at this point— and ask Safia if there's more.

The next few hours pass slowly. I can't get rid of the nausea—the wine isn't helping—and group familiarity pushes me out unless I'm reaching into the middle for cheese or a cracker, but I stay, anyway, drinking free wine and veiled in enough drunken confidence to eat the free food. I listen with waning interest to inside jokes and anecdotes, hoping for more information on the protest. I've never been to one and would like details about time and location—if they mentioned them, I've already forgotten—but it doesn't come up again. I wonder what I'm supposed to wear and if I'm supposed to make a sign, but I don't ask. I don't want them to know it will be my first time.

If the one in the sleeves is right, this will be my only protest because the war will be over soon, and it could be years before there's another one.

Over.

Hot tears come and my breath catches and a scream builds in my neck. *Over.*

Frank catches me smiling and smiles back. I hurry around the table and squeeze him tight and he smells like sandalwood. I fill my glass with the last of the wine on the table and light a cigarette and thank Safia for inviting me, then run upstairs.

Chancey rubs his side against my shins under the desk while I wait for the internet to come up, then trots to the bedroom when my cigarette smoke drops to cat-nose level.

There's been no opportunity to check email for the past few hours, so there must be something waiting by now.

"No new messages" appears in the screen's bottom corner. The nausea crests and I shove my cigarette in the ashtray and run to the toilet.

Afterward, I pour out the wine and mix a drink I can handle and open a page to begin a new message. My fingers move like they're cold, landing on the wrong letters, and strands of my hair fall into the small, black crevasses when I lean in to better see the keys.

To: Jake.Lakeland@army.net
09 May / 10:23pm
Subject: You!
Jake,

You haven't written back, so you must beb on a mission. You can't be that mad, can you? You would'nt ignorn me, would you? Sometimes I thingk you're lying when we say "I love you'. Are you ever think we stayt toghethr because we're all we know anymore? Your lasst letter—letter, not emoil—you seemed I dno[tn know. Ih thought you dind't agree with us ebeing over there/? Oh well! Diesn't matter bercuase the wir is overl! Jake, you hear me? OVER! I finally feel like I can breathe and like smiling without caoution won't get you shot. They didn't sayk on the news that it's over, but you can tellk by the stories. I cant'n wait to seew you agai, Jaike. We'll gfet a new houske with no trees and nop spiders and live happilyyj evern after,. You wnt new, you got new. You want wall to wall carpting? You got well to weall carpetingl. You want a bababy? You gotr a babay. Antyhing youi watn, Jake, because you fought in a war. A WAR. Aand I didn't nothing but sit here.
Love ferver,
Mia

I send it and turn on the news and fall onto the couch. Images and anchors' faces slip by like pictures on a View-Master, making me dizzy, so I turn to a movie channel and settle back and feel something poking my skin just above the waistline of my jeans. Some digging behind the cushion turns up a bent picture of Jake that came in the stack Denise brought. He sits with a skinny, big-headed puppy on an uneven but sturdy-looking wood-planked patio in front of a square brown tent. A sandbag wall surrounds the tent and everything else either is dirt or matches the dirt. He is smiling and his hand rests on the puppy's back. I remember his hand. I remember it holding mine. Stroking my arm and curling around the back of my neck in the hangar before he left.

I put out my cigarette and close my eyes. *No rushing this*, I tell myself, fighting the random images pushing their way through; daydreams speed forward like they're on a movie reel, but this I want to experience in real time. He walks across the hangar toward me, one side of his mouth slightly higher than the other, his eyes steady on mine. I hear his feet hitting the ground, his pants rubbing with each step, his voice when he says, "God, I missed you," and, "You're smoking again, aren't you?" I mumble no, I put it out, *See?* and I only get as far as circling my arms around him before falling asleep, the first easy sleep I've had since he left. In a hazy dream, we hold one another with forever behind us and I see his hands in mine and feel his chest against my cheekbone.

Screwdrivers climb up my throat.

Between flushing the toilet and returning to the couch, I check my email.

Nothing. I write *I can't wait to see you* and turn the TV to the news, falling back into sleep without hearing any of it.

"…PRESIDENT WARNING THE neighboring nation that…" I listen without opening my eyes, thinking it just another recommendation from the President that the countries bordering Iraq behave. Sunlight shines bright on my eyelids and the news anchor reads, word-for-word, a not-so-veiled threat to Syria: if it doesn't *something something* and it doesn't even matter what it is because it's just another something the President wants, and we—we?—will do whatever is necessary to protect the interests of America, he says.

We.

Same as before, the same speech he gave before Jake left, and I feel sick again, the remaining vodka and orange juice rebelling against any lingering red wine, but I clamp my hand over my mouth and will it away. When I feel like I can, I open my eyes.

"Many of the country's natives rejoicing in the streets, but still others—Americans included—arguing against occupation. The President saying, in response, 'It's a democracy. You're entitled to your opinions.'" Gray hair and a carefree smile—aimed at a well-groomed purebred—replace the anchor on the screen, whose voice continues behind the image. "Up next: The First Dog getting a special birthday tre—"

Small sparks light, then disappear, and thick chunks of glass spray out like fireworks from his face. Cigarette butts and ash litter the floor in front of the TV stand. The ashtray, unbroken, rests lopsided where the President's face once was. Or was it the dog's face? I don't remember. They're gone, now, disassembled like a child's puzzle and strewn across the hardwood, and when the anchor's voice still manages to break through the hole in the box ("…and to this, Trippy barking an enthusiastic 'Woof!'"), I roll off the couch and squint in the sun stream, blinded, but find my way to the television and pull out the ashtray. I push and pull the stand until it tips over and the TV lands with a piercing, heavy thud and shards from the screen shoot around my ankles. The cord snaps from the outlet. I smash the ashtray—solid, heavy glass—into the back panel again and again and stop when smoke seeps from ventilation holes and the voice inside dies. I stare at it, half aware of my heavy breathing, and last night's drinks—how can any be left?—come up so violently my nostrils sting. I run to the bathroom with my hands cupped over my nose and mouth to catch what I can't keep in and bend over the toilet, kicking the door shut with my foot. I heave myself empty and crawl to the sink to rinse my hands, then use them as a cup and suck down water until the taste is gone.

I rest my elbows on the edge of the sink, rest my chin on my arms. The sink is too white. And all the walls are white and the sheer curtain hanging in the window is white. I tug the curtain until the cheap, plastic rod springs off its metal hooks nailed to the window frame and clatters on the tile. I angle the window blinds to block out the blue sky and all the light and lie on my side by the heater, my knees pulled tight to my stomach. The discount-store throw rug is plusher than I thought, even downright comfortable, and I hadn't noticed the red spots before. I touch one of them and it stays on my finger. I check my hands and face and arms, then twist to look at my feet. Blood-soaked bottoms, both of them. TV glass.

Funny. It doesn't hurt.

I let my feet down and rub my cheek against the rug and stare at its loose coils, tall as mountains close to my eye but shrinking from row to row.

"Mia!" Safia knocks, out there, out in the hallway. "Are you okay? I heard a loud noise."

I pull the curtain over me and tuck it under my chin and, with my fingertip, rub a cotton-and-nylon rug loop one way, then back again. Over and back. Over and back. My breathing comes in a shallow, bursting rhythm and the loops turn blurry and warm tears bridge my nose and wet my temple and drop to the rug. I can't breathe through my nose, but I don't want to. I don't want to do anything. I don't want to blow my nose and I don't want to close my eyes and I don't want to stop plucking the rug and I don't want to stand up or even move. My body is at rest, not counting my finger and my lungs, and this is the way it is. This is where I am and this is my rug and this is my—

"Mia! I will call the landlord. Or the police!"

"I'm okay," I say, but nothing comes out, so I say again, louder, "I'm okay," and she says, "If you are sure," and I hear her go down the stairs.

I imagine her in her sunlit apartment with the yellow mug I left outside her door and that white hair, eating a piece of toast or a banana, dancing in her living room or putting together her things before leaving for a fun day of…whatever it is she does during the day. She's already forgotten me and here I still am, my body a rock, despair confined to the bathroom instead of bleeding under the door into some kind of collective unconscious, as I believe it should. Are we not connected, after all?

Chancey pokes half a paw under the door. I reach out a finger and he clutches it, then lets go. He must be looking for something. A toy, a string. I scratch the door with a nail and watch his foot searching for the source of the noise. Through the floor, I hear Safia humming cheerfully over running water. She taps something—her toothbrush?—and the water stops, her song fading with her footsteps as she walks to another part of her apartment.

Not for the first time, I hate her.

Chancey accidentally snags my skin and I pound a fist on the floor and say, without as much force as I feel, "Chancey." The pounding scares him enough and his back claws slide on the slippery floor when he scampers to hide. I want to smash his little head, but I don't, not really, and tears start fresh when I think of his paw drawing away from me. "I'm sorry, sweetie," I say. "Chancey, baby. Chancey." I shift focus from the rug to the gap under the door and see his nose, mouth, and whiskers. "Hi," I say. I stick my finger under the door and he backs off.

"Chancey! You shitbag little shit. Sit under the goddamn bed until you die, for all I care."

I pet the rug. Stare at the floor. Take out one of my earrings and roll it around on the loops.

Lying here isn't enough, anymore.

I throw off the curtain and stand up, dizzy. The sink keeps me steady until the spinning passes, and then I open the door. Chancey, who had only gone as far as my bedroom door, skulks—his stomach an inch from the floor, shoulder blades jutting like fins from his back—into the closet. I follow only as far as the vanity and take William's lighter—the only one I haven't lost—from the bowl it's been in since Brian's visit and bring it to the living room.

The Christmas tree stands in a perpetually tilted state, most of its dead needles still clinging, branches holding strong under the light weight of decorative balls and ornaments. No water pools in the stand because it has long since evaporated or been lapped up.

I can't have the tree out back in the woods, so close, a reminder of him, or of him and me. I read somewhere, once, that death doesn't really exist. It's not an 'end,' but energy's change in form. If there is any energy left in the tree, it must be struggling to escape the cage of dried, damaged bark.

I don't bother to remove the decorations before holding a flame under a low branch. One of Jake's ornaments, a hard molded teddy bear stuffed in a camouflage knit stocking, blackens at the heel and is quickly followed into the fire by one of mine and, in an instant, the full tree. *Whoomp!* I tear out my earring and toss it in, then hurry for the one still on the bathroom floor and throw it in, too.

The flames are tree-shaped, wide base to narrow tip, and dance to a melody I can almost hear, if I turn my head just so. In seconds, the tree will disappear completely, and might never have been here at all. With no remaining evidence—like the bird Jake hadn't been able to save from Chancey the first and last time we'd let him outside, beak and feet and bones all barbarically ingested—who can confidently say that it ever was? that it ever sat in our living room under cheerful white lights with presents—my earrings, my not-engagement ring—decorated in Santa-faced paper and piled around it on the floor?

I run to the closet and tear through the Christmas box until I find the crushed star, accidentally stepped on after I told Jake I thought it was the ugliest thing I'd ever seen, but then saved by Jake in case it could be salvaged for next year.

I toss it into the flames. It burns fast.

"Star bright." That strikes me as funny. I giggle.

In the distance, a smoke alarm screams and someone is pounding on a door and voices ramble incoherently. I squint at the firelight and scoot back a few feet from the heat, and the cliché of hypnotic flames proves true when I find myself jolting at a sudden grasp on my shoulder.

"…are you doing?!"

There are five or six, including Safia and Paul, but only Paul thinks to grab the small extinguisher from where it hangs in the kitchen. The others stand out in the hallway, craning their necks to look into the room, while he sprays the shelves (which latched onto the flame pretty early and continue to burn) and the wall behind where the tree once stood, until half of my living room is covered in foam.

I listen for sirens, angry that one of them probably called the fire department. I don't want to be bothered with all of that.

"Are you okay?" Safia kneels beside me, and the rest of the neighbors—strangers to me, people I have seen once or twice each in passing, except for the red-haired girl, who might be smiling—file away with sideways glances at me.

I nod and say, "I'm okay," and, "Did anyone dial nine-one-one?"

Safia shakes her head. "There was no time, and now everything is okay."

Paul carries the extinguisher into the kitchen, then comes back out to stand behind his wife.

"What happened?" she says while looking at the downed TV.

"I don't know," I say. "It was an accident. I was lighting a cigarette, and I guess I was too close to the tree."

Paul says, "They go up like tissue when they're dry like that."

"You are sitting there," she says. "just beside the tree when we come in. Why did you not call out or answer the door? We could *all* have died."

"Shock, I think," I say. "But thank goodness you all showed up. Thank you. You saved my life. And Chancey's, too. I can't thank you enough."

"It was nothing," says Paul. "You need us to do anything? Want to come downstairs and take a breather from the smoke?"

"Oh, no," I say. "I'll open a window. And I should clean up and make sure there are no…uh…embers. I'm okay."

He laughs. "No embers here. I foamed the hell out of that fire." He lightly tugs Safia's hair. "Ready?"

She nods and gives me a brief hug. "Please, come if you need something."

Her accent bothers me today, and I don't know why. The more I hear it, the more pronounced it seems and I'm starting to wonder if she's faking. "If you don't mind," I say, "where are you from, anyway?" The 'anyway' made me sound rude, but there's nothing I can do about that, now. And I guess I don't care.

She tells me, then waits for me to respond.

"What made you come here?"

"What do you think?"

"What town?"

She tells me.

"That's where Jake is," I say, barely registering how utterly strange it is that, with a whole country at the situation's disposal, Jake is in the same town where Safia grew up.

She blinks and pats my hand. "Again," she says. "If you need something…"

"No. Really. Thanks."

She gets up and takes Paul's hand and they leave.

The wall and a quarter of the ceiling are a beautiful gray-black and the air smells like evergreen and soot. Dried foam covers much of the floor.

I hear the door to their apartment close and their voices murmur through the wood. I get on my hands and knees and put my ear to the floor.

"…didn't you just tell her why you came?. . . 'Why do you think' will make her…"

"…fine," she says.

"…curious. So bad…came to live here for me?"

Silence, then, "No, it is not, but…"—they move to a room where I can't hear them, and then they return, their voices louder—"not the only reason, and you know."

"Of course I know. We…week without being reminded. How about a thank you? 'Thank…help, Paul.' That's all I want."

She says, with exaggerated enunciation, "Thank you for your help, Paul."

A door slams, and then another. I shuffle on my knees to the window. Paul slides into his car and shuts the door and sits there for a long time before starting the engine and pulling onto the street.

I wonder what 'help' means and why she *did* come here. I hadn't thought about it before. People move to America for any number of reasons, and I must have assumed hers was to be with Paul. But, what of that other reason?

She could be a sympathizer, but that requires no help, unless…

That she is a woman means nothing. They've been as likely to work alone as they have to work with or for men.

Her clothes, her hair, all gradually altered to make her indistinguishable in a crowd. Who would notice—or be suspicious of—a blonde in a baseball cap?

I used to think the warnings were silly propaganda that brought to mind a passage from a book on Jungian philosophy I was assigned to read in college. The subject matter focused on the methods governments use to gain the public's backing for war. Something about degrading the enemy's moral character while painting them as omnipotent so the public is encouraged to believe they must be stopped at any cost. Should there still be any doubt, the supposed and likely exaggerated threat of their power is used as a reminder to us that we must kill them, and that while we're doing it, there's absolutely no reason to feel guilty. We're just defending ourselves, after all.

The textbook specifically referred to the Soviet empire as the enemy in question, but how do I know the writer's intent wasn't to turn Americans against their own government? To have Americans, at the very least, questioning their faith in the administration they created?

My lack of faith is beyond the questioning stage, and yet…yet…Safia could—but, *could* she?—be one of the people they warn us about. *Be aware of your surroundings*, they say, because *another attack is imminent*, but they don't know where or when. *It could be in a city, or it could be in sleepy, small-town America. Your small town.* And this town, while small, is home to one of the country's most historically famous Army divisions.

The door to Safia's apartment opens, then closes, and I hear footsteps on the stairs.

I get up and lock the door. My socks stick like gauze to the dried blood on my feet. She knocks and says, "Mia?"

I hold my breath.

She knocks again. "Mia, are you there?"

I feel her standing out there, waiting.

"Here," she says sliding a folded piece of paper under the door. "So you do not forget. Please come." She waits for another moment before going down the stairs. Her feet fall in soft scrapes like she's wearing slippers.

Her door closes and I pick up the protest flier and affix it to the refrigerator with a Times Square magnet.

To: Jake.Lakeland@army.net
10 May / 5:09pm
Subject: Answer me
Jake,
Are you okay?
Don't play with me, anymore. I have to know you're out there. You don't know what it's like not hearing from you. Part of me wishes I'd never found out about email. I'm more worried now than I ever was, but not about your safety. About us. Is there still an "us"?
I hate not knowing.
Mia

p.s. I did something. It's almost all gone. We still have what we need, but I just couldn't have it around, anymore. You know? So, I finally got rid of the tree, and the TV won't be upsetting me. I think it's important to have no television, don't you? They make you crazy with it.
M.

p.p.s. I forgot about the one in the bedroom. It's taken care of now, too.

WRRR, WRRR. Paul's remote control car jumps a mound he made from surrounding dirt in the lot across the street, then speeds out of control and slams into a light pole. He rushes over to check it for damage. I watch a car resembling Brian's pass under my kitchen window and catch a glimpse of Brian inside. He stops at the stop sign and revs the engine while he waits for the intersection to clear. I make out a set of smooth knees in the passenger seat.

I wonder if Denise knows.

She must be back by now. It's been over a week.

I take my glass with me to the phone and dial her number.

"Hi—it's me….Just making sure you're okay—you know, after everything…I just saw you and Brian passing by in his car, in case you're wondering how I knew you were home…That was you, right?. . . Give me a call—we'll have a drink, or something."

"Mia! Hey, girl…You ever hear that song, 'I once knew a girl named Mia…'?" A chuckle is followed by the tap of a glass being set on a table. "It ain't Mia, it's Maria, but don't you think it's got a good ring to it?. . .Yeah, I'm still livin' it up at the resort with my masseuse and a pretty cabana boy…That enough to get you to visit?…Anyway, c'mon over or give me a call. I've got somethin' for you. This is Donny."

I pick up the phone to call him, then put it back down. Later, maybe.

A note waits just inside the door, having been slipped under the crack.

Mia. The handwriting is more masculine than feminine. Paul must have written it. *Because we want to make sure we have many people in attendance, the date of the protest has changed to June 10th, but the location will stay the same. —Safia*

COLD COFFEE LEAVES a fuzz coating on my tongue, but I drink it anyway while watching smoke from my cigarette inch toward the flame of an oil lamp balanced on the windowsill. Not for light, but for the hint of a breeze. 'Uncharacteristic warmth,' they called it on the news. The weight of humidity alone should have snuffed the flame, but it burns steady.

I look at the clock—ten in the evening, his time—and give myself ten more minutes before leaving for the grocery store. The change jar has been depleted of all but fifteen cents, and I'm hungry again. This morning I finally dug Jake's card out of the junk drawer and tore off the strip of paper he taped to the back with his PIN number scratched on it. The number was easy to memorize: nine, one, six, nine. His birthday followed by mine.

I sit with my back to the living room so I can ignore the television, still facedown on the floor.

The filter slips from my lips, slimy from random crying, and I catch it before it falls into my lap, but burn the skin between my fingers. I dry my face with the back of my hand and wipe my hand on my shorts.

Denise calls to ask if I'd like to stop over later for dinner. "I'm sorry I haven't called sooner. I just got back three days ago," she says.

The grocery store doors slide open to the smell of rotisserie chicken. I roll through the produce section, snatching fat red grapes and shiny, green apples, then head for the meats and fill up with top-cut steaks, double-thick pork chops, lamb chops, and a small rack of ribs. After the meats come the sides: boxes of seasoned stuffing, macaroni and cheese, and a narrow bag of rice pilaf because Jake and I always wondered what it was.

I snack on grapes from the bag sitting lopsided in the child seat until more than half are gone, then switch to Jake's crackers because the box will ring up the same price, empty or full. I go back to the produce section and exchange the grapes.

Jake would want candy, so I go to aisle nine—CANDY, COFFEE, CHIPS, SOFT DRINKS—and look for the bag Olivia tossed into the cart, "Jakey's favorite": lollipops. Holding the bag of candy to his chest, Jake once explained the importance of variety before setting the lollipops on a bag of bagels so they wouldn't get crushed. Once home, the bag's seal broken, he would pluck out a yellow to start the cycle. Lemon was always the first to go, followed by orange, then grape, and finally—his best saved for last—cherry. Cherry is my favorite, too, and when Jake caught me biting at one of the plastic wrappers, he said, "What are you doing?" and watched me, waiting for me to take it out of my mouth and drop it back in the bag. "What?" he said when I stared at him. "They're mine. You get all the chocolate-chip ice cream."

I shift the bag from one hand to the other and it droops over the sides of my palm. I wait for something to happen—a surge of sentiment, anything—but all I feel is annoyed.

Still no emails, and if he has no time to write, I have no time for a trip to the post office.

I weave through the store and, item by item, return what would have gone in his care package to the shelves where I found them, then bypass the pharmacy—not today—and pick out some of the most exotic-smelling—and expensive—lotions and shampoos and drop them in the cart. This is the first time I've bought them without smelling them first. My stomach can't handle it today. But I remember. They smell good.

The air works well in Denise's house. Too well. My hands, when they're not holding a fork and knife, are tucked under my thighs. My hot kitchen would feel pretty good.

"Thank you for bringing the pilaf," she says with odd formality, cutting into a tender slab of swordfish. "It turned out to be the perfect side, don't you think?"

I don't know what the perfect side for swordfish is and didn't know Denise knew, either. "It's good," I say.

"I thought about spinach, but I wasn't sure you would like it." She wipes her mouth with a small corner of her napkin.

"Raw or cooked?"

"Cooked."

"No. I wouldn't have liked it."

She takes another bite of fish and looks at me while chewing, then swallows. "Have you had any luck finding a new job?"

"You were only gone a week."

"That's not enough time?"

I wonder if she left anything in there with William. I would leave something with Jake, I think.

There's no sign of a flag, anywhere. The one they would have given her.

"You look good," I say, and she does. Not like a widow, or the way I'd imagined a widow would look. Her hair is back to perfect, her makeup dark and overdone the way it always was, shirt stiff and creased and buttoned low, fake nails applied and painted the color of blackberries. When she opened the door, her smile was wide and she said I had to come in so she could show me her souvenirs from D.C.

"I look okay. Life goes on, right?" she says.

Life goes on. Life goes on goes on goes on. *Goes. On.*

The pilaf turns blurry. Or not. Too hard to tell, so I look at the fish. The fish is blurry. I nod and poke my fork around on my plate.

"No," she says. "No, I don't mean that. That is, I do—because of course life *does* go on—but it's not as easy as that. What I mean is, it goes on whether or not you…" She sighs, exasperated. "It just goes on, regardless.—Are you okay?"

I take a bite of food, say "Fine," and chase a clump of rice with my fork and wait for my eyes to dry. Yesterday, maybe the day before, whoknowswhocares, I started worrying about me. *I* might die before he comes home. A car wreck, an aneurysm in the shower, choking on swordfish bone.

An apartment fire.

And what if he moved on the way Denise has? What if he were okay?

If Jake dies and, like Denise, I end up moving on, what will that mean?

"You just do what you do," she says and takes a deep breath. "Anyway. Do you like the fish?"

"Fuck the fish."

I am about to apologize—I hadn't expected to say that—but I don't, because Denise goes on to tell a story about a girl she knows, a friend of a friend, who died in a car accident two weeks after her husband left for Iraq.

"You never think it will happen that way," she says, shaking her head. "He gets a month home, and then he has to go back."

Would a month be enough? Could Jake go back to work after a month? Pity for the girl's husband turns into pity for Jake when I remember the fire, that it could have happened to me, to us. That I might have actually *killed* myself. I might have killed the neighbor whose newspapers I stole, killed Paula and Safia and their cats and Chancey, all of us choking and melting and clawing at the burning walls.

"I think it tastes a lot like regular steak," she says. "Don't you?"

I look around at Denise's walls, white, cool, and not burning, and think of my own, gray but sound. And Paul and Safia and the red-haired girl are alive. I'm alive. Chancey was there this morning to pull at my toe. But it could have happened. Everything else aside, so much bad could have happened and didn't.

Did I even say that? About fucking the fish?

I laugh. And I tell her I don't usually like fish. "But this is good." I tap it with the tip of my knife and then get up for a paper towel—

"Want one?"

"Please."

—and notice a thick stack of collapsed moving boxes wedged between her refrigerator and the counter.

She takes the towel from me when I sit down and another bite of the fish confirms it is the most flavorful fish I've ever eaten. Between chews, between swallows, my focus has drifted from myself and the time on the clock to the things that are missing around her house.

"Moving?"

She nods.

"When?"

"Soon."

"Where?"

"Home. Not with my parents; I'm buying a house."

"Buying? How?" I wonder if we'll get a house when he comes home. A small one with yellow siding and a cheerful face—the way doors and windows can make a face—and a mailbox with "Lakeland and Sharpe" stenciled on the side.

She flattens some rice into a patty, then uses her fork to press a criss-cross pattern into the top. "Insurance." She doesn't look at me.

"How much?"

"I don't know." She shrugs. "About two-fifty."

"That's ridiculous. You don't even have kids."

She shrugs again.

"Are you keeping it all?"

"What else would I do with it?"

"I don't know. Give it to his parents?"

"Right," she says. "I didn't think about that."

We look at one another across the table.

"How soon is 'soon'?"

"It depends on when the money comes through," she says.

"What about Brian?"

But she will not talk about Brian, so I ask instead for more details on her trip to Virginia and she answers without mentioning the funeral. I learn that the temperature was slightly cooler. The grass was very green and the sky seemed to her to be a different shade of blue from what we have in Tennessee. (I try to imagine how the sky can be different shades of blue from state to state.) She tells me the Metro is "so fun, and so efficient! The rest of the country would truly benefit from public transportation like that," and that someone, "the most beautiful man you've ever seen," helped her onto the platform by reaching out for her hand. "I would never sleep with someone just after meeting him, but if he hadn't disappeared into the Metro, who knows?" She winks, then says, "You know I'm only playing."

"Sure." I mix some rice with some fish and blend it with the smallest taste of wine. As Donny's friend Judy might say, *heaven*.

"I even bought a hotdog from a street vendor near the Mall," she says. "I asked for everything—ketchup, mustard, sauerkraut, onions. He called it 'the works.' Then I added chili. Everything. Have you ever had a hotdog from a city vendor?"

"No."

"It was awful." She laughs. "The worst hotdog I ever had. But I had to eat the whole thing. You know?"

I don't. "No," I say. I drink more wine and the nausea builds. Damn it.

"Anyway," she says. "Virginia was beautiful. And there were the most heart-ripping paintings on display at the Mall, all of them being sold by veterans. There was one..." Her eyes tear and she wipes them without hiding. "I forget what it was called. A man in a briefcase leans forward with his hand against the Wall—you know the Wall?—and on the other side, in the reflection, are…well. You'd have to see it. I can't—you would really have to see it."

I have no idea what she's talking about because I've never been to D.C. and haven't seen the painting, but I listen, anyway, and sit quiet when she stops.

"Do you like the wine?" she says.

"It's fine."

"William's mother knows wines, and this is her favorite. It's brisk, I think, and nice and light."

I taste it again. Light? Sure. Brisk? I have another sip, but can't taste the briskness.

"I've been meaning to ask you," she says, "about William's lighter. Did you ever find it?"

"I didn't."

"You'll let me know if you do?"

"Sure."

"His father gave it to him on his twenty-first birthday." She twirls her own lighter in her fingers like a coin. "William used to smoke. He started at sixteen and thought he'd hidden it from his father for all those years, until he unwrapped the lighter. He quit that day."

"I'll be on the lookout." I say, "Brian was worried when I couldn't find it."

She turns in her chair to open a drawer in the hutch behind her and pulls out a pack of cigarettes and lights one. She hands one to me and lights it for me. "He knew how important it was," she says, leaning to open the window, the cigarette hanging from her mouth.

"What were you going to do with it?"

"I wanted his father to have it."

"Do you think he would want it?"

"Probably. Wouldn't you?"

He carries a state quarter in his pocket, the one with St. Louis's Arch on the back. I gave it to him one Valentine's Day because it reminded me of our first weekend away. A bride and groom had been having their pictures taken in the downtown square, and we'd sat on the stairs and watched. Later that night while we waited for pizza to be delivered to our hotel room, I asked Jake what he thought of the bride's dress (I'd thought it frilly). He said, "I don't remember. I was watching you."

That quarter, a simple twenty-five cents, belongs to him and getting it back would be the same as—or worse than—having never given it to him.

It was the right decision, not handing over William's lighter.

"You have it, don't you?" she says.

"Hm?"

"William's lighter."

"What would I want with his lighter?"

Denise leans back in her chair and crosses her legs and her arms. "I'm not sure, Mia. What *do* you want with it?"

"I don't have it." I hold her stare until I think she believes me.

"Well. If you do find it—"

"Absolutely," I say.

"I'll give you my parents' address." She takes a deep drag from her cigarette, so deep I see her hide a gag when she flicks off the ash. Her face is contorted and ugly when she exhales.

For what might be half an hour we make empty conversation. She asks again about my job hunt and nods uninterestedly when I tell her I'm on the verge of finding something.

"Where?" She studies an acrylic nail.

"The paper," I say. "They're looking for a proofreader."

"You'd get to use your degree again."

I want to tell her that any moderately literate moron could be a proofreader. "That's right," I say. But it's a good idea, actually, and I make a mental note to look into it. She tells me there were a lot of jobs in the D.C. classifieds, then tells me about the professional "aura" of the city, the exciting lives they must all lead.

"Surely not all of them."

She ignores me and goes on about the day she spent with William's parents. They dressed like "rich city people" for lunch at an expensive restaurant, and then they changed into "street clothes" to visit Mount Vernon.

"Thank God it's the last time I'll ever have to see his mother," she says. She taps a finger on the table. "You know what, though, Mia? She wasn't even that bad. All the complaining I did, all the whining—I was incredibly immature. Once I realized she was no longer my mother in-law, I started to see her differently. As a woman instead of as William's mother. And she's a pretty wonderful lady."

I want to ask her, I need to know, *what does dead look like*, because until you see it, it can't be real, can it? "How was she? At the funeral, I mean."

"Crying. Sad. What else?"

"Did…uh…how did—? William?"

"What do you mean, 'William'?"

"Sorry. I mean, was it an op—"

"Oh. No." Her look says *Don't ask* and so I don't. "I still can't get over it," she says. "Do you know what I mean? *An accident*. It could have happened here! He went all the way over there to die in some…" she shakes her head, searching, "…some foolish accident. He should have been shot down," she says. "That would make more sense than flying into wires. Then again, he was the only one who ever said he was a good pilot. How do I know if he was or not? Maybe he was the worst they had."

"Jake always said he was very good," I say, which is not true. Jake said nothing about William's flying one way or the other.

She shrugs. She shrugs a lot, and I never noticed. "It doesn't matter now, does it? Dead is dead." She refills her glass, then mine.

"Brian said William asked for it," I say. The wine is good. Too good. My glass holds all that remains of the Pinot, and the nausea hasn't left, but I'm getting better at ignoring it.

She sets down her glass. "No, he didn't."

I tell her about Brian's visit, the things he said.

She shakes her head. "He didn't mean it that way. You would have to know Brian."

The way she says Brian—vowels drawn out, soft—and the way she strokes her glass…it was her. In his car, on my street.

I think about his hand on her thigh, repulsive just days after William's funeral, and on the heel of my disgust trails an odd sexual excitement, the same conflicted—and fairly recent—thrill that swells when, considering a possible future, I imagine Jake attracted to someone else. He smiles at her, some anonymous beautiful woman, and kisses her in the dark of a helicopter on the tarmac at night. I hate him in those moments and believe I could probably kill in a passionate instant. I'm also inexplicably aroused. But only for a second. It must be a consequence of all this abstinence.

"Brian dodged the war."

"He didn't 'dodge,' Mia."

"Close enough."

"I guess that's it, then!" she says, throwing up her hands. "I officially dislike him, now." She lights another cigarette. She's been smoking them quickly, one after the other. She used to space them out, unless I count the night she found out about William. "What do you think? Do you think we're two strangers who've spent the last few years sweating under the sheets without a word to one another? We know each other, Mia. Do you understand? It's not a torrid tryst, not some cheap *affair*. You and I have already talked about this."

"I know." Still, there is a determination to destroy her confidence in Brian's devotion, her easy acceptance of William's death. It's not at all fair to her. She fell out of love, is all, and maybe he did, too, at some point. Can it ever be only one person who falls out of love? William had to have let go, to some degree, or he couldn't have stayed. Not without destroying himself.

I say, "I just don't understand how you can be okay."

"I'm not 'okay,'" she says, "but, I am better than I could be. I don't want to go into why, if you don't mind. But I do have my reasons. Do you trust that I'm not evil, not cold?" She pauses while I nod. "What about you?" she says. "How are you?"

"I'd rather talk about you." Which is true. Since I arrived, I haven't thought about the messages Jake hasn't sent.

She lays her cigarette in the ashtray and comes around the table to hug me. Her arms are thin and her shoulder bone is sharp on my cheek. The closeness is awkward, but even so I want to hold her close far longer than she stays.

We don't look at one another again until she's back in her chair on the other side of the table. "He'll come home," she says.

Before leaving, I pretend to have to use the bathroom and snatch one of her souvenirs, a porcelain model of the White House, from a shelf in the hallway.

Outside, after goodbyes and when I'm sure she's not watching from the window, I set it in front of my tire and listen for the pop of the hollow glass when I pull away from the curb.

MAY 20, TUESDAY TO MAY 26, MONDAY

THE LOCAL NEWSPAPER'S editorial office will call if something becomes available, but for now, the woman says, they think they're okay.

I want to tell her they're not, no, and that in the space of four days I found two misplaced apostrophes, four typos, two errant commas, and at least seven sentences lacking parallel structure.

"No one pays attention to that stuff," Denise says when we meet one afternoon for coffee. I tell her they should, that attention to detail is part of what keeps us civilized.

She does not ask about her White House.

I use Jake's card to buy a new television, a small thirteen-inch, and put it in the bedroom for the nights I can't sleep. Without it, I lie awake listening to Chancey moving between rooms, pawing at his litter, scooping water with his tongue. Listening to the computer humming and waiting for the email chime to ding.

Time, too much time, passes with no word from Jake, no visits from Denise, not even a call from Olivia, and I wonder if I am dead. If, as in some movies, we die and aren't conscious of our deaths until a spirit guide takes us to see our lifeless bodies, bloodied and grotesque, or pale, limp, and peaceful. I might have had a stroke in my sleep, it occurs to me, and the days I move through are not real, but are instead my own creation, something I continuously conjure to ease the transition into the eternity I'll be spending here on the second floor of this nondescript apartment building. The real panic comes when even Chancey ignores his name being called and I can't find him anywhere, and when I hear a voice outside—Safia!—I thrust the window fully open and say "Hey!"

A long few seconds pass without a reaction and I start to feel weak, but then she turns, looks up, and waves, and Chancey walks in with a string of dust hanging from his whiskers.

Jake's card also buys more darts for my gun. During press conferences, I hold it the way Jake instructed when we visited a range a few years ago. His chest bumped the back of my neck and he held his arms straight against mine to demonstrate. "You have to not be aware that you're pulling the trigger." His hands cupped my hands. "It should be as natural as breathing, and your breathing should be even and relaxed. Squeeze, actually—don't pull—slowly toward you—slowly—and when the bullet fires, you should be surprised."

The gentle-squeeze method doesn't work well with the toy gun; the trigger is stiffer and clicks roughly into place. But my aim is improving. I've made some dead-on shots, even from the kitchen doorway. Chancey chases the darts that bounce off the screen.

I send Jake one more email: *I need you.*

I don't know that I do.

Shellie pets her Chihuahua and coos "Aw, Puddin'" when he stretches his black and gold neck for a treat she holds in front of his nose. "I don't see why not," she says to my returning to work. "Lionel ain't hired no one else, and Charlie sure would like to lose the extra days you left him."

I tell her I didn't mean to do that to Charlie. That I just had to leave. Hard times, all that.

"I know, sugar. I know. It's all right." She sets her dog on the floor, says, "Lionel won't like it, though, if you do like you did, callin' in all those times, so be careful." She pulls out a traced calendar where she writes the schedules. "Same days okay?"

"Same days are perfect." I look at the cheerless walls, the grimy windows. I had thought she might say no. Better that she said yes— I'm respectable, now. Not a disappointment to Ja—to myself. Not someone different, or worse, from who I was.

I slide the chair out. "I guess I'll see you tomorrow."

"Where you goin', girl? Cab's right there." She nods her head at the wide blue car parked outside the window. "Charlie took today off to run his errands."

Before it's time to for me to go home, ten people slide in and out of my cab. One asks if I'll buy his food stamps, because some diapers he needs for his little boy aren't covered by the program. "Eighty dollars oughta do it," he says. I look at the red marks on his arms and neck and tell him that I'm sorry, I don't carry that kind of cash.

Another, a woman dressed up to go nowhere, tells me I should take more care with my looks. "No excuse, a lady goin' out without a little makeup. Always try to look pretty." She says my hair is okay, but that my face looks like "some zombie" she saw on cable TV. "Now is when you got to be takin' care of yourself, child," she says.

No tips. After eight hours, I leave with thirty-five dollars. I stop for a coffee on the way home and avoid the coffee boy's eyes. He looks good today.

To: msharpe@email.net
27 May / 1632
Subject: re: Hi, there!
Mia,
Let me start with I love you.

Sorry I didn't write sooner, but I've been unbelievably busy. And, yeah, I also wanted to think a little. I don't know. I read all your emails. I try to understand what you're going through, and I do understand as much as I can without going through it myself. I know it's tough. I just hope that when you sound like you don't like me it's because you're upset and having a hard time. Not that I want you to have a hard time. You know what I mean.

It's really starting to suck over here, if that makes you feel any better. Misery loves company, right? The only time I feel like I might not go nuts is when I'm either planning or flying a mission. Every day is the same thing and my eyes feel like sandpaper. We change it up every now and then, play volleyball or have a cookout, and it's great for morale, but it only lasts so long. Then the days get back to normal. A week takes a month to go by, and I feel like I'll never really come home. Do I even live there, anymore? I don't, you know. This is where I live. Everyone says they're deployed here because it makes the stay seem shorter, but I've lived places for less time than I'll be here.

Are you real? I wonder if you're real. The words I get from you are black and white with no hair or lips or hands. I wish I could see you for five minutes just to know for sure.

Speaking of seeing you, we had a meeting today. No chance, it looks like, of us getting out of here in under a year. I know. I probably shouldn't tell you. I don't want to know, either, but if I know, you should know. It's selfish, but I want to go through the shit of it with you.

On a more positive note, I'm getting lots of flight time and having a blast flying. You know about William, by now. Thanks for not asking about it in emails and for not pushing. It was hard, and I miss having him around and flying with him. But I don't want to talk about it much, if you don't mind.

The last thing I'll say about it is that he didn't die for nothing. He was doing something he believed in.

I have a lot of time to write, today. Not much to do and no one's around. I don't know where they are, but they're not here, so I'm sitting in my foldout chair on the deck I built and writing this on my laptop. I'll paste it into an email later. It feels so good to talk to you that I could spend all day writing. I would call, but—honestly, M, I don't want to. I don't know what we would say. Maybe, for now, one-way talking is best.

I thought a lot about us and about you when I got your emails and because you asked, I wondered too if we only stay together because we've been together so long. This distance makes it easy to look at things like that. How I go on without you and how you go on without me. I guess neither of us can ignore my changing thoughts about the war. I'd like to think we can agree to disagree about that.

Being here, getting shot at (not to be too dramatic, but it happens), knowing I might not come home, it makes me think about my life. I have no control over my life, here. I don't get to come home until they tell me, and between now and then, I fly the missions I'm told to fly and while I'm not scared while I fly, I am more than vaguely aware that flying can get me shot down.

I can't use the phone when I want or without someone standing behind me, and I can't usually send an email without having to wait in line, and even then I might only get off a couple of sentences before someone behind me starts coughing and grumbling.

I don't know if I'm making sense.

Thing is, M, I know that when I come home, I'll be somewhere I can make certain choices. Life is too short, they say, and they're right. You learn that kind of thing in a way you never really understood before when someone close to you dies doing the same thing you do a few times a week. You learn that you want to make your life mean something while you're living it instead of after, and that there's no excuse for settling into a life you're not sure is the one you want. Nothing but the best, if you can do it. Which I can. Which you can. Do you understand?

I want to be happy. I want to stay in the Army and keep flying. What do you think about that? What would you think if I stayed in for life? It sounds crazy after everything I wrote up there about not having control over my own life, but part of the control I want is deciding what I want, and though much of my day-to-day control is in the hands of the Army, I have to remember I gave them that control when I signed up, and I did it for a reason.

I know we talked about me getting out when my time's up, but the longer I'm here and the longer I'm in, the more right this feels. I felt a little of this before I left but was afraid to tell you because I thought you would leave. Now, though, I kind of think I have to do what's right for me, and you'll either understand and stay with me, or you won't. It's not that I don't care. Please don't think that. I love you and you know I do. But we have to do what's right for ourselves whether or not the other agrees with it. And, M, I don't want you to stay with me if you don't want to. Guys talk a lot of shit about 'supportive' wives and girlfriends, and a lot of times that means the women give up their own lives to be nothing but support systems or appendages. I wouldn't want you to do that. Never give up something that's important to you just to follow me around. My life, my job, isn't any more important than what you would do if you found something that meant something to you. What I hope is that I can do my thing and you can do your thing and somehow our things will work together.

And now I'm thinking about sex. Great. But that reminds me that I wanted to ask if you'd send some KY.

Anyway, as for the very hard to read email you wrote after a whole lot of drinking (you wrote about "well to wall" carpeting and a "babay" – funny), that's the kind of thing I don't want you to do. You never wanted a brand new house, and you were never too on-board with the baby thing. Don't give in just because of my life choices, okay? One of the things I love most about you is that you know exactly what you want and you don't buckle to anyone. My being here is no reason for you to change who you are. My choices are mine alone.

On a similar note, you also asked me to marry you in a letter you sent early on. I haven't mentioned it because I figured you would say you didn't remember writing it. Anyway, remember or not, I have it. Proof. It's taped to the lid of my tuff box so I can take it from the envelope whenever I want to read it. Sometimes I read it before going to sleep. I also look at the picture I brought with me of you on the fence and say 'good morning' to it. Weird? I can't help it, though. The sun is behind you and your hair is all over the place and your face is so beautiful. You are so beautiful, Mia.

No one has ever asked me to marry them before. You talked about it often enough before I left, but it seemed like you were waiting for me to ask. Well, even if it was just the result of an emotional outburst, thanks for asking. You know, until just now, I hadn't thought about what I would say if you actually meant it. The idea of marriage is one thing; being asked is something completely different. If you were serious, I'm really sorry I didn't get back to you sooner. Now I'm scared you feel rejected or something. I swear, M, I didn't think you meant it. Tell me if you did, and I'll give you a better response. And don't feel bad if anything I've written (about my plans) has made you change your mind, either. I would understand. I'd be destroyed, but I'd understand.

I wonder how you are. I think about it a lot. What you're doing, how work is, if you're going out with Denise at all. I hope she's doing okay. Some of her letters were left behind and I kept a couple so I could send them back to her. Hold on—I'm going to get one so you can read something she wrote. Tell me what you think she might be talking about.

Here it is: "You are right in what you wrote. You are so often always right, William and that is one of the things I like about you. No one knows me like you and, I don't know if someone ever will."

After that, she just goes into some crap about the weather. It's warm there, I guess. Boo hoo. Anyway, did you notice anything suspicious? It sounds like she's saying something nice, but he didn't like it at all. He muttered that part a couple of times out loud while reading it, then threw it on his cot and stomped out of the tent. You know anything? It's the last letter he read from her. Another one came about two days after the accident. I read it. I shouldn't have, I know. It didn't say anything. Just that she was putting together a package for him and that she hoped he was doing well. His package isn't here, yet. I don't know what to do with it when it gets here. Maybe give it to someone who doesn't have anyone at home to mail them stuff.

I might not be able to write for a few days. We have to make a trip. Nice change from the everyday platoon meetings, mission briefings, workouts (you should see me now), etc. I can't tell you where I'm going, obviously, until I get back, but it shouldn't be bad. I just don't want you to worry if you don't hear from me. I hope what happened to William hasn't made you worry more. If it helps at all, it was really a freak accident, and it's encouraged me to be even more careful. I want to come back. To you. No. I don't want to. I have to. A few nights ago I was in my cot and everyone else was sleeping. I lay there in the quiet staring at the dark, and suddenly I was afraid something would happen to you. Not that I think something will, but I thought, "What if?" What if you broke up with me? What if you got hurt? What if you died? My chest constricted and I felt like I could cry. I can't lose you, M.

Don't worry, though. I don't think about things like that very often. I couldn't. It would cripple me. When I fly, I don't think about you at all. All I think about is flying. Sometimes, it's impossible to think of anything else, even if I want to. You get so overwhelmed by the fun of the flying itself. Last week I made a quick trip and ended up doing a hundred knots at fifty feet over a river in this narrow valley between the mountains. I loved it!

People are starting to come back, so I think I'll end this and get it to you. It's a long walk to the email tent, and it's damn hot out. Oh! Sometimes you'll see these huge, scary-as-all-fuck-looking spiders, called camel spiders, running across the sand. Yesterday, there was one in my boot! You have to check your boots every morning before putting them on. Have you ever seen a picture of a camel spider, or heard anything about them? You wouldn't want to find one in your shoe. Sometimes some of the guys will take a camel spider and put it under a bowl with a scorpion. They call it "The Arena of Death." I don't condone it, but I really hate those fucking spiders, so I'm not too sad when they lose.

Hope to hear from you soon,
Jake

P.S. If you could, M, would you put something together for me? Just the regular. Chips and cookies and jerky, things like that. I loved the coffee cake you sent. And those mimi donuts. I appreciate it. Just take whatever you need from my card. Hey, did you quit driving? I went to check my accounts a few days ago and (I'm not accusing you or complaining, because we had an agreement) I noticed I'm not saving as much as I thought. No big deal, I just wondered. Again, take what you need, but just do me a favor and don't go crazy.

P.P.S. Um, I did tell you about Shelbi, you psycho, in the beginning. And I tried to call again, too, but no one answered and the machine didn't pick up.

JUNE 2, MONDAY TO JUNE 3, TUESDAY

SHELLIE CALLS FOR me over the radio and I take another hit from the joint I bought from Lenny during this morning's shift change. "At least this time you're payin' for it," he said.

"Miss Mia. Where you at, girl?"

I pick up the radio and push the button and say, "Pshhchk," and set it back on its base.

The sun is out, the sky cloudless, and smoking has eased the upset stomach I had this morning. The tree I park under bursts with fat, shady leaves and cools the breeze coming through the window. A man on the radio sings a promise to his love that someday she will die, but that he'll be close behind, he'll follow her into the dark. I turn it off and look for whatever it is I hear jumping around in the tall grass outside. Grasshopper. I found two in the kitchen yesterday, but Chancey had found them first. One was missing a leg, the other a head, which I found stuck to the bottom of my foot.

When half the joint's been smoked, I wet the tip and close it in the ashtray and go over what I've written, so far.

~~I'm glad you decided what you want to do.~~
~~Thank you for telling me~~

I toss the tablet and pen onto the passenger seat, then recline my chair and look out over the green field. It brings to mind movie portrayals of Vietnam, and I imagine bent-over soldiers plodding through the wheat with damp cigarettes held tight in their lips, weapons ready. I see them cross in front of me—almost hear dried stalks crunching under their boots—and then, one by one, they disappear over the horizon and into what is, to me, a mystery. I wonder if the women left waiting during the Vietnam War knew it was really a war, or if they thought they couldn't possibly be hanging on the fringes of what they'd only read about in school texts, if they thought war was an abstract, or at the very least, something meant for the older generations. When I was ten and first learning world history, I pictured war in black and white, explosions rocking my front lawn and tall, shadowy men coming to kill me, everything happening fast, battles continuous and simultaneous. Not this slow-paced and random series of attacks in a country painted green on my world map.

If this were history, Jake would have been one of those men pounding through the grass or sitting hot and scared under a wide cluster of jungle leaves, listening for footfalls and fighting to see through sweat.

Just over a week until the protest, and I think I might paint my name on my shirt in red. Maybe the president's people will watch the media coverage, and maybe they'll tell him my name. I wonder what Jake would think. I wonder if they're able to watch the news.

Where are you, he wrote in an email I opened this morning. *When I came back, you hadn't written, and now I've been back for two days and still haven't heard from you. I tried to call yesterday, but there was no answer and the machine didn't pick up. Let me know you're alive. Love you, M. –J.*

I've left his long letter open on the screen since the day he sent it. In the same number of nights I have emptied a bottle and a half of vodka, hoping the alcohol would free the right words to tell him *I can't. I can't do this again. And again. And again. Even one more time will kill me. If you stay in, I will leave you.*

Or maybe he's already left me.

I grab the paper and pen.

I am broken.

~~*I am broken.*~~

The flame in William's lighter is getting low, but there's enough there to set the tablet on fire before I toss it out the window. Black smoke curls up through bowed, green blades.

Shellie says, "Mia, you hear me, yet?"

I slouch down and close my eyes for a short nap, but I know I won't sleep.

To: Jake.Lakeland@army.net
June 2 / 6:36pm
Subject: re: Hi, there!
Jake,
I'm alive. I'm glad you're back from your mission, and I'm happy you wrote because I like knowing you're safe. Got a new answering machine, fyi.
Mia

p.s. As for Denise's letter, besides her punctuation, no, I don't see anything 'suspicious' and I don't know what she might have been talking about. I'm sorry I'm not much help. Sleep well daily.

To: msharpe@email.net
June 3 / 0709
Subject: re: Hi, there!
Mia,
What's the matter with you? Your email was weird.
Jake

To: Jake.Lakeland@army.net
June 2 / 10:12pm
Subject: re: Hi, there!
J-
Nothing's the matter. I'm just working a lot of hours because I'm driving again, and when I get home I'm too tired to write very much. Why is it that you can be absent for weeks, but if I don't respond for two days you get hostile? Jesus.
-M

To: msharpe@email.net
June 3 /0819
Subject: re: Hi, there!
Mia-
I wasn't hostile. I was worried. Okay? I thought maybe you were mad about my letter, or something. Why haven't you said anything about it? I want to know what you think about the things I say. Why do you think I write them? Stop fighting with me. I'm not mad at you.
- J

To: Jake.Lakeland@army.net
June 2 / 11:22pm
Subject: re: Hi, there!
Jake,
Is you is or is you ain't my baby? Gokadllad. Decode that.
You really can taste the briskness in Pinot Grigio, once you know to look for it.
Me-a.

To: msharpe@email.net
June 3 / 0824
Subject: re: Hi, there!
Hey, M! Your email just came in. I'm at the computer right now. Which means you sent it, your time, at about eleven-something. I'm glad you're still up!

To: msharpe@email.net
June 3 / 0828
Subject: re: Hi, there!
Mia, you there?

To: Jake.Lakeland@army.net
June 2 / 11:31pm
Subject: re: Hi, there!
I'm here, but just ran out of something and have to go get more.

To: msharpe@email.net
June 3 / 0835
Subject: re: Hi, there!
I'm working on the code, but I haven't gotten it yet. I think I'm close. Don't go. I want to talk to you. What do you mean, you have to go get more? Right now? Can't you wait for a little bit? What did you think of my letter? Tell me before I have to give up the computer to someone else. Not too many people here right now, but a lot will be coming in from this 29-ship mission that just got back. Actually, it was a lot bigger than that. I think there were 104 in all from different countries and units, but only 29 were ours. You wouldn't believe the sound when they flew in. Wish you could have heard it.

To: Jake.Lakeland@army.net
June 2 / 11:38pm
Subject: re: Hi, there!
I thought your letter was very well written. A literary joy.

To: msharpe@email.net
June 3 / 0840
Subject: re: Hi, there!
You know that's not what I mean.

To: Jake.Lakeland@army.net

June 2 / 11:43pm
Subject: re: Hi, there!
Do you mean what you said about staying in the Army?
(There's not really a code.)

To: msharpe@email.net
June 3 / 0844
Subject: re: Hi, there!
Yeah.
(Then why did you say "decode that"??)

To: msharpe@email.net
June 3 / 0846
Subject: re: Hi, there!
Mia?

To: Jake.Lakeland@army.net
June 2 / 11:48pm
Subject: re: Hi, there!
Whatever you want is what I want for you.
(I said "decode that" because…I don't know! I was playing. Forget it.)

To: msharpe@email.net
June 3 / 0849
Subject: re: Hi, there!
Come on, Mia.

To: msharpe@email.net
June 3 / 0852
Subject: re: Hi, there!
You there? I have to go in a minute. Where are you?

To: Jake.Lakeland@army.net
June 2 / 11:53pm
Subject: re: Hi, there!
I'm not feeling well, Jake. Sorry. I hope you have a good night. Take care.
Love.
M.

"HEY, M…What is up with the machine? I thought you said you got a new one. I tried two days ago, but no answer, no machine. At least it's working now…Uh, anyway, I hope you're out doing something fun for your birthday…Was hoping I'd catch you, especially today, but I guess…Well, happy birthday, birthday girl…I wish I could try back later, but there's a mission, so…I love you. Email me, okay? Tell me about your birthday…Bye."

JUNE 10, TUESDAY

I RIDE WITH Safia and Paul to the college. Posters and banners in the back seat spill over onto my lap, and I try to keep them smooth and unwrinkled. Safia sings with the radio, her white-blond hair blowing around her face, and Paul, his elbow resting on the door through the open window, taps the car roof with the drum beat while he circles the lots.

"Look how packed it is. Good sign, huh, Saf?"

He finds a spot near the science building. Safia smiles at him and throws open the door, then comes around to gather the posters from the back seat. With her arms full, she asks which one I want to carry. I choose the one reading, ANYTHING WAR CAN DO, PEACE CAN DO BETTER, because it seems the least inflammatory. The one under it demands an end to a war started by men who would not fight in a war, themselves. "This one is mine," she says, patting it. "Paul, help me?"

When we get to 'the bowl,' a low, circular stone wall in the dip of a vast lawn between buildings, we find a crowd of close to fifty standing in small groups of three or four and holding posters or signs at their sides. Safia and Paul walk ahead of me and stop at one group, shake hands, thank them for coming, and move on to the next. I recognize some of the people from their dinner standing in their own circle, and when Rose and I make eye contact, she looks away as quickly as if she didn't see me. Maybe she didn't, and if she did, I'm grateful to her for not wanting to wave me over. I hate small talk.

I move through the clusters and avoid eye contact, pretend I'm headed somewhere, looking for someone I'm meeting. Most of them are younger than I am and wear old sandals and loose-fitting knits that smell of patchouli. "Sorry," I say when one of them, stepping backward, ends up on my foot. He touches my arm and apologizes and asks if I'm okay, and I tell him yes, fine, fine, and continue through the crowd, stopping when I see Denise and Brian sitting on a far wall. *Over*, she said. She nudges Brian, who searches until he finds me and then nods. Denise beckons, but I turn around and weave back through the crowd to the other side.

"…have your attention," I hear Paul shout. The group quiets for his announcement that it is time, and will they please raise their signs. I raise mine, feeling foolish, but—after catching onto what they're saying—I chant along with them, anyway, feeling more foolish, then, because the chant isn't inspired, or even original.

"What do we want? Troops out! When do we want it? Now!"

"What do we want? Troops out! When do we want it? Now!"

I look around at others' posters and find them to be a combination of sentimental (YOU CAN HAVE MY GUN WHEN YOU PRY IT FROM THE FINGERS OF MY COLD, DEAD CHILD), humorous (a leashed dog wears a T-shirt warning that "Bombs kill puppies"), and ironic (WHO WOULD JESUS BOMB?). The crowd skirts the inside edge of the bowl, and on the other side is a scattered crowd of onlookers.

The words keep coming from me, and the more I say them, the more I mean them. I do want the troops out. I do want it now. I do want Jake home, safe, regardless of our future together, and I want it as soon as possible. I want them *all* safe as soon as possible, because they are all someone's Jake. Or Jennifer.

I want the troops out. I want it now.

A woman howls from the center, "The military is nothing but a murdering instrument for the government!"

The transformation comes instantaneously; the energy changes form. People shout and shove and signs I hadn't read, hadn't seen before—

A.R.M.Y.: AMERICA'S REASON TO MURDER THE YOUNG

and

WE SUPPORT OUR TROOPS WHEN THEY SHOOT THEIR OFFICERS

—fly high over the rest and this is not what I came for, not what I believe, not what I think Paul and Safia had in mind. The din of shouting drowns any one message and all that is clear is that there is no agreeing about anything. The calm gathering has become a rally of screaming, spitting, hatred, and rage. Signs soar and fists jab through the space in front of me and someone yanks my hair. I pull it free and back my way out of the pit, stopping to jump on—and bend over to tear in half—a sign calling to SUPPORT OUR MUTINEERS! I rise just in time to see Brian with an arm around the neck of one of the men who helped carry the banner reading WE SUPPORT OUR TROOPS WHEN THEY SHOOT THEIR OFFICERS. Denise stands by, watching, shouting something with her teeth bared, then swipes at the man's face and leaves three dark, red lines. He struggles to get free and Brian punches him in the stomach. Denise smacks the man again, smearing the blood from his cheek to his mouth.

The onlookers have changed, too, protesting the protestors, calling us traitors and un-American, jumping into the bowl to fight. I push through them, my sign since dropped so I could use my hands to guard my face, and I see Donny standing just outside the wall, shouting with his fist in the air and his mouth open wide, eyes invisible in his angry face.

I wave, and his arm falls when he sees me. When I move toward him, he steps back and screams something at me I can't hear. I hold up my hands and move closer, but he takes yet another step back and the way he looks at me makes me want to fall to my knees. He points at a sign raised high above the commotion, rocking side to side in the struggle: AMERICAN MILITARY: PROOF NAZISM IS ALIVE AND WELL IN THE USA.

"I'm not one of them!" I scream. I scream it so loud I cough, but he waves me off and trudges up the hill. I start to run after him, but trip on a sign in the grass. By the time I'm back on my feet, he's gone.

I crawl to the top of the hill until I'm at a safe distance from what looks like a mosh pit in the bowl, and I wait for a ride home.

A camera crew films the scene from the granite steps of the library. I hope they caught the first peaceful minutes before the fanatics took over.

"…anti-war protestors rallying in what the university refers affectionately to as 'the bowl,' anger and violence marking their anti-war, anti-military sentiment." Cut to a young college boy holding out his T-shirt, the picture a dead American soldier, the caption reading, "The only moral soldier is one who's been stripped of his weapon." Cut to a still of a crumpled banner: VICTORY TO THE ENEMY; DEFEAT TO OCCUPYING SOLDIERS.

A commentator in a red tie says, "Would you look at that, Janie and Tom?" He gestures at the image. "These anti-war types are ruining our country and destroying the morale of our troops. Look at that sign. Disgraceful. They're anti-America, is what they are. Protestors! They hate our military and they're enemy sympathizers, every last one of 'em. We ought to try the lot of 'em for treason."

Beside me, the bowl of rubber darts empties steadily.

Load.
Fire!
Load.
Fire!
Load.
Fire!

Chancey's paws fly at the air.

DENISE'S PLACE IS quiet behind the front door. I put my ear to the wood and hear movement, so I knock again. "I saw your car," I say. "Open up."

The day of the protest, I didn't see Denise and Brian again before Safia and Paul came up the hill, banner dragging behind them, and told me to get up because they were going home. I studied Safia's face for a betrayal of amusement or satisfaction—maybe she got exactly what she wanted—but she was crying. "Those assholes ruin it for us all," she said, more angry than sad. "They want to hate, hate, hate, and they think they have sense, but they are the same as— Paul, where was that? Those people with the funeral?"

"Indiana?" he said, breathless. The walk to the car was more of a slow jog.

"Screaming to the top of their lungs at the funerals because the soldier is gay. I do not like this war, you know. You know this. But I do not like it because of the politics. The people—the people are only doing what they are told, even if they do not agree. They work hard, they die, and you have more assholes—" (I think 'asshole' is her favorite English word)—"telling the families at the funeral that they are *glad* they are dead, only because they are gay! Stupid asshole people and—"

"Shhh, Saf." Paul rubbed her back and she leaned into him.

I hear the bolt slide and when Denise opens the door—"I don't have a lot of time," she says—her eyes are pink and swollen and she's wearing baggy sweatpants and a man's stained white T-shirt. "I'm packing."

She doesn't wait for me to come in, but leaves the door open and walks around a corner. I close the door and follow her into the living room, filled with boxes packed and taped. A few more are open, their contents obviously haphazardly chosen. Throw pillows and rolls of toilet paper and pens in one, books and coffee mugs and scarves in another. Written on the boxes in black marker is simply, "Stuff."

"They won't give you movers?"

She straddles the coffee mug and scarf box and folds down the flaps, drags the tape dispenser along the seam. "Of course I get movers. They couldn't come until Monday. I have to do something between now and then, so I'm packing it myself." Her back is to me. The waistband of a pair of boxer shorts rises above the elastic waist of her sweatpants. "Besides," she says, "you can't count on them to do it right."

"So, you got the money."

She swipes her hair out of her eyes and turns to look at me, one hand still on the box. "What's up, Mia?"

"I just mean, if you're able to leave, they must have—"

"What brings you here? Today."

"I don't know. The last time I saw you, you and Brian were…lecturing…a guy."

"And?"

"I'm just making sure you're okay."

"I'm fine."

"And, I haven't called since we had dinner. You know. To see how you are."

"I know." She smiles, but not really. "Thanks for making up for it."

"Do you want help packing?"

"No, thanks. It keeps me busy." She stretches and laces her fingers over her head. "A break would be nice, though. Wine?"

(She follows this with asking me to take the rest. "Will you please take the rest? It's too nice to waste, Brian hates white, the movers won't take it, and there's no room for it in my car. I bought the case last month when I didn't know just how soon I'd be leaving.")

"The money isn't here, yet," she says. "My parents are helping out."

"That's nice of them."

"I'm giving most of it to his family."

I say nothing.

"I *thought* that would make you happy."

"It's none of my business."

"I know it isn't." She circles her hand around the base of the bottle and rotates it little by little on the table.

"Why did you decide—"

"They—those *people* at the bowl—turned him into some kind of villain. You know that? William, a bad guy." She laughs. "How ridiculous is that?" She looks outside when a gust of wind punches the window. "I was only there to watch, you know. I'm one hundred percent for the war." She looks at me. For a reaction, I think. "Anyway. I have to get out of here."

"I wasn't one of them," I say.

"I know, I know." She clears her throat and concentrates on her glass. "Do you mind coffee, instead? I don't feel like wine."

"Have whatever you want."

"Do you want coffee, or not?"

"Yes, please."

She carries our drinks to the counter and sets them in the sink, then fills the carafe and pours it in the coffee maker. "Brian asked me to marry him."

"Oh," I say. I have no feeling about this, have no emotion whatsoever. I wonder if I've run out. Ordinarily, I think this would affect me.

"I thought it was a little more interesting than 'Oh' when he asked."

"Did you say yes?"

"Of course," she says. "Actually, the entire conversation you and I just had—about me moving, making a change—was contrived to lead to this shocking surprise. Are you shockingly surprised?"

"Yes."

"For crying out loud, Mia." She gets a cigarette from the hutch and tosses one at me.

"I shouldn't."

"Why not?"

But I'm not ready. I light it.

She points hers at me. "Why aren't you at work today? You said you started again."

"Day off," I lie. I called in sick. Shellie said she hoped I would feel better tomorrow and that I should get plenty of rest and chew on some garlic.

"I suppose I'll have to get a job, now," Denise says. "Do you know how long it's been since I worked?" When I don't answer, she says, "A long time."

I put out my cigarette half-smoked. "What *did* you say? To Brian."

She turns away to check the coffee's progress, using it for avoidance the same way I do. No wonder we love our coffee. "I told him to go home," she says. The pot's filled a quarter of the way, so she pulls it out and fills our cups, then slides it back onto the burner and sits across from me. She rests her chin in her hand and says again, eyes filling, "I told him to go home." Her mouth quivers and she groans and uses a rough hand to wipe at the tears on her cheek. "I am *sick to death* of crying. I don't know how you handle everything so well."

It takes me a minute. "Sorry?"

"Look at you." She waves her hand. "Nothing gets to you."

"If you thought I was doing so well," I say, "why didn't you tell me they had email?"

She shakes her head. "I don't know. Jake made William make me promise. So I promised." She sniffs. "Jake couldn't stand to think of what it would be like for you if you didn't get an email you were waiting for, or how much you would worry if he went on an unexpected mission and couldn't write you for a week. I think he was wrong to do it. I think you would have handled it just fine. You handled everything else."

"Well." My hair has grown a few inches in the past months and hangs in my face. I pull and hold it back. "I haven't really handled it all that well, Denise."

"So, you broke some knickknacks. Big deal. If you didn't have at least one day like that I would kill myself."

She uses the bottom of her shirt to wipe her eyes and says, "Excuse me," then gets up from the table and follows the hallway to the bathroom. After she closes the door I turn around in my chair to look at myself in the black reflection of one of her artsy posters. I don't know what she sees.

She comes back with her face washed, damp hairline-hair clinging to her cheeks. "Ignore me," she says. "Everything is okay. Everything is fine. Things happened the way they were supposed to happen, and they could have been worse. Right?"

I shake my head. I don't know.

"Right. Right, right, right," she says. "I know you didn't do it on purpose, but I'm glad you lost William's lighter. If I'd had it, I would have given it to his father, like I told you. But now when you find it, I can keep it. His father doesn't have to know. I need it, and it's my right as his wife. Do you think it's still somewhere in your apartment?"

"I'm sure of it."

She closes her eyes. "Good."

I look out the window. There isn't much to see. A square lawn with no trees, a wire fence separating it from undeveloped land overrun by tangled grass and weeds. Three mourning doves peck around in a clearing a few yards out. "You know," I say, "I don't mean to beat this to death, but I can't let you just think I'm handling everything the way you think I am. I haven't done well at all."

"You just don't think you have."

I let it go. Maybe she needs me to have handled things.

I ask her, if the movers are coming on Monday, when she'll be leaving.

"Same day," she says. "Bright and early. Or, as William would say, 'at the ass-crack of dawn.'" She looks out the window again. I wonder if she is thinking it's also something Brian would say. They all say it.

I tell her she should stop by before then, and she assures me she will. "Monday," she says.

Before I leave she reminds me to take the case of wine (five bottles are left, and I do the math—she's been drinking as much as I have), and then to be sure I don't leave it with her, she carries it to my trunk.

"What's this?" She uses her chin to point at a gift-wrapped box tucked between the jack and a jug of wiper fluid.

"Co-worker's birthday tomorrow."

I don't go straight to Donny's. Instead, I drive the opposite direction on route seventy-nine past my apartment and follow the road out to nothing. I've been this way a few times to pick up fares, but haven't really explored the highway on my own. Small houses with slanted porches line one side, and on the other, acres of trees are interrupted now and then by patches of red clay where roots have been torn up for a future gas station or strip mall.

The wind feels good on my face, thick and hot as it is, and I don't turn on the air. I pass cows that don't look up from their grass, horses tall and still in the shade, a stand-alone pizza place with a full parking lot.

Jake is away—*It'll be a few days again, M. Mission. Miss you. Hope to have an email from you when I get back to a computer. – Jake*—and I wonder where. I send a quick safety wish and turn up the radio and think instead about Denise and that she'll be gone in a few days, not even halfway through the deployment, and that I've grown to like her, for whatever reason. She was also the only woman I had. Jake would tell me to contact someone in the Family Readiness Group for companionship, and he would remind me that he already told me before he left that they're great for information and support. "The last thing I want to do is sit around with a bunch of women and talk about everything," I told him. *You're doing it to yourself,* he would say to any admission of being lonely without Denise. *Don't complain about being by yourself if you're not going to do anything to change it.*

The trees end, and I spot a brown sign announcing the entrance to Fort Donelson. I pull in and drive around until I find the parking lot, then get out of the car and grab a bottle of wine from the trunk and start down the hill.

History, taught as an annoying series of dates to memorize— 1492: Columbus. 1773: Boston Tea Party. 1963: Kennedy—always bored me in school. But here, this, a history I can smell, and touch, and…and why I should care about walking the very same trail as a Civil War soldier, I don't know. (If one of them could read my thoughts, he might say the trail I walk is not their trail at all, not by a long shot.) But here they stood, here they ate and walked and died and laughed and complained about superior officers. Here they *lived.*

A minivan passes, its occupants pressing faces to the windows while studying a map. *This happened here, that happened there.* How can they hope to feel it from their air-conditioned pod?

Sweat dampens the pits of my tank top and my hand is slippery around the bottle's neck. I stuff the wine in a deep overall pocket and pass by a family having a picnic on a trench, blood from the past carnage hidden deep in the soil under their checkered blanket, the scuffle a fifty-word narrative on a pole-mounted marker. I read it, then climb to the top of a different trench, separated from the family by a curve in the path, and stand beside a cannon and close my eyes. I imagine it is February of 1862, cold and bare, trenches active with cannon and gun fire, orders echoing in thin winter air. The men I'd paid little attention to when reading about them in high school stood here, fighting in freezing snow. Union losses numbered two thousand, eight hundred thirty-two, said the marker. Confederates: over sixteen thousand. This piece of land seems too small and too quiet and too green to have seen over nineteen thousand injuries and deaths, all those bodies turning blue in the cold.

I pull a clump of grass from the trench and put it in my pocket.

The next clearing is circled by a path and some benches, and a monument stands alone on a shallow mound. Before climbing up to it, I read the marker positioned at the base of the hill:

BECAUSE THEY HAD FOUGHT AGAINST THE UNITED STATES, CONFEDERATE DEAD WERE NOT REBURIED IN THE NATIONAL CEMETERY. THIS MONUMENT, ERECTED BY THE UNITED DAUGHTERS OF THE CONFEDERACY IS A MEMORIAL FOR THOSE MEN.IT WAS ERECTED IN 1933.

I notice and ignore the missing comma. So many years later, and still. *Still.* No wonder Donny is convinced he never came home. These battles don't end.

I take the stairs to the monument and sit on a bench in the sun. Heat warms my shoulders, my face, my arms, and the worn denim of my overalls cling to my thighs. I stay for a while, at first trying not to mind the heat, but then welcoming the little bit of suffering. Running to my car for the air would be rude, in this place. This park.

A car door slams and jolts me awake. I get up and move on to find a place in the shade where I can open my bottle.

Down the path is an old log cabin, and at the bottom of the slope behind it, a cluster of trees. A good enough place to sit, but to get there I have to go up another hill, this one identified by a marker as a place where more Confederates lie, "Exact grave locations unknown." The hill is standard for the park: longish faded grass, a shallow incline, and like a trench, but wider, and ending at a line of trees. I stop halfway up when I realize I'm stepping on, essentially, graves, but something at the edge of the trees and sitting part in the shadows and part in the sun gets me curious. "Sorry," I say, tiptoeing. "Sorry, sorry."

A flower. Just a purple flower, growing alone on the trench.

I reach out to pick it, then rub the petals, press them gently between my thumb and finger.

Better to leave it. It belongs here, the way they do. The way they did.

I head to the trees behind the cabin and toss the bottle behind a tree. "Bottoms up." I don't have a corkscrew, anyway. I lie on my back and look up at the trees and imagine I hear their voices, smell the campfire and the breath of their horses.

When I wake up an hour later, I take the long walk back to the car and get on the road to Donny's, stopping at a grocery store bakery on the way.

Turquoise paint chipping off of the motel's façade reveals the original pink. I pull into the spot in front of his room. Next door, shades open, and then they close.

"Donny," I yell, standing outside his door.

"Who is it?"

"Mia."

"I don't want to talk to you."

"I have something for you." My hands are full, so my knock is a kick. I kick three times, hard.

"Go away," he says.

"Didn't you hear me? I have something for you."

"I don't care what you got. You're dead to me."

"Then why are you talking to me?"

"When I call someone my friend, I mean it. You—you betrayed me." He's shouting now. "You was s'posed to be different!"

"From what?"

"Don't be a goddamn smart ass."

"I'm serious."

"From everyone. You understood me. You came over. You drank my bourbon in my house and I told you 'bout my wife. And you betrayed me."

"Let me in."

"You know what you did."

"I didn't do anything."

"Goddamn. . .you're…goddamn bitch. Right."

"That's not nice. Are you drinking?"

"Don't talk to me like I'm some damn kid."

"Don't act like one."

There are a few seconds of silence, then, "I have a gun."

"Oh. Well, are you going to shoot me?"

"No."

"What are you going to do with it?"

"They called the police on me, but they couldn't take my gun. They got no right."

"Who called the police?"

"John."

"Who's John?"

"He's in room six. He came over and saw the gun and called the police, told 'em I was goin' to shoot myself. But I've got a license."

I kick the door again. "Donny, just let me in."

"Door's open."

"My hands are full."

"With what?"

"Just open the goddamn door!"

He opens it and peers outside. "You alone?"

I push past him into a smoke haze and he slams the door behind me. He has plants, now. Vibrant and well cared for. And a jar filled with water to feed a tied bundle of alstroemerias.

He looks out the window. "Can't trust no one out there." He follows me to the table where I am setting down my things: his cake, the box that was in my trunk, a bottle of wine. "What's that?" He points at the cake in the plastic pan.

"It's a cake."

"I see it's a goddamn cake." He picks it up, then sets it back down and takes off the cover. "For me?"

"This, too." I slide the box across the table. He leans forward to grab it and staggers.

"Donny…"

"Doctor Donaldson," he says and slams his palm into his chest. His eyes are flat, dark.

"Do you drink wine?"

He shakes his head. "What're you…? When've you seen me drink wine? Bourbon! Bourbon, bourbon."

He makes his way to the rear of the room and brings back two glasses, one full, the other half full. I take mine and sit in one of the chairs at the table. He sits in the other. Behind him, a young spider plant gets light through the window.

"How long are you going to live here?"

"As long as I got to. Why? What's the matter with it?"

"Nothing," I say, and he laughs.

"Nothin'!" he says. "I was just playin' with you. This place is a crackhead shithole. You know. Next door, guy sells crack. Whores come day and night for it so much I can't get sleep unless it's durin' the day, but they come even then. It's just that I'm so tired by the time two o'clock comes 'round that I can't stay awake." He picks at the plastic tray under the cake with his fingernail. "I don't know, though. Yeah, as long as I need to, I guess. Wife ain't comin' back." He drags his sleeve under his nose. "Won't do it. I tried. I called her and wrote her a letter, and…"

I look around now and then while he's talking, impressed with the plants, which are healthier and sturdier than anything I could ever grow. The pepper plant is already dyi—

I hold my breath when I see it—the smooth, pristine snow on the driveway is unmistakable—tucked behind the chair.

"…says I drink too much, but what's she want? I didn't drink this much before, and I told her if we got back together I'd quit it all. I swear I would. What, you don't believe me?"

"No. Sure."

"What're you lookin'—" He turns, sees it, and jumps out of his chair. "You didn't call back. I told you I had somethin' for you."

"I thought maybe it would be a free *TV Guide*."

He lifts the canvas. "Why would I give you that?" He carries it over and sets it in front of me. "What, you think I'm goin' to stand here and hold it up for you? Take it."

I take it.

"Almost didn't give it to you after what happened. Didn't know what to do with it, though, since I already took it back from that place even though they said they had somebody interested. They get a commission, you know. Fifteen and a half percent."

"What did they say?

"I don't care! It's my goddamn painting. Wait," he says. He slides off his chair and crawls to the bed, reaching underneath to pull out his drawing of me. "Take this, too." He rests it against the other and sits down again. "Read it."

I check the back for a message.

"No, no. The front." He reaches out for it. "It's on the—on the front!"

"Okay." I slap his hand away. "Christ."

A note spreads across the chalk-streaked strands of my hair in looped, elegant writing: "I love you today—and pray for you tomorrow." His signature is a scribble.

"Thank you. Thank you so much."

"I ain't got no use for a picture of you."

"I mean, for both of them."

"Yeah. You're welcome." Donny turns his cake and looks at me and smiles. And there, nineteen years old, there he is. In there somewhere, always, but so quick to leave. So quick he's already gone.

"First, this." I hand him the wrapped box and he tears at the paper, swipes it to the floor. He pulls out a clear plastic cube with 'USA' floating in the middle, each letter made of air bubbles the size of pin-pricks. He raises it to eye level and turns it in a circle, reads the letters, then sets it down.

He holds out his hand to shake mine, and when I give it to him he squeezes, releases.

"Now this." I nudge the cake. I get up and walk over to him, lower to my knees on the floor in front of him. I spread my arms the way Jake does, and Donny hesitates, then leans into me. Over his shoulder I say, "Welcome home," and his fingers tense and curl to clutch my back and his chin presses hard into my shoulder. "Thank—" he says, but the rest gets caught somewhere. He pulls back just enough to cup my face in his hands and pushes my bangs away from my eyes. "You are my angel." His thumb strokes my cheek and he kisses me.

His mouth is unexpectedly soft.

There should be something I feel, right now. Anger, embarrassment, disgust. Thrill. But all I notice is his mustache pricking my upper lip and that I'm trying hard to pretend he has the long hair, the torn jeans. That he's even younger than I am.

Before too long, he pulls away and falls back into his chair. "What the hell're you doin'?"

"Me?"

"What the hell—what the hell was...?" He brushes his hair off his forehead.

I say, "What was what?"

"Oh, you think I'm that drunk? Think you can trick me?"

"Let's have some cake." I look for something to cut it with, but he has no utensils. I settle for a sturdy envelope, unopened, an attorney's address in the upper left corner. "I would have put something more on it—a decoration, something about where you were specifically—but I don't know any of it."

He rubs his foot on the floor. "You do somethin' nice for me and I tell you it's nice and now you think I want somethin' from you. Because I kissed you."

"Forget the kiss. I don't think you want anything from me."

"Bullshit." He shakes his head. "Bullshit." He looks at my glass. "You ain't had a drink. Why're you bein' such a little girl?"

"Donny. Can you *please* just be nice?"

He lights a cigarette. "I don't know what the hell just happened." He looks through the smoke at his cake, then back at me. "You got me a cake," he says, jabbing his cigarette into the space between us. He tilts his head and looks at me, his face softer. "I love you."

I smile and take a taste of the bourbon, just a layer to numb my lips.

"I do," he says. "You think I don't mean it? Why're you smilin'?"

"When someone says they love you, you smile."

"Naw," he says. "You're laughin' at me."

"I'm not laughing at you."

"You're goddamn laughin' at me."

"Donny."

"Forget it." He stands up to look out the window.

"That's a nice plant," I say.

"Forget it. It's a fuckin' plant. Who cares? I won't ever get out of this place."

"Aren't you still working?"

"Do I look like I'm workin'?" He turns back to me. "What, you tryin' to help me? What do you think you can do? I ain't gettin' out of here 'cause I got fired. All that shit with Emily. I told her to take the house, but she wouldn't, and I don't got the money to pay what's left of the goddamn mortgage." He finishes off his glass and says, "I'm out. Take me to the store."

"'Take me to the store'?"

"Aw, well," he says and bows, but only a little before he has to grab onto the table. "I'm so sorry. Mia, my darlin' angel, will you *pleeeease* take me to the store?"

I drive him to the nearest one, a dingy building the size of a kiosk with a blinking 'Q' on the sign and a skinny man in torn jeans standing by the front door. I forget his name, but he lives on Lucy Drive. He nods at me and I nod back.

When we get back to the hotel parking lot Donny says, "You comin' in?"

"I don't think so." I haven't been home all day. I want dinner on my bed with a movie playing on TV, Chancey purring somewhere I can hear him.

"Come in. I got cake." He smiles.

We eat half of it. I drink water because he doesn't have milk, but he sticks with bourbon until he can't stand at all, anymore, without having to steady himself on a chair or the table, or slide along the wall to the end of the bed.

"I've had it," I say with my hand on my stomach. "Time to go."

"You're leavin'?"

I check my watch for show. "It's late."

"Aw, it ain't late. C'mon. Have a drink."

"Donny, I'm really tired."

"Five minutes! Stay five minutes. I have to show you somethin'. From the war."

"What is it?"

"It's a—well, damn it, you'll see what it is when I show you. You keep askin' me where I was and so I'll show you. If you stay."

"Okay," I say. "Five minutes."

"Five minutes! Well, that hardly gives me enough time to—"

"Five."

"Have some more cake. You only had a little bird bite. Lookit that."

I stand. "I'm going."

"Wh—? What for? Are you mad 'cause I kissed you?"

I'd let it slip my immediate memory, but now that I'm reminded, I don't like the way it feels. Not quite as uncomfortable as having been molested by an old family friend, but maybe as uncomfortable as having been flirted with by that old family friend. "No. What do you have to show me?"

"Damn. Why're you in such a hurry?"

"Because," I say. "I'm *tired*."

"Well, you don't got to be like that." He takes his time lighting a cigarette. "Ain't you goin' to sit down?"

I sit and fold my arms on the table.

"I miss my wife," he says.

"I know you do."

"She's gone."

"I know."

"What d'you mean, you know? I'm tellin' you."

"Donny, you already told me. We talked about this ten minutes ago." I get up and push my chair under the table. Through the window the sky is purple-blue.

"Where're you goin'?"

"Home."

The canvases are awkward to carry with one hand, but I can't count on him to open the door for me. I set the smaller on top of the larger and flatten my hand against the bottom, a server with a tray.

Donny leans forward in his chair. "I'll take those back."

"You can't. You already gave them to me."

"I can take 'em back right now."

"Nope," I say, turning the knob. "Too late."

He kicks over a chair. "You can't do that. You can't take a present from someone and leave. Ungrateful. Bitch!"

"Nice try." I open the door. Even if he won't remember any of this tomorrow, I say, "I'll come over again soon, okay?"

"Sure. Soon. Right. But, where're you goin', now? What do you have to go home for? You hear from your husband lately?"

"He's not my husband."

"Awww," he says. "I see. I see. How long's it been? Days? A week? Month? What, d'you think he's out bangin' someone else? Some of them soldier girls ain't bad lookin'. Wouldn't want you to worry, though. C'mon. Talk to me. Tell Donny."

"Fuck you." I toss the drawing across the room. A corner of the canvas ricochets off the wall and my face lands undamaged on the bed.

"Hey!"

I step outside, cut him off when I slam the door.

I set the painting against my car—carefully—and check on him through the motel window. He sits at the table in dim lamplight with his legs out straight, drink balanced on a narrow thigh. He picks up the remote control, points it at the TV, shakes back his hair and watches the channel guide.

"MIA, HON, IT'S Olivia. Are you there?... I'm just checking in to see how you are...You know, this kind of thing can be very stressful...Anyway, hon, I hope you're well and that you've started eating better...Oh, and thank you for sending Jakey that last package...That's one less trip to the grocery store for me! So... ...Okay...Well, you take care, and make sure to tell my Jakey that I love him...See you soon, all right?"

July 14
Jake,

I get up to heat my coffee, then sit back down and move the candle to spread more light on the paper. Normally, late morning sun would light the desk, but today's clouds and rain make the apartment dark, dreary, cozy.

I'm looking at your letter on the computer screen. I know. I should have responded to it long ago, but I couldn't.

Thanks for the message you left on my birthday.

In truth, Jake, I put off writing you on purpose. How was I supposed to talk or write you without saying something about what you wrote about the Army?

Oh, and I'm sorry about ditching you when we were emailing. I was avoiding you.

But I'll tell you now.

At first, I was angry. You were sure you were getting out, you said. I told you how I felt when you first joined, and you said you felt the same way. It was something you needed to do, but there was also more we wanted to do together that included being rule-less, remember? And then I got your email and I felt like I was being grounded, or something. How many more years did I want to have to rely on you getting weekend passes any time we wanted to leave the area (I know, they're not hard to get, but still, you have to), or let the Army decide where we live? All of this affects me, too. I thought we were going to see the country before finding a house somewhere. Yes, the Army moves us around, but we wanted to make all those choices that are made for us now.

I know people change and minds change and I can't count on anything, but I thought I should at least be able to count on you. (I'm not trying to make you feel guilty; I just want you to understand what I was thinking when I was avoiding you.) I thought I should have been able to trust you to not do anything to hurt me. But then you told me about your decision to stay in the Army, and I actually hated you for a minute.

I scratch out the last sentence with heavy lines and loops so he can't make it out even if he flips over the page to read the backward pen impressions.

But then you told me about your decision to stay in the Army, and it hurt.

Now it's the creamer in my coffee making me nauseous (can I drink nothing I like, anymore?). I go into the bathroom, bend over the toilet, vomit, flush, and brush my teeth. I bring the roll of toilet paper with me to the desk.

Now, though… I'm not mad, now. I saw this flower, Jake, this one purple flower just growing there all by itself on a trench at a Civil War battlefield. The petals were so vibrant and soft and beautiful and I almost, almost picked it and took it home. The same way I picked a clump of grass from the trench and stuffed it in my pocket. Do you know what, though? What if a piece of a soldier's soul was in those blades of grass? What if it's all there because that's exactly where it's supposed to be?

The thing is, Jake, I understand. I really do understand, now. Before, I would have tried to get you to quit the Army. If you can't empathize, it's easy to ask for all kinds of unrealistic and unfair things. (I still wish you would have asked me what I thought before you decided to stay in. In case you're thinking, "But, I asked you what you thought," your asking me after the fact is a little different from having asked me about the possibility, before the decision had already been made.)

And I understand your thoughts about marriage, too. People shouldn't get married unless it's because they want to. Nothing, no outside force, should push them into it.

Which brings me to this: It won't work for me, you staying in the Army. I can't…I can't, Jake. It sounds crazy, but I love you too much to be with you through that many more years of Army life. I'm just not cut out for it. Some people aren't, you know. That's forgivable, isn't it? Maybe if we knew for sure there would be no more deployments… (Well, okay—that's a ridiculous line of thinking.)

You don't know what I've gone through, what I'm going through. I know – you're going through things, too. And I know, they're bad. You're the one doing war stuff, you're the one who lost a friend. I'm not discounting that. But this, right now, is about me. And I think my stuff is just as hard, but in a different way.

But it's okay. You were right. Your life is yours, and my life is mine, and we need to live them the best way we can. Everything you wrote in your letter

I'm interrupted by the phone. Shellie asks if I've started feeling any better since calling in this morning.

"I wish I did. I know you guys are short."

She tells me to keep up with the garlic, and in the background, before she hangs up, I hear Lenny say, "She's a liar. She ain't sick."

makes sense. Which is why I know we should

I wipe my eyes and blow my nose, and the force of it presses everywhere inside my head. Lenny was right. I am a liar.

not be together anymore. We got a little practice these last few months, so it's not like much will change, right? Jake, I don't want to hurt you. I never, never want to hurt you. I love you so much.

Love,

Mia

p.s. I hate that I already feel better. I had hoped I would be wrong.

The mailman—early, today—arrives in his white truck just as I'm about to put the letter in the outgoing bin. Denise follows him up the walk.

He opens the door, nods, "Mornin'," and sticks out his palm. "Goin' out?" He points at the envelope while wedging a foot in the door.

Denise says, "Excuse me," and squeezes past him and waits behind me on the landing.

"Sure," I say.

He takes the letter from my hand, then deposits incoming mail in the boxes on the wall. Mine stays empty.

The rain starts fast, falls heavy, and he runs to the house next door.

"Sorry," Denise says, her hands in her back pockets. "There's nothing worse than an empty box, is there?"

We look at each other. Her mouth twitches.

"No," I say, "there isn't."

We're still laughing when we get to my kitchen, and I learn that Denise tends to snort.

"Coffee?"

We sit at the table with our hot mugs, neither of us saying much. Denise's bronze-brown lipstick collects at the corners of her mouth and in the thin lines of her lips.

"Isn't that…?" Denise points behind me at the far livingroom wall where Donny's painting hangs.

"Yeah."

She laughs. "But, *why*? It's so…it's so…well, you like it, so never mind. How did you afford it, anyway?"

I tell her I got a deal.

She says, "I do miss snow. Looking at that reminds me of what winter is supposed to look like."

Rain splashes from the sill onto my arm, and since Denise hasn't lit a cigarette, yet, I close the window.

"Anyway—" she says, and from downstairs we hear, "You ready?"

"In one second!" Safia screams.

"The door is open."

"Asshole!" she yells. "We cannot go without my Visa, and you know."

"Call me an asshole again and we won't go at all."

"Oh, Paul, you do not mean that. You know I love you, my bear." We listen through the pause. "I found it!" she shouts.

"Well, hurry up," he shouts back.

Keys jangle in their lock, she pounds down the stairs, and the main door slams.

"What was all that about?"

"I don't know," I say, though, now I do. I wonder if they'll pass. We watch their car speed to the intersection, wipers on high to fight the downpour.

"Anyway," Denise starts again, "if Brian comes by—"

"Why would Brian come by?"

"I don't know. He's crazy. He calls all the time and begs me not to leave."

"Well, you're leaving today. He'll have to get over it."

She nods, her eyes on the painting. "I guess he will."

"You were saying, though, that should he come over…?"

"Oh. Right. Don't answer the door, if he does. He'll trap you in a sad story and won't leave for hours. He's done it to Marc—do you remember Marc from that party?—and Marc has called me to plead on Brian's behalf. It's pitiful, really."

"I think it's kind of sweet."

"That's because it's not happening to you." She holds out her cup for more coffee and I point at the machine. She gets it for herself. When her back is to me, she says, "Maybe it is kind of sweet, huh?" She sits back down and says it's too late, anyway. The movers came this morning and by early evening, she'll be somewhere else, hours away.

I want to ask her if she already gave him the driving directions.

We talk about her plans, which include not only buying a house, but a new car. "A used new one, because you really have to think about depreciation. Can you believe how responsible I sound? Do you even recognize me? And I'm going to have a child by the time I'm thirty-two—in case I want two, you know, because after that," she says, munching a cashew from a tin I set on the table, "your eggs dry up little by little. It's true. You can't even sell your eggs after twenty-nine because they're practically worthless. You have to sell them while you're young. Like you."

"I'm not much younger than you are."

"Three years is three years."

I get up for a glass of water and she watches me walk from the chair to the refrigerator and back to the chair.

She says, "No one wears overalls anymore. What is this, ninety-seven?"

"They're comfortable."

"I bet." She tosses a nut in her mouth. "So?"

"I'll be right back." I go to the bathroom and close the door and run the sink. I hear her chair slide back from the table and her weight shifting the floorboards as she walks around, browsing the way she does. Hallway, bedroom, hallway, living room. Then the noise stops. I flush the toilet and turn off the water and open the door. Denise sits at the computer with her fingers on the keyboard's arrow pad.

"What are you doing?"

Her face is white, a reflection from the monitor. "He's so…*communicative*. William was never able to express himself very well in letters."

I walk over to the desk and see that she hasn't read beyond the first screen.

"William didn't really write much about what he felt. Just, 'I woke up at this time, then I had breakfast, and then I went to a meeting. The meeting was boring.' I don't know how long it would have taken me to find out about the twelve-month thing." She shrugs. "I enjoyed getting his letters, but I wish he would have…I don't know…told me more." She presses the down arrow until the next page comes up.

"If you don't mind," I say, turning off the monitor before she can read Jake's question about her letter to William.

"No, no. I'm sorry. I had no business…really." She gets up and smoothes her pants and asks if she can stay a while. She gets pretty sore sitting on the floor for more than fifteen minutes, she says, and she never knew she could miss her furniture so much. "It hasn't even been a full day!"

I sit on the oversized chair and she curls up on the couch and I ask her if she wants to watch television.

"Anything but the news," she says, so I find something equally mindless, but more upbeat. We laugh when we're supposed to and sit quietly during commercials until she says, at the end of an advertisement for a new plastic mallet-and-bolt set, "I envy you."

Two hours later, Denise and I are folded in the quiet peace of an hours-long rain, warm and dry inside while, outside, occasional lightning strikes whiten the room, and strong winds whip branches against the side of the building. Denise snores on the couch, turned toward the wall in a fetal position, and I watch TV while falling in and out of sleep, a screamer in the laugh-track audience pulling me from fleeting dreams. When I open my eyes, it's to the painting, always the painting, and I can't help but imagine Emily in her slippers and robe and the man standing at the end of the drive and that, someday, his big boots will disturb the snow on the way to ring her doorbell.

"You take care, Len! Y'hear?" The yelling—and next, a slamming car door—is loud enough to be heard through closed windows.

I lift Chancey off my lap and get up to look outside. Donny squints up at the building, wet hair stuck to his head. I watch him waver on the walkway to the building and disappear through the door, then hear him dragging up the stairs, stopping now and then to, I imagine, check numbers on doorways.

When he knocks, I am already at the door and watching through the peephole, but I don't answer.

"Mia! Mia, you here? I got to talk to you. Mia! You home?"

His voice echoes through the stairwell and the red-haired girl across the hall opens her door to glare at him, then slams it.

Denise comes up behind me and whispers, "Who is it?"

"Mia!"

I open the door and pull him in. Rainwater rolls off his hair, drips to the floor. "You can't just scream at someone's door," I say.

"I have to go, anyway." Denise stands against the hallway wall. Donny holds his hand out to her, and she shakes it. "Denise," she says.

"Donny. Donny Donaldson, Doctor."

"Oh, really," she says, then looks at me.

"Vietnam," I say.

"Ohhh." She nods. "How nice."

"You don't believe me?" he says. "I got proof."

She waits.

"Not here. What, you think I carry it with me? It's at home. Come over any time, I'll show it to you."

"I believe you," she says, and Donny stomps his foot on the floor, says, "Goddamn it, don't you patronize me. I was a goddamn doctor. Doctor Daniels."

"Okay. You're a doctor." She looks at me again.

I tell her not to bother.

"Two minutes," he says, "but I made sure they felt no pain those two minutes. Me. I did that for them, and they'd tell me, they'd say, 'Doctor'—and I told 'em, 'Don't you dare call me Doctor' 'cause I don't want formality when I'm holdin' their heart, their life, in my hands—'Doctor,' they'd say—'Thank you.'" He grabs her hand and squeezes it, and I see her wrist turning to get free. "'Thank you,' they'd say. They knew. Y'see? They knew they was dyin'. We all know, just 'fore it happens. And thanks to good ol' Doctor Donaldson, they went peacefully. Maybe even while havin' some fun." He rolls his eyes and smiles, bounces his head around like he's drugged, high. He laughs, then stops abruptly and steps closer to her, having to look up. Denise is pretty tall, for a woman. At least five-nine. "Point is, I don't got to show you no goddamn proof."

"Donny," I say, "the living room is right through there. I'll be there in a second."

He dismisses her and says to me, "Thank you." I hear him grunt when he falls onto the couch.

Denise backs against the wall and holds herself. "Mia."

"Yeah?"

"Do you think William knew?"

"No. I don't."

She nods. "Okay. Right. Okay." She pats her hair and moves away from the wall, toward the door. "But, not just about that." She puts a nail in her mouth, and then must taste that it's fake, because she lets her hand fall. "I've been wanting to ask you, and then I didn't want to ask because I didn't want to know because it's— because, if I knew, that would…that would—"

"What is it?"

"Did Jake—? I wrote him—William—this letter, and—believe me, I know it wasn't the right thing to do. I know that now, anyway—but in the—I've been relying on the idea that it didn't get there until *after*, you know? But what if he read it—"

"No," I tell her. I make it sound strong, sure. "Jake would have said something. William told him pretty much everything."

"You're positive?"

"I'm positive."

"Do you promise? That's stupid, isn't it? Asking you to promise. But you can't lie in a promise."

"No, you can't."

"So? Do you promise?"

"I promise."

"Pinkie swear?" She laughs. "I'm kidding." She hugs me fast and tight, then lets me go. "Thank you. I've been so—'What if?' You know? What if my letter was what—"

"You did what you thought you had to do."

"No," she says. "I was selfish.—Don't. I know what you're going to say, but I should have waited." She looks at things on the walls and runs her hands over her back pockets. "Anyway. I have to get back and pack my clothes."

We hug again—this one longer—and make promises about emailing. But the door closes behind her and I don't expect to hear from her, or to write her.

"Mia! She gone? Hey, what happened in here? Fire?" The sound of a hand slapping the wall. "I'm thirsty. You got any water?"

"Coming."

I pour a glass and bring it out to him. He sets it on the table without drinking any. "I wanted to say…I wanted to tell you, with my whole heart, I'm sorry. You're an angel. You know that? You are."

"It's okay."

"You don't even know what I'm sorry for."

"For before. I know. It's okay."

"Damn, girl," he says. "Here I am, comin' out in the rain and payin' ten dollars—it ain't cheap comin' here, 'specially when Lenny makes me pay more for an address—and you act like you want me to leave." He pulls a pack of cigarettes from his shirt pocket, then searches his pants, back and front. "Got a light?"

Donny smokes in the passenger seat and I tell him to open the—

"I know, I know." He rolls it down, but the smoke comes in, anyway. He offers one and I say no. There's not even a craving.

"Where we goin', anyway? I live the other way."

"I already told you."

"No, you didn't."

"Damn it, Donny, yes. I did. I told you twice."

"Well, I don't remember. I'd jus' like to know where we're goin', is all, and on a dark and rainy day with you drivin' like Andretti, I don't think—"

"My friend's. We're going to my friend's house, and then I'm taking you home."

"Take me home first."

"No, Donny. I already explained—"

"Take me home! I want to go home. Take me first, then go see your friend."

I pull over in the lot of an abandoned tire store. Faded red paint advertises a close-of-business sale, sixty percent off, and a tangled chain hangs from the door handle. The windows are smashed, jagged, and we're stopped where others aren't likely to stop. "If you want to get out, get out."

"Shit. I was just kiddin'. Why're—can't you take a joke?"

I pull out of the lot and he falls quiet.

Kudzu drapes roadside bushes and trees, and miles down the sky the cloud line ends.

"…helicopter crash this morning killed its two pil—"

I punch the button, search the stations until I find music.

"Wait! I wanted to hear that!" Donny reaches out and I catch his hand, say, "*My* car."

I don't know if I'll stay here, and if I do, I don't know for how long. I suppose I might save for a while—there's plenty of time until Jake comes home—and use the money for a truck and first month's rent somewhere. Somewhere I've always wanted to go. Only, there's nowhere I've always wanted to go.

It hits me, then, that I can go anywhere and that there's no one to stop me or to choose my destination for me. Not Jake, not Jake's Army.

I'll go north. That much I know. Somewhere where there's snow.

Denise doesn't answer her door and her lights are off, but her car is outside (as is Brian's), so I know she'll get William's lighter before she leaves. I drop it through the mail slot.

On the way home after dropping off Donny, I stop at the grocery store to pick up the snacks Jake asked for, plus some. I'll add a note to the box: *Friends?*

I turn onto my street, and though everyone else is at work and the street-side where I park is bare, my tire bumps up against the curb, then rolls back down. I open the door and float to standing beside the car until I'm looking over the roof, and I can't remember how to breathe, or that I do breathe, and the mess behind my ribs lurches like I'm on a ride and I remember what Denise said about leave and that his mother said tell Jakey something or something and I steady myself on the door and I think I am smiling, I'm sure I am smiling, and there's some noise, like a donkey braying, which is strange, and I think I say, "Oh…" and my next thought is the baby, I have to tell him about the baby, but I don't want to tell him because then his whole visit, so short already, will be focused on the stupid baby, and I have to warn him about the letter, too, tell him it's bullshit, all of it, that leaving him won't make it better, but later, I'll tell him later…

He pulls me from the space between my car and the door and closes it for me, then steps closer and circles me with his body and says, "How're you doing?"

ABOUT THE AUTHOR

KRISTEN TSETSI has been an adjunct English professor, a newspaper feature writer and columnist, a cab driver, editor of the literary journal *American Fiction* (New Rivers Press), and an instructor of creative writing, playwriting, and screenwriting. Her other novels are *The Age of the Child* and, under the name Chris Jane, *The Year of Dan Palace*.

Her website is kristenjtsetsi.com.